D1094380

BOOKS BY

EMILIE LORING

THE TRAIL OF CONFLICT
HERE COMES THE SUN!
A CERTAIN CROSSROAD
THE SOLITARY HORSEMAN
GAY COURAGE
SWIFT WATER
LIGHTED WINDOWS
FAIR TOMORROW
UNCHARTED SEAS
HILLTOPS CLEAR
WE RIDE THE GALE!
WITH BANNERS
IT'S A GREAT WORLD
GIVE ME ONE SUMMER
AS LONG AS I LIVE
TODAY IS YOURS
HIGH OF HEART
ACROSS THE YEARS
THERE IS ALWAYS LOVE
WHERE BEAUTY DWELLS
STARS IN YOUR EYES
RAINBOW AT DUSK
WHEN HEARTS ARE LIGHT AGAIN
KEEPERS OF THE FAITH
BEYOND THE SOUND OF GUNS
BRIGHT SKIES
BECKONING TRAILS
I HEAR ADVENTURE CALLING
LOVE CAME LAUGHING BY
TO LOVE AND TO HONOR
FOR ALL YOUR LIFE
MY DEAREST LOVE
I TAKE THIS MAN
THE SHADOW OF SUSPICION
WHAT THEN IS LOVE
LOOK TO THE STARS
BEHIND THE CLOUD
WITH THIS RING
HOW CAN THE HEART FORGET
THROW WIDE THE DOOR
FOLLOW YOUR HEART
A CANDLE IN HER HEART
FOREVER AND A DAY
SPRING ALWAYS COMES

SPRING ALWAYS COMES

SPRING ALWAYS COMES

EMILIE LORING

LITTLE, BROWN AND COMPANY
BOSTON · TORONTO

LIBRARY OF CONGRESS CATALOG CARD NO. 66-16685

FIRST EDITION

Published simultaneously in Canada
by Little, Brown & Company (Canada) Limited

PRINTED IN THE UNITED STATES OF AMERICA

SPRING ALWAYS COMES

ONE

CONSTANCE Wyndham was only dimly aware of the audience around her in the darkened theater, of frequent outbursts of laughter, of the actors moving across the lighted stage. She might as well have been separated from them by a glass wall. She heard nothing of the crisp, sparkling dialogue that had been so enthusiastically praised by the critics; she saw nothing of the brilliant acting that had made the play a smash hit.

Automatically, over and over, she drew her long white kid gloves through her fingers, trying to sort out the jumble of her thoughts. Once she shook her head impatiently. She had to think things through, make up her mind about the future.

How could she have drifted so long, put off the time of reckoning until it was upon her? Always she had been aware that, sooner or later, she would have to leave behind her the luxury and protection of John Kent's great Park Avenue apartment, that she would have to face the world on her own feet, using what abilities she might possess to build her own life.

Up to now, she had made no preparation beyond learning to type and to take shorthand during her last year in college. The truth was, she confessed to herself, that she had always hoped, in some secret corner of her heart, that something would happen, some miracle that would make it unnecessary for her to work, that would enable her to go on living this pleasant, cushioned life. Hoping that her future would be like Sandra Kent's, luxurious, sheltered, free of worry.

Once more she pulled the long soft gloves through her restless fingers and Sandra turned, trying to make out her expression in the darkened theater. Connie kept her eyes on the stage, pretending not to be aware of her friend's movement. Friend? Of course Sandra was her friend. From the day when John Kent had offered to send Connie through college, had taken her into his spectacular duplex in New York City, had arranged for her to spend her summer vacations with him and his only child, his daughter Sandra, the latter had adopted her as a sister. Not once had she ever made Connie feel like an outsider; not once had she ever been condescending; not once had she ever implied that their futures could not be alike.

Could not be. That was the point at which Connie had refused to look honestly. Sandra's father was an immensely wealthy industrialist; Connie's father was a guide in the Maine woods, a man who loved three things: his daughter, the well-worn books on the shelves that lined the walls of his living room, and what he called the "wild air" of the woods.

Four years earlier, John Kent had been advised by his physician to get away from his responsibilities and to spend a month hunting and fishing in Maine. No two men could have been more different than John Kent and Bill Wyndham, whom Kent had hired as a guide, but they had developed a mutual esteem and, to their surprise, a warm and steady friendship.

Toward the end of that month, Kent, restless and impatient at having his actions directed by someone else, had insisted on going off by himself, against Wyndham's strict orders, had sustained a serious injury, and his life had been saved by Wyndham.

The latter had dismissed the incident as of no importance, simply a routine part of his job. But Kent was a man who never forgot his obligations, a man who always paid his debts. He not only set Wyndham up in a camp called Stony Brook but he educated his daughter, an expense that Wyndham could not have afforded because of the extravagance of his son.

When Wyndham had received Kent's letter, offering to provide Connie's education, he had handed it over to her, smiling at some thought which amused him.

"What's the joke, Dad?"

"John always does the right thing."

"What's wrong with that?" Connie laughed.

"Nothing, of course. But when a man is always right he becomes a little inhuman. He demands too much of others. He loses his understanding and compassion for human mistakes."

She had read the letter and cried out impulsively, "Oh, Dad, how wonderful! A good college and a Park Avenue apartment and New York City. A great metropolis to live in, things to do and see and experience, instead of this —"

The brightness had died out of his eyes, a shadow of disappointment had passed over his face. Seeing his expression, she had broken off abruptly. She would have given anything to retract the spontaneous words and undo the pain they had inflicted.

It was, she knew well, her worst fault, this tendency to speak without thinking. Why couldn't she learn to think first, to avoid the words that so often brought pain with them?

"It's your decision," he told her quietly. "You must do what seems right for you."

Connie had made her decision, and for four years she had lived in a world of glamour and wealth. And now it was all over. The telegram had come just as dinner was being announced: FATHER VERY ILL URGE IMMEDIATE RETURN. It had been signed JEFFERSON GRAY.

Father very ill. It was difficult to picture Bill Wyndham incapacitated, let alone seriously ill. A lean, bronzed man in his early fifties, he had a hard, disciplined body that was as powerful as it had been at thirty. He had never in Connie's memory been ill.

It couldn't, she assured herself, be anything serious. Perhaps he had broken a leg. Accidents were always possible in the woods. By the time she got there he would be recuperating and probably he would be annoyed because she had been summoned. For all his deep devotion, or perhaps because of it, he had never made any demands on his daughter. Connie was aware that he had always hoped that she would share his love for the woods, but he had never tried to persuade her to remain with him.

After the arrival of the telegram, Kent took charge of the arrangements, having his secretary make plane reservations, instructing Sandra's maid to do Connie's packing. But it was Sandra who, after a look at Connie's white face, had insisted that they go to the theater that night as they had originally planned. That would be better than sitting at the apartment brooding, or waiting alone at the airport.

During the first act of the play Connie recalled her childhood in the Maine woods. Her mother had been a city girl who had never become reconciled to the long, harsh winters of Maine, but who had stayed there out of a sense of duty when all her efforts failed to persuade her husband to take a city job. Connie recalled clearly how her mother had hated the cold and the isolation of the winter; how she had talked, huddled close to the blazing logs in the fireplace, of the lights and warmth, the gaiety and excitement of city living.

When the first intermission came, the two girls joined the crowd that thronged the theater lobby. As usual photographers snapped pictures of Sandra, who was always news because of her father's prominence and the power wielded by the many interlocking businesses he controlled. Sandra waited passively until they had finished — it was an ordeal she always dreaded — and then she drew Connie away from the people who had inevitably turned to stare.

"So he is still there," she said unexpectedly.

Connie looked around the lobby. "Who is?"

"Jefferson Gray. The man who sent you the telegram about your father. Still at Stony Brook."

"You know him?" Connie asked in surprise. She had not even wondered who the man was, she had been too startled and dismayed by the import of his message to think of anything else.

"He is one of father's most promising young executives. Father has great hopes for him. But he works too hard; he was run down and too thin and not sleeping, so Father —"

Sandra's father was a stickler for formality; she had never dreamed of calling him Dad.

There was a deeper color than usual in her face. "Father suggested that Jeff go up to Stony Brook to rest, because it had done him so much good. That was nearly a month ago. I was wondering why I hadn't heard from him. I thought maybe —" Again the color deepened. "But he is still up there. You'll like him, Connie."

"You like him, don't you?" Connie said, struck by the glow on Sandra's face, a kind of radiance.

"Yes," Sandra said softly, "I like him. When you meet him you'll understand why. He's a wonderful person."

"Attractive?"

"Wildly attractive."

Connie's face glowed with delight. "Sandra! Is this serious? You mean you have found the man who is right for you?"

The glow faded from Sandra's face. "What would be the use of finding the person who is right for me?"

Connie was startled by the unexpected bitterness in Sandra's voice. "What on earth do you mean?"

"My father wanted a son," Sandra told her. "Instead, he got — me. He never really overcame his disappointment. He wants someone who can carry on the business for him. I've tried as hard as I could to please him. Honestly I have, Connie. But it has never been enough. There is only one thing left. I'll have to marry to please him. Marry someone who can carry on the Kent Enterprises and eventually take the load from my father's shoulders as a son would have done. Of course, it wouldn't be quite such a bleak prospect if it should turn out to be someone who is devastatingly attractive, someone like — someone I could like."

"But you can't do that, Sandra! You can't marry without love," Connie cried out in protest.

"Why not?" Sandra said drearily. "Let's face it, Connie. I might as well marry to please my father. No one has ever been interested in me except for my money. So why not make my marriage satisfactory to my father as long as it can't be to me?"

"Oh, Sandra, that's all wrong!"

"Is it?" Sandra pulled Connie around so that the two girls faced the long mirror in the theater lobby.

For a long time they looked at their own reflections and then at each other. Connie was tall and slim, with russet hair that swung in soft loose waves, deep brown eyes, hollows under the delicately molded cheekbones, a passionate red mouth whose softness contradicted the firmness of her chin. The first impression she made, even before people noticed her stunning beauty, was the vivid impact of her personality.

Beside her Sandra seemed colorless, though her features were good, her blue eyes really beautiful, her brown hair thick and glossy. She was, Connie thought, like a negative that had faded in the light. Behind her face there was no acceptance of life, no vibrancy, no assurance.

"All you need is to believe in yourself," Connie told her firmly.

Sandra laughed, still with that note of bitterness in her voice. "You are wrong, Connie. All I need is to have someone believe in me. To have someone find me attractive in myself, just as I am."

"But people do," Connie insisted.

"People like Jim Baker?" Sandra said.

The previous evening the girls had double-dated. Before the end of the evening Sandra's escort had asked Connie for a date. She had refused, of course, but she realized now that Sandra had overheard; that she had, understandably enough, been hurt in her self-esteem, if not because of the young man himself.

Remembering all that the Kents had done for her, Connie felt wretchedly guilty about causing Sandra any pain, however unintentional it might be on her part. The worst of it was that the incident had not been the first of its kind. Frequently Sandra's dates had shown a preference for Connie. Never again, she vowed, would she permit any man in whom Sandra was interested to pay her the slightest attention.

While she was wondering what she could say, Sandra gave her a quick smile. "Forgive me. I don't like self-pity. I don't know what got into me tonight. Just feeling alone, I guess. Now that you are leaving, I have no one but my father and he always seems so far off."

"I have only my father," Connie pointed out, "and now he is ill."

"He's going to be all right. And you have Nick, of course."

"Oh, yes, there's Nick."

"Do you ever hear from him?"

"Not unless he wants something," Connie said dryly.

Nick Wyndham, her father's son by an earlier marriage, had been a problem all his life. It didn't seem possible that anyone as fine and as honest as Wyndham could have had such a son. He was always in trouble of some sort, trouble that seemed to become more serious as the years passed. He drank too much; he didn't like to hold a steady job; he was continually out of work and making demands on his father.

Up to a point Wyndham had done all he could to help his son, steadily impoverishing himself and stripping Connie of her fair share in order to provide the money Nick needed so urgently. The breaking point came when Nick struck a child while driving under the influence of alcohol. He had driven on, been caught, and had managed to wriggle out of a jail sentence by some plausible story, which had convinced the judge but failed to convince his own father, who knew him too well.

Wyndham had sent for Nick, had faced him across the big table in the living room at Stony Brook. Connie could still remember the flickering light of the fire on the two faces that were so much alike and yet so different: her father's lean and purposeful, her half brother's flabby and vacillating.

"I've carried you too long, Nick. Propped you up whenever you began to sag. But from now on it is up to you; unless you can learn to stand on your own feet now, you never will."

"You mean," Nick demanded, concerned by only one factor, "you won't give me any more money?"

"I mean I won't give you any more money," his father told him.

Nick had slammed out of the lodge without saying good-by. Later he had hitched a ride away from the camp. After that, Connie had had only three indications that he was still alive: once he wrote from Portland, saying he needed a small loan to tide him over for a few days. Once he telephoned her collect from Boston to demand a hundred dollars immediately, this time dropping the fiction of a loan. Once she ran into him in Times Square in New York and he swerved out of her way as though anxious to escape recognition.

But he would show up again. Sooner or later, he always did.

Connie was so deep in her memories of the past that she was startled by the storm of applause. She had paid no attention to the play. Now the curtain was falling on the bowing cast. The house lights went up. She drew on the long white kid gloves. Beside her Sandra was pulling an ermine coat over her smooth shoulders.

"There's plenty of time," she said reassuringly. "Your plane doesn't leave until twelve o'clock."

"Midnight," Connie said. "That sounds more romantic."

Sandra laughed. "Won't you ever grow up? Never mind, I like you as you are."

"Just the same, we had better get out of here," Connie said, worried. "I may have trouble getting a cab just when all the theaters are closing."

"*You* may have trouble? Constance Wyndham, did you think for one single minute I'd dream of letting you go off by yourself, with no one to say good-by? Don't be ridiculous. I'm going to the airport with you. Father is having George call for us both here."

As usual the Broadway district was a blaze of light when the two girls went out of the warm lobby. Theaters were disgorging their audiences, taxis were crawling along the jammed streets picking up passengers. There was bustle and excitement everywhere. On the sidewalks crowds of people were hastening toward Times Square and the subways. Kent's long dark car moved smoothly toward the curb and the chauffeur opened the door for them. As they sped away toward Long Island Connie wondered bleakly when she would see all this again. If her father were really ill it might be a long, long time. It might be — never. A knife seemed to pierce her side at the thought and she made a tiny strangled sound.

Sandra's hand covered hers. "Don't worry," she said gently. "He's so strong. He's always been so healthy. Whatever is wrong with him, he has the strength to fight it, and with you there he'll have a better chance. It's going to be all right, Connie. Really it is."

Connie forced a gay smile. "Of course it is."

George had stopped the car, was opening the door for her. This was the end, the very end of her New York life. The clock had struck midnight for Cinderella and she must go back to her corner and the ashes. She did not want Sandra to see the tears she could not conceal.

"Don't get out," she said quickly, "and don't wait for the take-off. It's bad luck to see people go away. And thank you, Sandra. For four years you've been all that a sister could have been to me. I'll never, never forget it. I wish there were something, one single thing, I could do for you."

Sandra smiled. "There is. Give Jeff my love."

TWO

FEELING somewhat conspicuous in the evening dress she had had no opportunity to change out of, Connie pulled the collar of her coat closely around her throat, fastened her seat belt, and looked out with the pang of excitement she always felt just before take-off.

It's going to be all right, Sandra had assured her. All right. Of course. It had to be all right. Nothing could go wrong with Dad. Not possibly. It would have to be all right.

The ground fell away, the plane roared through the star-studded night. Connie unfastened her seat belt, leaned back, and then was aware of the feeling that someone was staring at her insistently. Idly she turned her head and saw the man across the aisle, saw his amusement when she recognized him. It was, she realized in shocked disbelief, her half brother.

"Nick! I didn't expect to see you."

"Why not? He's my father, too, or have you forgotten?" There was an edge of anger to his voice and then he smiled mockingly. "Evening dress, yet! It's a wonder to me you'd bother with Stony Brook. No nightclubs, no opera, no millionaires. A waste of time for you, isn't it?"

Connie felt a surge of familiar anger and fought it down. "Let's not quarrel the minute we meet," she said wearily.

"What have you been doing, Nick? I haven't heard from you in months."

His eyes wavered. "I've been busy," he said at last.

"Working?"

"That doesn't concern you, does it?"

She made no reply, turned her head away, closed her eyes.

"Listen," he said urgently, "I want to have a talk with you before we get to Stony Brook."

"There's nothing to say we haven't said a thousand times before, is there?"

"Just what do you know about Tomas Nuñoz?" Nick demanded.

Her blank stare answered him.

"So Dad never mentioned him to you. Well, there was always a chance." He turned his head away and went to sleep.

Connie sat staring into darkness. Tomas Nuñoz? She was positive that she had never heard the name before. Why was it so important to Nick? What did the man Nuñoz have to do with her father, or, more important, with Nick?

There was no answer to be had. She found herself wondering uneasily why Nick was returning to Stony Brook, which he loathed. She was bitterly aware that he would not return simply because his father was ill. He cared no more for his father than he did for his half sister, or for anyone else except himself. She hoped that he would not add to his father's problems at this time.

Something about her half brother frightened her. He had changed in some intangible way. His mouth seemed weaker, less decisive than ever; his eyes were shifty and yet they had acquired a certain hardness.

She wondered what he had been doing in the months

since she had heard from him, where he was living; above all, *how* he was living. He had always hated having to work; he had resented it. There was a dark corner in his life of which she knew nothing but, warm as it was in the plane, she found herself shivering and pulled her coat more tightly around her.

They were the only passengers to alight at the little airport. The night air bit through Connie's thin evening coat. After the plane took off, the big lights were switched off and the field was dark and empty. Silent as the grave. No, not quite silent. Somewhere there was movement, furtive footsteps.

Connie looked at Nick in alarm, touched his arm for comfort, for protection. He had not heard the sounds.

"Where's that taxi?" he asked irritably. "Get a few hours away from New York and there's no civilized living at all."

In the distance there were headlights that grew nearer and brighter. A car was pulling into the airport. She started toward it in relief.

"Don't move," a harsh voice said. "I have you covered."

Connie stood motionless. Her feet seemed to be rooted to the ground, the blood in her veins had turned to ice. Beside her Nick was breathing in deep gasps, his fingers hurting her arm as they dug in.

"What is it?" she whispered. And saw his face. The color had drained out of it.

"We've got to get away from here," he said, his voice pitched low but betraying his alarm.

"All right," said the harsh voice, "I've been waiting for you. That woman at the lodge said the plane would stop here. I got to talk to you. Let the girl go. I don't want her. But I want you. I mean business. See?"

Although the man spoke with a strong lisp there was something as menacing about his voice as about the words he spoke.

Someone was racing toward them, feet pounding. Connie found herself falling as she was knocked to the ground; there was a heavy blow, a grunt, men were fighting.

Afraid to get up, she turned her head cautiously, heart beating wildly against her side. Nick was crouching, face gray-white, staring at the two men who were pummeling each other savagely. Then one of them broke away, raced across the field, and disappeared in the shadows.

The other man got to his feet, brushed himself off, picked up something, looked at it for a moment, and then shoved it into his pocket.

He came toward them slowly and Nick got to his feet. He was humiliated by the poor part he had played in the struggle and characteristically tried to throw the blame on someone else.

"If the taxi hadn't been so late that guy wouldn't have had a chance at us," he snarled. "What held you up?"

The other man surveyed him without comment. Then he bent to help Connie. "Miss Wyndham, I didn't mean to hurt you. I just wanted to get you out of range of that revolver."

She sagged, blackness coming over her mind, receding, coming back again in waves. He picked her up in his arms and lifted her into the front seat of the car, which was not, she realized, a taxi but a Cadillac. His cheek brushed against hers and she heard him catch his breath. As his arms released her she found herself clinging to him, her only safety in this sudden violence. For a moment, an electric moment, his arms tightened, held her close. Then he released her.

"You all right, Wyndham?" he asked.

"Yeah." It was a grunt. "Let's get moving."

"You might have been killed," Connie sobbed. "He had a gun."

The man laughed softly. "He was too quick in trying to put it away and it caught on his pocket. He couldn't pull it free. Anyhow, I doubt if he planned to use it. Just shock tactics to scare Wyndham."

"But we can't just let him go. We'll have to call the police."

"Forget him," Nick said sharply from the back seat. "Anyhow, you ought to be in bed."

"But—" The words died on Connie's lips as the man who had saved them switched on the dome light and turned to look at Nick. It was a queer, appraising look. Then he turned to Connie. He was a tall, thin young man with blond hair and long narrow eyes. He wasn't in any spectacular way handsome but he was, she thought, quite the most attractive man she had ever seen. For a moment their eyes met and held, questioning each other with curious intentness. Then he smiled.

"I'll get you home at once," he said, and Nick, in the back seat, let out a shaken sigh of relief.

For a few moments the car moved swiftly through the night. Little by little, Connie's breathing came under control, though her thoughts were whirling.

Unexpectedly Nick exclaimed, "This isn't a taxi! Who are you, anyhow?" There was something close to panic in his voice.

"I am Jefferson Gray," the man behind the wheel told

him. "It's hard to get a taxi out here at this time of night, especially after the end of the tourist season, so I told your father I'd come for you." He turned to Connie who was trembling. "Are you all right?" He sounded anxious. "I'll get you to Stony Brook as quickly as I can."

"I'm all right. But what was that all about?" she demanded.

"I think you'll have to ask your brother," Gray said coolly.

"Just what do you mean by that?" Nick demanded. "It was some fool attempting a hold-up."

"But he said —" Connie began.

At the same time Gray exclaimed, "At a deserted airport? He was waiting for someone and that someone seems to have been you, Wyndham."

Nick laughed, an unconvincing sound. "What nonsense!" he said easily. "The whole thing was just a disagreeable incident. It had nothing to do with us."

"Let's hope so." Gray turned off the main highway and followed a winding dirt road through the forest. Here and there, through a clearing, Connie could catch sight of mountains in the distance, dark masses against the early light.

Her heart began to thud again. Nick was lying. He had known the man at the airport. He had been petrified with fear. What had he been doing?

Jefferson Gray had made clear that he did not believe Nick's claim that he did not know the man. He had not attempted to hide his suspicion of her half brother.

"What are you getting at?" Nick was belligerent.

"I mean that we don't want anyone storming around Stony Brook making trouble. Not while Mr. Wyndham is ill. And in my book an armed man means trouble."

"I thought I saw you pick up his revolver."

"I did pick it up."

"Hand it over." There was an arrogant tone in Nick's voice that whipped angry color into Connie's cheeks. Jefferson Gray had saved them both from an unpleasant time if not from something much worse. He deserved courtesy, gratitude, as the very minimum.

"I wouldn't dream of it," Gray said pleasantly. "But get this straight, Wyndham." His voice had hardened. "Keep your friends away from Stony Brook."

"I tell you I don't even know who the man was!"

"Someone has been prowling around Stony Brook, scaring Mrs. Kennedy half to death. Someone tried to break in. Someone asked her tonight whether you were coming up by plane or train. Stood out of the light so she couldn't identify him."

"No one knew I was coming."

"Everyone in town knew after I sent the telegrams. And that guy has been around for several days."

"Damn it, this doesn't concern you," Nick exploded.

"Quiet." There was authority in Gray's voice. "Sounds carry at night and your father needs his rest. I intend to see that he gets it." He shut off the motor and coasted quietly down the steep driveway to the entrance of Stony Brook, a big sprawling lodge, which at this hour was dark and seemed deserted.

Nick got out of the car, carrying his own luggage and ignoring Connie's.

"Is my father — very ill?" she asked, her voice catching.

"You'll do him a world of good," Gray said, avoiding a direct answer. "Before I met you I suspected that from the way he talked; now I am sure of it." He picked up her suitcases.

The air was frosty and, in her evening dress and satin slippers, Connie shivered and pulled her coat more closely around her.

A light flashed on inside and the door was opened cautiously on a chain.

"Who is it?" a woman asked rather nervously. "Oh," as she caught sight of Nick, "it's you, is it?" She opened the door wide, revealing herself to be an elderly woman in a flannel bathrobe. "Well, come on in, but don't make any noise. Your father is sleeping."

She saw the slim girl behind him and her tired face brightened. "Connie, child! I'm that glad to see you, that relieved."

"Got a drink in the place?" Nick asked.

When Mrs. Kennedy shook her head he shrugged his shoulders and went upstairs, carrying a suitcase.

"How is Dad?" Connie asked.

Mrs. Kennedy led the way to the big living room, which, with the kitchen and her own room, took up the whole of the main floor. The room was pine-paneled, with a huge stone fireplace on one side, three bearskin rugs on the floor, a long trestle table with a hanging lamp over it, several shabby couches and nearly a dozen chairs, which, like the draperies that covered the windows, were of dark red. Except for the windows, the wall space, from floor to ceiling, was completely filled with bookshelves.

After switching on lamps, Mrs. Kennedy took a quick look at the white-faced girl and bent over to shove a Cape Cod lighter under the logs in the fireplace. She struck a match.

"Now," she said, "you curl up on that couch and pull the Indian blanket over you. I declare to goodness that dress has no more warmth than a butterfly's wing, though it's just as pretty. The place will be warm in no time. I'll turn up the thermostat, but there's nothing like an open fire for cheer, and I'll make you some coffee."

She looked at the girl's white face. "You're like a ghost. I guess hot milk will do better. Then you can go right to bed and sleep as long as you like. I gave your room a thorough turnout and the bed's made up for you." She hastened out, almost like a woman in flight.

Connie turned to Jefferson Gray, who stood before the fireplace looking down at her. His long narrow eyes held hers in a look that was like recognition, that was warmth and comfort such as she had felt when his arms had held her. Upstairs her father lay ill, perhaps dangerously ill; a half hour ago an unknown man had been lurking with a revolver, waiting for Nick. But for the moment everything faded in the brightness of that long look.

She broke it at length. "Mr. Gray—"

"We're going to be friends, you know," he told her in his easy, relaxed manner. "My name is Jefferson, but Jeff is even easier."

"Jeff." Her hands gripped the blanket Mrs. Kennedy had pulled over her. "I want the truth, please. How bad is Dad's condition?"

He sat on the edge of the couch and his hand covered hers. He spoke very gently. The damage to Bill Wyndham's heart had not been detected in time for treatment.

After a long time Connie asked, her voice choked, "How—long?"

"Perhaps weeks. Perhaps only days. He suffers very little."

"Does he know?"

"Yes. Like you he insisted on learning the whole truth. He has been magnificent. No struggling against the inevitable, no self-pity, no gloom. Why, he has kept the place bright for all of us! He says he has had a good life, rich and rewarding, and he is grateful for it. And he says that death, too, is an adventure, one about which he is intensely curious."

"Thank you," Connie said huskily, "for telling me, and for telling me in the way you did."

Mrs. Kennedy bustled in, gave Jeff a grateful look when she realized that he had broken the news, and after coaxing the girl to drink the glass of hot milk, took her up to her room, helped her undress, and tucked her into bed.

Connie lay staring up into the dark. "Dad," she whispered to herself, "oh, Dad." She turned to bury her face in her pillow, muffling the sobs that shook her slender body.

ii

It was nearly ten o'clock next morning before she awakened. After the noises of the city, even muted as they had been on the fourteenth floor of John Kent's apartment, the deep silence had been restful, the balsam-scented air a delight in contrast with the exhaust fumes of the city.

For a few minutes she lay, half asleep, half awake, gradually becoming aware that her nose and ears were cold. She opened her eyes and remembered that she was in her old room at Stony Brook, and that she had forgotten how chilly late September can be in northern Maine.

Then in a wave of sharp memory she recalled her father's critical condition. Tears welled up in her eyes but she forced them back. She must not cry now. When she faced him, it must be as he would want her to be, courageous, gallant, helping him to maintain his own courage instead of weakening it by any sign of her own grief.

Surely Nick would not dare to worry his father now.

Nick! His terror the night before. He had known who the man with the gun was. He had known what the man wanted. But he had not wanted him pursued, caught, arrested. And Jefferson Gray had been aware of all that, too.

Jeff with his prompt action, his cool courage. Jeff with his arms around her. Into that glowing moment came a chilling memory. Sandra was saying, "Give Jeff my love."

She has given me so much, Connie thought, and that is the only thing she has ever asked of me. For a long time she stared at the ceiling and then, with a determined gesture, she tossed back the soft warm comforter and got up.

Already her luxurious bedroom and bath in the New York duplex seemed far away; they belonged to another life. She looked from the patchwork quilt on her bed to the homemade dresser, from the bearskin rug on the wide floorboards to the rocking chair, from the gay curtains at the window to the view beyond.

She ran to close the window and then stood staring, unaware that she was shivering in her thin pajamas. The sky was a deep cobalt blue against which maples flamed with color, red and yellow, russet and bronze, scarlet and crimson. The spectacular beauty of autumn caught at her breath and, unmindful of the chill in the room, she stood absorbing the magnificence of nature's pageantry. Her heart lifted. While there was so much beauty, the world must be good.

Shivering, she dressed hastily in a soft green wool skirt and matching sweater, slid her slim feet into sturdy Oxfords; brushed her hair until it shone and caught reflections of red.

When she opened her door the house seemed very still,

with the hushed silence that accompanies serious illness. Walking softly, she went downstairs and found Mrs. Kennedy in the huge sunlit kitchen, making pancakes and talking in a low tone to Jefferson Gray.

"Sit here, child." Mrs. Kenney put a cup of coffee before the girl, served a plate with pancakes and crisp bacon. "I declare I don't know how you keep going with so little flesh on you. I'm going to fatten you up if it's the last thing I do. And don't talk to me about keeping your weight down and being fashionably slim and all that nonsense. For nonsense I call it. Your energy and your well-being come from the food you eat and while you are here, young woman, you'll eat hearty or I'll know the reason why."

Connie hugged her, aware that the older woman was determinedly maintaining a cheerful atmosphere.

"Anyhow," Mrs. Kennedy rattled on rather nervously, as though it were safer to keep the conversation in her own hands and under her own direction, "you're built like your mother. You could eat like a stevedore and not gain a pound. But you are more beautiful than your mother ever was. You always were the prettiest girl in the State of Maine but now you're a raving beauty. Not," she added with an attempt at severity that would have convinced no one, "that you're to preen yourself, mind. You aren't responsible for your looks so far."

Connie smiled. "*So far.* What on earth is that supposed to mean?"

"Remember that story about how Abraham Lincoln didn't like a certain man because of his face? And another fellow said that, after all, the poor man wasn't responsible for his face. And old Abe, who always hit the nail on the head, said no young person was responsible for his face but everyone over forty was, because by then the face mirrored all that the person had thought and felt and been up to then. He had made his own face, like it or not."

"What a terrifying thought! Has Nick come down yet?"

The housekeeper shook her head. "You know Nick. He'll probably sleep until noon."

Connie glanced at Jeff, her brows arched, and he answered her mute question by shaking his head slightly. He hadn't told Mrs. Kennedy about that appalling and terrifying experience at the airport. He intended to remain silent for Nick's sake. Again her heart sank. This time Nick was in terrible trouble.

"Is Dad awake yet?"

"Not yet. He sleeps a lot. Best thing for him, of course."

"Then I think — until he wakes up — I'll take a walk."

"May I go with you?" Jeff asked.

For a moment she hesitated, aware of how comforting it would be to have him at her side. Then she remembered the vow she had made to herself.

"Do you mind if I go alone? Oh, I forgot, I have a message for you."

"A message?" He was surprised.

"Sandra Kent sent you her love."

A shadow passed over his face. Then he said, "That was very nice of her."

Hands thrust deep in the pockets of the heavy plaid woodsman's jacket she had found in the hall closet, Connie strolled through the woods, her feet sinking into the soft bed of pine needles. She walked steadily until she was tired and then sat down on a log. For a long time she breathed in the aromatic air, smelling of balsam and pine, feeling the deep stillness of the forest first as a healing balm, then as something more vitally real than anything she had ever known. Her feet were solidly planted on the rich earth.

She caught her breath in delight as a fox stole out from the underbrush and stood with the sun turning its coat red, nose pointed upwards, sniffing for danger. Then it disappeared as silently as it had come.

This was the world her father loved, the world that had filled him with such vast contentment, that had taught him not only to value life but to accept death as naturally as he accepted the change of seasons. Why, she wondered, have I always felt so alien here? She realized abruptly that she had not looked at Maine through her own eyes but through her mother's. She had accepted her mother's feelings as her own.

The immemorial peace of the woods filled her heart. This is where I belong, she thought in profound surprise. I have come home.

She got up from the log, brushed a golden leaf off her skirt, and started back to the lodge. While her courage was still high she went quickly up the stairs and tapped on the half-open door, smiling.

"Hello, Dad."

THREE

WILL Wyndham, propped high on pillows in the big, old-fashioned bed, turned away from the window and held out his arms.

"Welcome home, dear! How lovely you've grown but how metropolitan and sophisticated. You've become more Park Avenue than Stony Brook."

"Don't you believe it!"

His thin arms closed round her, he brushed her cheek with his lips and then released her, smiling. "At least nothing has changed those clear, steady eyes of yours." He turned his head toward the window. "Look at that little fellow, Connie. I've been watching him. Isn't he a beauty?"

Connie looked from the familiar and beloved face, unchanged except for its thinness, to the bird feeder hung outside the window on a long branch of a maple tree, and saw the bird beside it.

"Of course," Wyndham boasted with his old grin, "I set a darned good table for those birds."

She laughed as she kissed him and settled down on the side of the bed. "I've been for a walk," she said gaily, "looking at all the improvements you've made at Stony Brook since I've been away."

"About Stony Brook," her father began. Stopped. "I've left the place to you, Connie." He put out a thin hand to check the words on her lips. "I'd like to talk about it," he assured her. "There must not be any more mistakes."

"Mistakes?" she echoed in surprise.

He nodded. "I've always loved the Maine woods. It seems to me the only real life. But, looking back now, I wonder if I was justified. Don't misunderstand me. It was what I wanted. I've been a happy man always. But there are other ways of life, more important, perhaps; more useful, no doubt; certainly" — and a faint smile flickered across his mouth — "more remunerative. Half a dozen times I was offered jobs that would take me down to the cities, give me a good income, but I always said no. I'd found my rightful place here, the life, at least, that was the right one for me."

"Then what worries you?" Connie reached for his hand, held it clasped in both of hers.

"Your mother. She was never happy here. I can see that now. She would have preferred the glamour of the city but she stayed here because she felt it was her duty."

"She loved you," Connie said softly.

"Love should not have to become a sacrifice. That is why I wanted to talk to you about Stony Brook. As I said, I have left it to you. Nick wouldn't have it as a gift except for what he could get out of it. Anyhow, my son has had more than his share, far more, and at the expense of my daughter." As Connie started to interrupt he said, "I know you have never complained about what I did for Nick. But your generosity should not be taken advantage of. It wouldn't be honest of me to permit it.

"What I want you to understand clearly is this, Connie. It's true I used to hope that either you or Nick would want to live here, but it's a long time since I've known that Nick hates everything about the place.

"So far as you are concerned, if you don't like it, really like it, I'd rather you sold out. There's a lot of acreage. Perhaps some rustic cabins could be built and the place turned into a really profitable lodge for summer people or hunters. But don't do anything hasty. John Kent will advise you. The place should bring enough to carry you for a few years, at least, if you decide to sell."

Seeing her expression, realizing how close she was to breaking down, he brightened with an effort. "Well, that's enough about that," he said cheerfully. "All over and done with and we won't mention it again. Now let me tell you about the wonderful thing that has happened to me."

Connie caught her breath. How could a man who had heard his death sentence speak like that?

"If you'll open the middle drawer of my desk, dear, you'll find a large package."

While Connie set it on the bed where her father could reach it easily, he went on, "You know how stamp collectors are." He stopped to laugh at himself. "But of course you don't. Anyhow, a correspondence frequently springs up with a fellow collector; less frequently some spark is struck out of those letters and a friendship develops. I have made at least three such friendships with men whom I have never met, but we have exchanged views for so many years that in some ways we know each other better than we do people we meet every day. And, of course, this is how I first came to know John Kent.

"Well, one of my correspondents was a charming Mexican, Tomas Nuñoz, a widower like myself, except that he had lost not only his wife but his children. It's a queer thing, Connie, how it came about. Here I am, a guide in the Maine woods. There he was, a great landowner and aristocrat, a man who had traveled widely and had been educated at a great university. You would think we had nothing in common. And we turned out to have just about everything in common. Everything that counts."

His fingers were fumbling with the cords that tied the package and Connie, vowing not to mention that Nick already knew about the Nuñoz collection, got scissors, cut the string, removed the wrapping paper, took out the stamp album and placed it where he could reach it without effort.

"Nuñoz had a bad heart," Wyndham went on. "One day I got a letter, written by his nurse, in answer to one of mine. She said he was very ill. I didn't hear again for some weeks. Then I was informed by the executor of his estate that Nuñoz had died and had left me his stamp collection. Only a few days ago this package reached me and I haven't even opened it yet."

He turned the pages eagerly. "Look at this, a Guatemalan stamp, showing a quetzal bird. Now the original value of that stamp when it was printed in 1881 was two centavos. Today, it would be worth about fifty cents. But some printer put the die together wrong and stood the poor bird on his head. Technically, that is called an inverted center. And because of the error, the stamp is now worth about fifty dollars."

For a few moments he sat staring at the stamp without seeing it. Then he said abruptly, "Connie, I'd like you to give my stamp collection, including this windfall from my old friend Nuñoz, to John Kent. You don't care for stamps and he does. Anyhow, it came to me from a good friend. I'd like it to be passed on to another. Is that all right with you?"

"Of course," she said huskily.

"Then I'll dictate the letter and you write it so that I

can sign it, will you? I don't think I ought to put things off too long." He closed the album wearily and Connie took it away.

When she went down to lunch she found Nick lounging in the living room, flipping the pages of an illustrated magazine. He seemed to have recovered from his shock and terror of the night before.

"Picture of your friend Alexandra Kent," he said. "Heiress to thirty million. Thirty million! The man who gets her will be sitting pretty. She could be a lot less attractive than she is and still be worth having."

"You barely know her," Connie said angrily. "You have no right to speak of her like that, as though she had no qualities of her own."

"Okay. Okay. Don't get excited. How's Dad?" He made no attempt to conceal his indifference.

"He's very weak but he is wonderful, Nick. He has been talking and laughing, just as cheerful as can be, acting as gay as though he didn't have a single trouble in the world. He even told me about his stamp collection."

"Stamp collection?" Nick looked up alertly, tossing the magazine aside. "Did he mention Tomas Nuñoz?"

"Yes, and he started looking through the stamps Señor Nuñoz bequeathed him, but he was too tired to go on. How did you know about it, Nick?"

"A friend of mine is a stamp dealer. He read about the Nuñoz collection, an article saying a lot of collectors had hoped it would come on the open market so they could bid for it, but he had left it intact to a fellow enthusiast, no less than William Wyndham of Stony Brook."

"Dad is terribly excited about it."

"He should be. Know what that collection is valued at? Thousands and thousands of dollars."

"For heaven's sake! I don't think Dad has any idea of its financial value."

"That doesn't surprise me."

"He hasn't had a chance to look at it," Connie said defensively.

"Well, at least," Nick said in a tone of satisfaction, "it will be something."

Connie's face stiffened. "What on earth do you mean by that?"

Nick looked at her, looked away, avoiding the challenge, the accusation in her eyes. "There's no sense in not being practical, Connie. There's nothing unfeeling in thinking ahead. We have ourselves to consider. About all Dad has to leave us is Stony Brook and that ought to be called Stony Broke, if you ask me. We'll be lucky to get fifteen thousand out of it, maybe not more than ten. But with this stamp collection we'll have something with a real commercial value."

"Dad intends to leave it to Mr. Kent."

"Kent!" Nick shouted.

"Quiet. Keep your voice down or you'll disturb Dad. He has every right to do as he pleases with his own property."

"Kent!" Nick raged, though he lowered his voice. "That guy has millions and we have peanuts. I'm not going to sit back and let that money go without a fight, I can tell you right now."

"It isn't your money. You won't do anything to upset Dad or his wishes." For once the full strength of her jaw was in evidence. "You've hurt him enough. Things are going to be done exactly the way he wants them done."

Nick's eyes narrowed. "Well," he said softly, "so that's it. You are going to play along with Kent, are you? Maybe you are smart, at that. But just remember one thing: you've got to count me in. Or else."

Outside the living room door Mrs. Kennedy said, "Oh, there you are, Mr. Gray. I was just ready to call you for lunch."

Nick's eyes leaped to Connie's in alarm. How long had Jefferson Gray been outside the door? How much had he overheard?

ii

On a crisp cold day, three weeks later, the minister concluded his moving words and sprinkled a handful of earth over the open grave.

Connie was aware of the unexpectedly large crowd that had assembled to pay its last respects to Bill Wyndham and of Jefferson Gray's comforting hand on her arm as he led her away from the cemetery.

He helped her into his car. "It will be warm in a few minutes." He turned to Nick, who had climbed into the back seat. "You still intend to go down to New York on the afternoon train?"

"I've got my luggage right here," Nick informed him. "There's nothing to keep me in this neck of the woods."

"There's Connie," Jeff reminded him. "It's going to be lonely for her here. And, of course, if you leave I can't very well stay on."

Nick laughed. "That's your lookout. And from what I overheard of that telephone conversation you had with Kent a week ago, I'd think you had overstayed your leave of absence and then some. All those explanations for hanging around up here, week after week, didn't seem to be going down very well. And as far as Connie is concerned, she has proved that she can look out for herself. Dad disinherited me and left everything to — guess who? If she's lonely at the lodge that's her headache."

Connie saw the anger in Jeff's face, saw him struggle for control. When he spoke his voice was impersonal. "There's another thing, Nick. You've avoided every effort I've made to discuss it, but I've got to say something now."

"What's that?" Nick asked tightly.

"That man at the airport, the one with the revolver, meant real trouble. Watch yourself."

"I never saw him before in my life," Nick said.

"How do you know?" Jeff asked softly. "It was dark on the field after the plane took off. Very dark. Except when my car headlights were directly on you, I could see you and Connie only as shadows. And you had your back turned to the man."

"Don't interfere in my affairs," Nick said. "I mean that, Gray."

Without further comment Jeff drove to the station. "Here you are, Nick. You'll have quite a wait but I want to get Connie back to Stony Brook as soon as I can. She's had all she can take."

Nick leaned forward, touched Connie's shoulder. She turned around, her face white, her eyes enormous, her lips quivering. Something in her expression checked him in what he had been about to say.

"Well, take care of yourself, Connie. Don't hang around the woods too long or you might be snowed in for the winter, and how you'd hate that!" He started to get out of the car and added casually, as though it were merely an afterthought, "Oh, by the way, what did you do with the stamps?"

"Stamps?"

"Yes, stamps," he said impatiently. "Dad's collection and the Nuñoz lot."

"I put them out of the way somewhere. After that one time, Dad was never able to look at them again, and Dad's lawyer told me not to send them to Mr. Kent until the estate is settled."

Nick's fingers tightened cruelly on her shoulder. "Remember what I told you, Connie. Don't try any tricks or you'll be one very, very sorry girl. That's fair warning." He picked up his suitcase and went into the station without a backward look.

"Some day," Jeff said, "I'm going to bring one right up from the floor and lay out that dear brother of yours. If he ever tries to make trouble for you, Connie, just leave him to me."

The car moved off slowly. Little by little, as it grew warmer, Connie relaxed. For three weeks she had rested little, rarely leaving her father's bedside. His collapse occurred the very morning after she had had her long talk with him but he had lingered on, day after day, sometimes conscious, more often sunk in a deep sleep.

Once Jeff put his foot on the brake as a deer leaped across the road. Otherwise the landscape was empty, gray and empty, the bare branches of trees reaching into the leaden sky from which scattered snowflakes were drifting. Already the dark days were on them and the light was fading from the sky though it was barely four-thirty.

"How desolate it is!" she exclaimed suddenly. "How bleak and sad now that the wonderful foliage is gone."

"At least," Jeff said, "when the leaves fall, the evergreens come into their own. Isn't that hemlock a beauty?"

"You sound like Dad," Connie said, and caught her breath on a sob.

Beside her Jeff moved, his gloved hand covered hers, held it comfortingly. During the past days Connie had, without realizing it, come more and more to rely on this pleasant young man with his unstressed charm and his quiet way of relieving her of responsibility, of being on hand when he was needed, of effacing himself when she preferred to be alone. Absorbed in her father's needs, she had given him little thought. Now she looked up and met the steady look in his eyes.

"I don't know what I'd do without you, Jeff. Nick — well —"

"Forget about Nick," he said brusquely.

"I can't forget about him. Dad was his father, too. Jeff, what's wrong with him? He has never let me speak about that terrible man at the airport. He walks out of the room or just tells me to forget it. But he — that gun —"

"I have the gun," Jeff reminded her. "I'll try to find out in whose name it is registered."

"What did the man want?"

"I haven't the faintest idea. Obviously Nick has been mixing in dangerous company. A lot worse company than he had any idea of. If he would just come out with it, tell the truth about what his problem is, I might be able to help him. But he seems to think he can handle it alone."

"And you don't think he can."

"I don't know," Jeff admitted. "The one thing I am sure of is that you must not be involved with Nick or his — friends. Not in any circumstances. I don't like having to say this about your brother, about Bill Wyndham's son, but he's not above making unscrupulous use of you to save his own worthless skin."

"I'll be all right," she assured him. "I heard the man say he didn't want me."

"He said that!" The words were almost a shout. Then Jeff cleared his throat. "Connie." He came to a full stop.

"What is it?"

"I don't want you to do without me. Ever."

FOUR

As SHE turned to him in stunned surprise he said, "I know this is a poor time to be talking about myself — about us — but now that Nick has gone I can't remain at Stony Brook unless I can stay as your husband. I love you, Connie. But you must know that."

Her eyes were wide, the passionate warm lips were parted in astonishment. "Jeff! I didn't know."

"That's why I've stayed on. I've been fully recovered for weeks but there was no one else to help you."

For a moment the world wheeled, then righted itself again. Jefferson Gray loved her. He wanted to marry her. After the heartbreak of the past weeks, when she had believed she could never be happy again, a miracle had happened. Jeff! The nightmare of the unknown future was gone, dissolved in sunlight. The future meant Jeff. Jeff to love her, to take care of her, to protect her. Jeff with his kindness and his gaiety, his gentleness and understanding, his devastating attractiveness.

His devastating attractiveness. His charm. Someone else had said that of him. She recalled Sandra's voice, speaking softly; Sandra with radiance in her face. Jefferson Gray, she had said, was the man her father designed as his successor. And she must marry a man who could take the place of the son her father had never had. She had said, "Give Jeff my love."

Always, always, Connie thought, I've hurt people I loved, people like Dad, like Sandra. I promised myself I would never do it again. Sandra has given me unstinting loyalty and kindness and yet, time after time, the men she liked have preferred me.

Now there was Jeff. Rebellion rose like a flame in Connie. She couldn't give up Jeff. She couldn't be expected to. He loved her. You can't turn love on and off like a faucet, she told herself. Even if she gave up Jeff, there was no reason to believe that he would turn to Sandra.

But that wasn't true. She was pretending to herself that marriage with her would be the best thing for Jeff. But would it? According to Nick, Jeff had already had trouble explaining to John Kent why he had remained so long at Stony Brook. Perhaps he had already endangered the future that promised to be so dazzling. And she had no reason to believe he could find happiness only with her. That was wishful thinking. Sandra was deeply attracted to him. When he returned to his office, when he was once again under Kent's dominating influence, he would be thrown with her more and more.

"I love Stony Brook," Jeff was saying. "I want to buy the place and run it, Connie. Run it with you, my darling. This is the rich, real life."

"You sound like Dad," she said again, fighting to keep her voice steady.

"I'd like to resemble him. He was the best and the wisest man I ever knew."

"Jeff —"

"Don't say anything now. I'll take you home, move to that motel in the village for the night, and tomorrow I'll go down to New York. When you have an answer ready, send for me and I'll come at once."

"New York?" She was startled. She was not prepared to have the break come so soon, to have it be so final.

"I'll have to explain to Mr. Kent, and that's not going to be the easiest job in the world after all he has done for me. It will be difficult for him to understand why I prefer this life to the one," and he smiled faintly, "he has all mapped out for me."

Connie's thoughts were whirling. Jeff had, she realized, been profoundly influenced by Bill Wyndham's personality, by the serenity that comes from a fulfilled life. But Jeff had not had time to learn whether, when her father's influence was removed, he would still find this quiet and almost primitive life as rewarding for him as he would the prestige and power and wealth of the life Kent had to give him.

For the first time in her young life the happiness and welfare of someone else was more important to her than what happened to herself. And staring through the windshield at the drifting snowflakes, Connie discovered, without preparation, without warning, that she had fallen in love. Fallen in love without even knowing that it was happening to her until it was too late.

Too late. Warm as the car was, her hands were cold. No, it was her heart that was cold.

You've got to make him believe you, she told herself. Aloud she said in a voice she did not recognize as her own because it was so contemptuous, "You mean you are going to throw away the future that Mr. Kent offered you, give up all opportunity of accomplishing something, of being somebody, give up New York for the woods, give up glamour and comfort and excitement for winter and cold and darkness?"

There was a long silence. When Jeff spoke at last he said

quietly, "I guess that's my answer. But there is something you forget, Connie."

"What's that?"

"You think of this life as though it would be a kind of eternal winter. But remember: spring always comes."

"It comes to New York, too," she reminded him. "I know Dad loved this life. But he was different; he was special. And he told me, the only time we really had a chance to talk after I came up here, that he didn't want me to be a sacrifice to his dreams as my mother had been."

"I — see."

She shot him a quick look from under long lashes, conscious of the pain she had inflicted, longing to heal it as only she could do, but aware that what she was doing was necessary for his own sake, to prevent him from ruining his life for what might, after all, prove to be only an impulse.

"Jeff," she said, "you could have a brilliant future. Sandra told me her father hoped that some day you would be in a position to take over the burdens for him."

"You'd like that, wouldn't you?" he said oddly.

Sandra would like that. The words trembled on Connie's lips until she was half afraid that she had spoken them aloud.

At Stony Brook Jeff helped her out of the car, spoke to Mrs. Kennedy, who came forward to take the girl comfortingly in her arms. In a very few minutes Jeff came down the stairs, carrying his suitcases.

Connie's heart dropped like a plummet. She did not want him to leave. She wanted to have him take her in his arms, tell her he'd never let her go. She wanted to say, in those beautiful words of Ruth: "Whither thou goest, I will go; and where thou lodgest, I will lodge; thy people shall be my people, and thy God my God."

He brushed his lips lightly over her forehead, a brotherly sort of kiss. "Anything I can do for you in New York?"

Head high, she smiled at him gallantly. "Give Sandra my love."

ii

During the next few weeks Connie, with Mrs. Kennedy's help, prepared to close Stony Brook. So far she had made no attempt to sell it. That could wait for the future. She could not bear to part with it, but without ready money it could not be maintained. Anyhow, Connie was forced to admit that she was unable to run it by herself.

As the lodge represented practically all that her father had to leave, there was the pressing problem of money for her support. If only Nick were different. If only he loved this place as her father had loved it, as she loved it, they could work together to build a future. But Nick had no interest in Stony Brook beyond any money that might come from its sale and he had been bitter when he learned that it had been left to her alone, in spite of the fact that he had already received far more than its value.

Where was he and what was he doing? For a few days after he had left, presumably to go to New York, Connie was haunted by fear for him. At night she dreamed of a shadowy figure that stalked him along the streets of New York. But he did not write, there was no word at all, and little by little, distance dimmed her fear. Perhaps the whole thing had been a mistake. Perhaps, after all, the man had not been looking for Nick, he had mistaken him for someone else.

Over and over, Connie found herself thinking of her father's idea of building rustic cottages to attract hunters and vacationers, but a man was needed to cope with the details.

There were times when all her will power was required to control the dreams that took possession of her mind, romantic dreams of Jeff sitting beside her, looking into the crackling fire; Jeff's laughter breaking the stillness of the house; Jeff's love turning the hours to magic.

It surprised her now to realize how profoundly she had changed in those few weeks at Stony Brook. While she still delighted in New York and missed it, she had discovered in that fleeting moment when she learned that Jeff loved her and wanted to marry her that she could be happy wherever he was. Perhaps only where he was.

No, she told herself sternly, don't even dare to think of that. You are going to earn your own living. You'll have to go to New York, after all. But not in Jefferson Gray's world. Never again in Jefferson Gray's world.

Jeff had not written. Every day she had waited for the mailman, had riffled through the letters, had turned back from the mailbox with a sinking heart, feeling curiously forlorn and deserted.

The only word she had received to feed her starving heart was the letter of condolence Sandra had sent about her father's death. After speaking sympathetically of Connie's loss, she had mentioned her debut and the resulting heavy schedule of social engagements. At the close of her letter she made a passing reference to Jeff.

"He looks well, I think. Better than he has for a long time. I am glad that his visit to Stony Brook did so much for his health, especially as he is working hard now to make up for the time he spent there.

"Of course we understand why it was. He couldn't leave while you needed him. After all, there was, as he says, no one else to help you. I do think he's the best-natured and kindest man I know, but I suppose, like most people of his type, he'll be exploited. Last night we saw the opening of *Black Plumes*. He mentioned you."

Connie had read and reread the letter. *He mentioned you*. Though not put into words, there had been an impression that Sandra and Jeff had become a closed corporation, one in which there was no place for Connie Wyndham.

And that, too, she reminded herself, was her own choice. She could have married Jeff. Instead, she had sent him away from Stony Brook, sent him back to Sandra and the future John Kent had planned for him. A brilliant future. And she had been right. Jeff's proposal had been an impulsive action, a part of his innate kindness. He had been sorry for her. And there had been no one else to help.

Connie plunged into the work of closing the lodge, keeping so busy that she fell into bed at night exhausted and too weary to think.

Early in December, when she had turned the key in the door of Stony Brook and said good-by to a weeping Mrs. Kennedy, she took the train for New York. When she climbed the ramp at Grand Central Station she emerged to lights and noise, huge advertisements, trundling carts loaded with luggage, people hastening toward the gates to their trains or lined up before ticket windows or crowded around the great circular information booth in the middle of the huge room.

For a moment she stood absorbing impressions in delight. New York! New York at last. Then, seeing the redcap pushing a cart that held her luggage toward the Vanderbilt Avenue exit and the taxi-stand, she ran to retrieve the suitcases and leave them in a coin locker. After she had removed the key she stood uncertain, fully aware for the first time that this was indeed a strange arrival in New York.

This time she was not being met by the Kent car. This time she would not be driven to the Park Avenue apartment to take possession of her old rooms. There had been no hint, no suggestion, in Sandra's letter that she would be glad to see Connie, that she expected her to return to New York. The past was gone. She was on her own.

Why, Connie thought with a shock of surprise, I don't even know where to go. She went out onto Forty-second Street as a taxi drew up at the curb and two girls got out.

"Plenty of time," one of them said. "The train for Greenwich won't leave for ten minutes."

"Connie!" cried the other. "Where have you been, stranger?"

"Hello, Mary. How nice to see you, Florence." Connie explained that she had just come from Maine where her father had recently died, and the two girls expressed sympathy.

"I saw Sandra just last night," the girl called Florence said. "I asked about you. She said she didn't expect you to be in New York this winter."

"Oh, well, it was a sudden idea."

"Sandra was with a dreamboat," Mary said. "Man named Jefferson Gray. It was easy to see what is going to happen there. She could hardly keep her eyes off him."

"Neither could you," Florence laughed.

"I'd try to cut Sandra out if I thought I had half a chance," Mary confessed.

"You mean they are actually engaged?" Connie managed to retain the smile on her lips. "She didn't tell me."

"Not yet, but the poor man hasn't a prayer. You should watch Sandra's father. He's always putting in an appearance at parties, which certainly has never been his line in the past, sort of looking on and watching the competition. He doesn't want his fair-haired boy straying. I'll bet if Jefferson Gray so much as dated another girl he would find himself joining the unemployed."

"And thirty million ain't hay," commented the other girl.

Connie was stung into blinding anger. "Jefferson Gray isn't the man to marry for money," she said hotly. "What's more, Sandra doesn't need to have her father keep an eye on her admirers to prevent them from straying. She is lovely and charming and she has always been terribly popular."

The two girls looked at each other awkwardly.

"I guess I spoke out of turn," Mary admitted. "I forgot how close you and Sandra have always been."

"Time for our train," Florence exclaimed, and they hurried away in relief.

"Give me a ring soon," Mary called back.

"Soon," Connie promised. But she knew she would not keep that promise. There was no place in the life of debutantes for a working girl.

FIVE

CONNIE fastened the collar of her coat high around her chin. The sky was as gray as when she had left Maine, but the air was many degrees milder. Instead of snow there was a chilly drizzle; instead of balsam the air smelt of exhaust.

She fumbled for coins, tucked under her arm with some difficulty the huge bulk of the *New York Sunday Times,* and turned into the nearest lunch room where she sat at a bare table and ordered breakfast.

After a cup of hot coffee her courage began to stream back. The depression left by her meeting with her two friends had faded. Through the rivulets of water on the window her eyes rose from the wet street, the plodding people in plastic raincoats or huddled under umbrellas, up and up the front of an office building across the street. It seemed, literally, to scrape the sky, to thrust its roof through the low-hanging clouds. She imagined the thousands of people who earned their living in that building, the countless ways of earning it, and excitement licked along her veins.

"New York, here I come," she told herself. "I'm going to conquer you. But I'll have to plan. First, I must find a place to live and then I'll look for a job."

She removed the Rooms for Rent and Help Wanted sections from the paper and began to mark ads. Half an hour later, aware that she had occupied her table much too long, she folded up the list of rooms that she had marked, and went out to face New York, head carried high, eyes shining, walking with the grace and distinction that had always characterized her. Absorbed in her thoughts, she was unaware of the many eyes that turned for a second look at the girl who went past, high of heart, eager to confront the future.

After the sixth disappointment, she realized that the description of a room as given in an ad and the reality were poles apart. "Completely furnished" turned out to mean a studio couch with broken springs, linoleum on the floor, and an electric plate for cooking, set in a tiny and airless closet in the room which served as bedroom and living room.

"Share kitchen" proved to be a kind of community scramble with five other roomers in a big, cockroach-ridden kitchen in an old-fashioned Pullman apartment.

"Walk-up" meant a sixth floor apartment at which she arrived panting, her heart pounding, leg muscles quivering.

Sometimes the block in which the apartment was located was enough to discourage her, a block that just escaped being a tenement section, with screaming children playing ball in the street, ducking agilely among trucks and taxis and buses, with grave risk to life and limb.

One by one she crossed off the places she had inspected. The next address was in the East Seventies and she climbed the subway stairs wearily and found herself outside a remodeled building with an old-fashioned minute lobby and a row of bells. Each one had over it a card bearing the name of a tenant. The one Connie was looking for was Debaney.

The advertisement read:

> Will share furnished apartment with another working girl. References exchanged. Cooking privileges. Private garden.

The address had been given and the name Lillian Debaney.

The prospect of a private garden had attracted Connie. She pressed the button and the inner door clicked. She stepped into a dimly lighted narrow hallway, out of which rose a steep staircase. Then the door at the back of the hall opened and a girl asked, "You looking for Lil Debaney?"

"Yes, I've come to see about the room you advertised."

"This way. The hall's always dark. Someday the landlord is going to put in more than a twenty-five-watt bulb and we'll all fall over in sheer surprise."

Connie went down the dark narrow hall, her coat dripping on the floor, shoes making a squashy sound, guided by the girl's breezy voice and a dim light at the end. The girl stood aside to let her enter the apartment.

"I'm Lil Debaney. Heavens, you are soaking wet. Here, give me your coat and sit over there. No, not on that chair; the springs are busted. Take the couch. I'll hang this coat up to dry and bring you some coffee. No trouble at all."

The two girls looked at each other curiously and appraisingly, and then Connie said, "Thank you," settled down on the couch, and looked around her.

Her first impression was that Lillian Debaney was very blonde, her hair done in an extreme style. She wore lounging pajamas of coral satin with high-heeled satin slippers.

She had a round face and more makeup than Connie was accustomed to, brown eyes, a small turned-up nose, and an exceptionally big mouth with a wide, warm smile, which was her chief attraction. It was hard not to respond to her smile.

The living room was small and shabby but cheerful, with bright cretonne covers for the chairs and couch. On one side there was a small kitchenette in which Lil Debaney was rattling cups. There were venetian blinds at the two windows opposite the door. Connie peered out through the gray rain onto a court, with the walls of apartment buildings rising to shut out the light on three sides. The small garden wasn't much bigger than the drawing-room carpet in the Park Avenue apartment. It contained a dwarf tree, some bushes in tubs, and a couple of canvas chairs that looked uninviting, soaked as they were with the rain.

"What's your name?" called the girl in the kitchen.

"Constance Wyndham."

"Working in Manhattan?"

"No, I'll have to start job-hunting tomorrow."

"Oh." There was a slight chill in the other girl's voice. "I've been getting eighteen dollars a week for that extra bedroom and kitchen privileges."

"That's fair enough."

"Paid in advance," Lil said warningly. She came in to set down a tray and serve coffee and cinnamon buns that were piping hot and dripping with butter. "I just took them out of the oven. Have some. These are my specialty." She looked rather dubiously at Connie. "The girl who has been living here got transferred out to Indianapolis. We got along fine."

Connie smiled. "I think," she said honestly, "that you'd

be easy to get along with." She was aware from her disappointing experience in room hunting that it would be difficult to find as pleasant a place as this for the money, especially a place where she could prepare her own meals, which would be a tremendous saving. She was aware, too, that there was a simple friendliness about the other girl.

Nevertheless, she hesitated. Those flamboyant lounging pajamas, so out of place in this environment; the extreme hairdo and the makeup, all aroused a kind of hostility and distrust. So she was surprised to hear herself ask, "When could I move in?"

"Today, if you like. The room's all ready. Want to look at it?"

There were two small bedrooms, each with a single bed, a chest of drawers, a small desk and straight chair, and an armchair with a floor lamp beside it. The narrow closet did not seem capable of holding a single day's changes of clothes for Sandra. But then, Connie reminded herself, she wasn't Sandra.

"Then I'll go back to Grand Central for my luggage and get settled so I can start job-hunting tomorrow."

"What kind of job are you looking for?" The question was not meant to be impertinent. Lil Debaney was genuinely interested and she revealed her interest as unabashedly as a child.

"All I'm trained for is typing and shorthand."

"Ever worked before?"

Connie shook her head.

"You know, Constance—what do people call you? Connie?—well, you know, Connie, with your looks I could maybe get you a job where I work. I model for Céleste. There's not an opening right now but with your looks and figure you could sell just about anything you put on. The work is hard but the pay is better than you're apt to earn as a beginner in an office, and you get clothes at a discount. Sometimes, even, if they've been shown a bit, you get them free."

She indicated the coral lounging pajamas. "Madame gave me these and they wholesale for sixty-nine fifty. And only a small rip in the fabric. You could hardly tell."

"Oh, I don't think —" Connie began.

"You should see Céleste's," Lil told her persuasively. "It's one of the smartest little shops off Madison. Glamorous. Wall-to-wall carpeting and nothing so common as clothes racks. Just maybe one smart dress on display. Paneled walls and foam-rubber chairs for the customers. And the customers! Why, honey, we get most of the Long Island crowd and a lot of debutantes and sometimes actresses from the movies and Broadway and television. Jeepers, you get so a celebrity means nothing to you. Just nothing. Part of the day's work."

Connie was about to say that she knew the shop well; it was one of Sandra's favorites, and she had often gone there with her, but she decided to say nothing. Of all the places in the world, she did not want to work where Sandra could see her, could feel sorry for her; a place where her presence might cause embarrassment for them both.

Nonetheless, there had been a warm-hearted kindness in Lil's offer, an unusual generosity to a stranger, and Connie felt the beginning of a real friendship.

"That's wonderfully kind," she said, "but I expect I had better stick to what I know. For a while, at least. When I get my feet under me, I'll know better what I can do."

Lil studied her, still with that open, childlike curiosity.

She was aware that, under a determined brightness, her new roommate was terrified of the ordeal ahead of her.

"It will all be easier than you think," she said encouragingly. "People are nice as a rule. If you let them be. And with your looks you are going to mow them down, though I expect you are used to that. Maybe I oughtn't to be taking in so much competition."

They were laughing like old friends when Connie left to get her luggage. As she braved the rain in the street again she was unexpectedly light-hearted. She had never before met anyone like Lil. She was aware that the girl was kind, that the small bedroom was clean and comfortable, that the little garden, dismal now, would be waiting when spring came back again.

Spring always comes, Jeff had told her. She must not think of that. She must not let herself imagine what it would be like to have him at her side now, to be planning a future together. Marriage with Sandra would establish Jeff's future. Anyhow, she had no right to take Jeff from Sandra, no right to spoil both their lives. She had made her choice and she must abide by it.

Late in the afternoon she returned with her luggage. Lil helped her unpack and stow away clothes and odds and ends of belongings.

After a light supper, which Lil insisted on preparing because it was her first night — ("Anyhow, I want to show off what a good cook I am") — Connie went to bed, aware that no one in the world, except for her new roommate, knew where she was. It was a curious feeling.

Her last thought was the surprised realization that the two girls had forgotten all about exchanging references. They had, after all, taken each other on trust.

SIX

AT ELEVEN the next morning Connie waited in an employment agency so big and impersonal that she wondered how a person could emerge feeling like himself and not merely like a piece of merchandise. She filled out forms and finally sat down beside a big desk for an interview.

Her heart was thumping and her hands were cold. In Sandra's world all that had ever been required of her was that she should be attractive, suitably dressed, and well mannered. Charm, personality, beauty were all extras. In that pleasant, comfortable world, no one had ever weighed her potentialities, her intelligence, her abilities. Now she was pitted against a new and hostile world. She would have to make her way with her own abilities. How would she measure up?

The interviewer was a tall, businesslike woman of middle age, who surveyed Connie keenly from the glossy hair to the simple wool dress, from the neat gloves to the trim shoes, before she looked at the application blank.

"A good school and good training," she commented, "but no experience." Unexpectedly she smiled. "Don't look so alarmed, Miss Wyndham. Anything we try seems frightening as long as it is strange to us, but trying new things can be an adventure, too. And remember that every single one of the countless millions who are working today had to start sometime." Her smile deepened. "And probably everyone of them was just as uneasy about it as you are."

Connie found herself remembering Lil's words: "People are nice, as a rule. If you let them be." She returned the interviewer's smile. "I guess I forgot that I'm not special," she admitted. "I'll try to remember that pretty much the same thing happens to everyone. The only thing that bothers me is that the application blank doesn't show very much. It doesn't seem to represent me at all."

"About all it can show is what a person is trained to do, not what he will do. That's where the most important factors come in: the willingness to work and the ability to get along with people. In the long run that is what counts most."

She filled out a slip. "I'm going to send you to a law firm, Emery & Emery, which has a vacancy in their stenographic pool. It's a pleasant place to work. They won't expect miracles the first day and they won't be upset if you make mistakes. Everyone makes mistakes in the beginning. Good luck, Miss Wyndham."

Impulsively Connie held out her hand. "Thank you for being so kind. You've propped up my courage."

It seemed to Connie a kind of omen that the address of the law firm of Emery & Emery was the tall building she had seen the day before on Forty-second Street. The great directory in the lobby seemed to contain as many names as the whole Manhattan telephone book. The law firm was on the thirty-sixth floor, where a smiling girl at the reception desk asked, "May I help you?"

Connie, feeling awkward and self-conscious, handed her the slip from the employment agency; she was directed to the office manager, a quiet-spoken, middle-aged man with a bald head. Half expecting some sort of inquisition, Connie was surprised when, instead of asking questions that were bound to reveal her inexperience, he spoke of her college and told her proudly that his daughter was a freshman there, studying on a scholarship. It was all unexpectedly friendly and informal.

In a shorter time than she would have believed possible, she was assigned a desk in a room with half a dozen other girls and provided with notebooks, pencils, and stationery.

The girl who had brought her the supplies said, "I am Jane Clark. It's awful being new, isn't it? Why don't you lunch with me today? There's a good cafeteria in the basement, not too expensive, and I'll give you the lowdown on Emery & Emery."

When they had slid their trays onto a vacant table in the basement cafeteria, they studied each other, half smiling. Jane Clark was a small girl with sandy hair, a puckish face with the corners of the mouth turned up, a scattering of freckles across her nose. She wore a simple but well-cut dress of dark green wool with a twist of gold metal that served for a belt and trim shoes with medium heels. The polish on her nails was pale and inconspicuous. She had a scrubbed look that was attractive.

While they ate their lunch she explained that she was a graduate of Barnard and that her job with Emery & Emery was the only one she had ever held.

"And so far as I'm concerned, I hope I will never have to change," she said. "The people are nice, most of them, and though they expect a lot of work, at least the other girls always help if you get loaded with more than you can handle.

"You'll be taking dictation from four men: the big boss, Stephen Emery; the junior partner, his younger brother Colin; Taylor Grant, a young lawyer who is just breaking in; and Tommy Beam, the office manager, whom you have already met. It's a small outfit but it has a very high standing. In fact, the present generation is the fourth to run Emery & Emery. Once you get used to the legal phraseology and the way they have of putting in all the whereases, you won't find it hard."

"Do you think I can handle the work?" Connie asked anxiously. "This is my very first job."

Jane laughed impishly. "It isn't a question of whether you can handle the work; it's a question of whether you can handle Junior."

"Junior?"

"Colin Emery, the junior partner. The big boss is slow and deliberate and dignified. He doesn't know we're alive except as impersonal machines. But his younger brother is a wolf. So watch yourself." She added frankly, "We've never had a girl as pretty as you are in the office so you can expect a conflagration."

That afternoon, seated at her desk before a typewriter and feeling both businesslike and nervous, Connie met the rest of the staff. There were several girls of about her own age and two women who were considerably older. The officer manager, whom everyone called Tommy, came around several times, bringing her forms to copy and giving her a few simple letters, endeavoring to make her feel at ease. The young lawyer, Taylor Grant, was a recent law school graduate and trying very hard to look as though he had years of experience behind him, which, of course, made him seem even younger than he was.

The senior partner, Stephen Emery, was a man of forty who looked like the advertisements of the Man of Distinction. He shook hands with her, wished her well on the job, and scared her half to death.

It was not until a few minutes before closing time, when

she was clearing her desk, that a voice at her shoulder exclaimed, "Who says there's no Santa Claus?"

The man who stood smiling down at her was about thirty-five, good-looking, with mocking eyes and the air of assurance of a bachelor who is successful with women.

This, Connie was instantly aware, must be Colin Emery, the junior partner, the wolf. She looked at him coolly, apparently unaware of his obvious admiration.

"Can I do anything for you, Mr. Emery?"

"You can indeed." He perched on the edge of her desk. "You can solve a deep and dark mystery."

His mocking eyes rested on her, certain of his charm, of his effect on her. He would, she admitted to herself, have been an easy man to like if he had not been so convinced of his irresistible charm.

"I have no talent for that sort of thing." She stacked papers and put them in the desk, closing the drawer with unnecessary sharpness.

"You don't even ask what the mystery is. Aren't you interested?" His tone implied that she must be interested. He waited for her to return his smile.

"Not particularly, I'm afraid." She looked at the wall clock, pushed back her chair. Across the room she saw Jane Clark watching in open amusement. At another desk one of the older women, Miss Ellis, a heavy-set woman with a thin mouth, watched curiously, waiting to see what Connie would do. There was a kind of anger in her face.

"You aren't leaving just when we are beginning a big, beautiful friendship, are you?" Colin Emery put out his hand, saw her expression, and withdrew it. "Aha, the Snow Queen. Well, I know what to do about that."

"I am inclined to doubt it, Mr. Emery." Connie picked up her handbag and walked past him toward the locker room. She was aware that the senior partner was standing motionless in the doorway to his private office, watching her walk down the room away from his brother. Unlike Colin's expressive countenance, which revealed both amusement and chagrin, there was nothing to be read in the older man's face.

Connie went down in the crowded elevator, through revolving doors onto the street. New York at twilight. A different city from the one she had encountered that morning. Lights blazing in a million windows, turning dross to magic, to fairyland. The roar and tension and excitement and pace of the greatest, most thrilling city in the world. Towers that yesterday had been lost in mist soared above the city, brilliant with light.

Then a plunge down the subway stairs, pressing through the turnstile into stale air and the thunder of trains speeding through narrow, black tunnels. Mobs on the platform, thrusting, pushing, fighting for position; weary faces drawn from a day's work; tired bodies swinging from straps; and finally the white glare of her station, squeezing through packed bodies that did not want to make way for her, and then the stairs to her street. Connie had ended her first day as a working girl, tired, confused—and triumphant.

ii

Nothing seemed stranger to Connie than the rapidity with which she became adjusted to her new life. As the weeks passed, she took dictation and typed with increasing speed and confidence, lunching now and then with one of the office girls, more frequently alone. She was aware that Taylor Grant, the youngest lawyer, admired her but that he was hesitant about asking her for a date because his job depended on the goodwill of the Emery brothers, and Colin had made it apparent that he had staked Connie out for himself.

There were minor difficulties, of course. Stephen Emery terrified her by his inhuman impersonality; Colin was a nuisance because of his persistent attempts to arouse her admiration; Taylor Grant stirred her pity because of his hopeless devotion; Miss Ellis made her uncomfortable because she never seemed to stop watching her, looking for something to criticize. She was the only employee of Emery & Emery who betrayed an open hostility. Not that she often addressed Connie herself, but she developed an annoying habit of talking at her. "Pretty girls," she would say with a sniff, "who don't try to work; just get by on good looks."

As a matter of criticism it was inexcusable because Connie tried as hard as she could to make good on the job. Miss Ellis was aware of this, as was everyone else on the staff.

"What on earth have I done to her?" Connie demanded at last.

"Poor old thing," Jane said unexpectedly. "No man has ever looked at her. She's jealous because you have all the things she wants: beauty and youth and as much male admiration as you can cope with. You can afford to be generous, Connie."

Over and over, the junior partner stopped at her desk to ask her to lunch, to suggest a theater, to leave a small bunch of fragrant violets, but Connie steadfastly refused to see him outside the office. For the most part, the exchanges between them were good-humored and light-hearted. Colin did not seem to be annoyed by her unvarying refusal of his invitations; instead, he was intrigued and increasingly interested in her. Her indifference proved to be a stimulating challenge.

Only once did Connie find herself trapped by her impulsive tongue, which she had tried so hard to guard. Colin had been more insistent than usual about her going to the theater with him.

"Don't be a little dope," he said when she refused the invitation. "You know what I think?" His eyes were laughing at her with a kind of challenge. "I think you are afraid you will find me too interesting."

"You are quite mistaken, Mr. Emery," Connie said, stung into annoyance by his confidence. "Playboys bore me."

A sudden crash made her start. She turned her head. Stephen Emery had knocked a paper weight off a desk near them. Her heart sank. She had been rude to his brother. She would probably lose her job. She left the office, still fuming with anger over Colin's assumption that any girl was his for the asking. And yet, just once, it would be fun to go to a theater, to be escorted by an attractive and attentive man, to break the monotonous routine of her days, the even more monotonous routine of her lonely evenings.

In spite of her promise, she had not, as she had foreseen, got in touch with the girls whom she had formerly known, girls who were, after all, a part of Sandra's world rather than her own. About Sandra's activities she was kept informed by the society pages of the *Herald Tribune*. Week after week, her picture appeared, attending an opening night, seen at a night club, sponsoring a charity ball.

Usually her escort was Jefferson Gray, looking unexpectedly remote and distinguished in evening clothes, not like the casual man in sweater and slacks whom she had known at Stony Brook. He had changed in other ways, too; he seemed older, graver; or perhaps the photographers had failed to catch him when his face was lighted by his engaging smile.

Several times, when loneliness clamped down on her, she was unbearably tempted to telephone Jeff, but she was stopped each time by her memory of Sandra saying, with that radiance in her face, "Give Jeff my love."

But she could not shut Jeff out of her mind and heart; she could not avoid the snares set by her imagination. She never walked along a street without thinking that Jeff, too, might be walking there. Always she was unconsciously watching for him. More than once her heart had lurched when the carriage of a man's head, his walk, the sound of his laughter had startled her into thinking that he was there, just in front of her.

The day of her impulsive outburst to Colin Emery Connie came home, tired and depressed, to find Lil busy getting dinner for them both.

"But we agreed that we would look after ourselves," Connie protested.

"You can pay your share, but I like doing it," Lil assured her. "I've been watching you. You just scramble eggs or open a can of soup. If I do say it, I'm a good cook. At heart I'm simply a typical housewife. You know, the kind they write about in the magazines for chain stores, the ones who care about what kind of soap powder they use, or floor wax, or the right lotion to keep their hands soft."

Connie laughed. Lil Debaney in black velvet slacks and a gold blouse with bishop sleeves provided by Céleste, hair a brassy blond, false lashes fluttering, was as removed from a typical housewife as anything she could imagine.

"It's true, just the same," Lil said soberly. "I wear these

clothes because Madame gives them to me, and they save my own, but I like to cook and keep house. I like looking after someone, don't you? I'd like to have a husband and three or four nice, healthy, noisy children. I'd like a house in the country that wasn't too grand for children to racket around in, and a great big yard where they could play without getting into traffic. I'd like them to know all the big simple things like horses and cattle and pigs and chickens before they learn about different makes of cars and planes. I'd like them to have toys they made for themselves and that stir their imaginations before they get guns and toy soldiers and trucks and things that go bang." She laughed at herself but her eyes were sober.

Connie remembered how her father had warned her over and over not to judge people too quickly, telling her that even when she was sure she knew all about a person there was bound to be a lot left over that she hadn't even guessed. She realized now that Lil had told her the simple truth. Under the sophisticated surface there was an essentially simple woman, warm-hearted and generous. She was popular, but though she had a great many dates she seemed to take seriously none of the young men who called her so assiduously.

"I'll know the right one when I see him," she told Connie. "I guess we all do. And I'm not settling for anything else."

The home-cooked meal and Lil's cheerful talk relaxed Connie. She was startled when Lil said unexpectedly, "You're the most beautiful girl I've ever seen and yet you never have a date. Why, Connie?"

"Well, I — my father died only a short time ago, you know, and —"

After a while she added, trying to speak lightly, though

her voice betrayed her. "I guess I'm a one-man woman."

"You've found him?"

"And lost him. To marry him would be to destroy his future and to spoil the life of the best friend I have in the world."

In an effort to escape from a dangerous subject, she plunged into an account of her problem with the persistent junior partner of Emery & Emery.

"Every working girl, and that means almost every girl, has to learn to cope with wolves," Lil said sagely. "It's a nuisance but what can you do? It's just part of the pattern."

"It's not Junior who worries me most," Connie confessed, "it's the senior partner. He heard me rebuff Colin today. It would be so unfair to lose my job because Colin Emery is a wolf on the prowl. I only hope his brother doesn't blame me."

SEVEN

EARLY next morning, Stephen Emery made one of his rare appearances in the stenographers' room. "Miss Wyndham," he said.

Connie's heart did a nose dive. *This is it,* she thought. She steadied her shaky voice. "Yes, Mr. Emery."

"I'll need someone in court this morning on the Brewer case. Will you come with me and bring your notebook, please?"

Her first thought was a surge of relief. She wasn't going to be fired. Then her heart quailed. Something in the senior partner's manner, unapproachable, inhuman, always terrified her. When she worked for him she was tense with nervousness. Then she told herself, "Other girls have done it, and they were frightened, too. I can do it."

In the locker room she straightened her hair anxiously, studied the lines of the simple gray suit, adjusted a tiny black hat, pulled on a black coat with a huge cape collar, black gloves, and pushed notebook and pencils into her outsize handbag.

"The boy stood on the burning deck," she recited to herself. Then she began to laugh. "And look what happened to him!"

The laughter relaxed her and she was completely poised when she went out to meet Emery. There was an unexpected glint of admiration in his rather cold eyes as he stood back to let her precede him into the elevator. The trip by taxi was a silent one.

When they arrived at the courthouse Emery explained what he required of her. She was not to make a verbatim report of proceedings. He could get all that from the court reporter. But he did want her to make notes of certain points.

Connie looked around her, wide-eyed. Up to now, law had been a matter of endless and perplexing documents of which she could rarely make head or tail. But in this place the law was put into practice; it became no longer paper work but the clash of interests between human beings which must be reconciled according to the rules of the land.

"Is this the first time you have ever been in court, Miss Wyndham?" Emery asked, seeing her absorbed interest in her surroundings.

When she nodded he smiled. "I hope you won't be disillusioned. People raised on Perry Mason expect fireworks. The overwhelming percentage of cases may be very dull proceedings. Anyhow, this particular case will wind up today and go to the jury. As a matter of fact, I won't be surprised if we get a verdict before we leave."

Connie's first impression was one of disappointment. Never having been in court before, she expected that the surroundings would have all the high dignity of the law itself. Having seen movies based on English trials, she would not have been surprised if the lawyers had appeared bedecked in wigs.

Instead, she found a drab and unimpressive room; a scattered crowd made up of people awaiting hearings in other courts, a few curiosity seekers and some, cold and pinched, who, she suspected, had simply come in from the street to rest their feet and get warm.

It was a bare, untidy room, with cigarette butts lying under the NO SMOKING signs, newspapers, and even a bag containing an empty carton and the remains of a sandwich.

As she opened her notebook she was aware that Stephen Emery was studying her. As though I were a butterfly on a pin, she thought in annoyance; just some kind of inhuman specimen.

"Not enough majesty?" he asked, watching her expression with some amusement.

"Well, not much, certainly," she admitted.

"The majesty," he said quietly, "lies in the law itself. Not in the surroundings in which we find it administered. Remember, Miss Wyndham, that law is man's bulwark against violence and injustice; it is his answer to anarchy and insecurity. It is the fruit of all our many, many centuries of groping toward civilization. It isn't perfect but it's the best we have. Making it better in its operation is the job of every one of us."

She nodded, frowning.

"Not convinced?" he asked with a smile.

"Well," she said uncertainly, "I was thinking of all the ways the law says no. Getting in our way. Slowing us up. Like 'Stop' signals, for instance, when we are driving."

"And that," he told her, "is where you are wrong. 'Stop' signals are the best justification for the law that I know. Traffic laws, Miss Wyndham, don't slow us up. They speed us up. Have you ever seen a traffic jam where there were no signals? What happened? Everyone tried to get ahead and as a result they were all blocked in complete confusion. Traffic laws keep us all moving faster — and safer."

When Emery's client appeared at the counsel table, he proved to be a thin, worn, worried-looking man of fifty. A helpless sort of man, this Gerry Brewster, Connie thought. One who would always do his best, one who was honest to the core, but gullible, easily tricked. He watched Emery with the look of a man holding on to his only firm support. At once Connie discovered a warm partisanship. She was firmly on the side of the client.

In spite of the setting for the case, this drab courtroom with paint peeling from the walls and a crack in the plaster on the ceiling, the atmosphere changed with the arrival of the principal figure. The white-haired judge, his face illuminated by the morning sun, seemed to her the incarnation of justice. The clerk of the court, the counsel at their tables, the policemen standing like sentinels, all took on a certain awesome dignity in his presence.

As the case unfolded, Connie was as deeply interested in it as though this were a play. She picked up threads of what had gone before, accusations and counter-accusations, listened to the evidence as it was brought out by the witnesses. For the first time she was aware of the intricacies of the law and of the power for good and evil wielded by a lawyer.

Watching Emery, she was aware that here was a man who had found the job that was right for him to do in life and who was doing it with all his heart. For the first time she realized that idleness, however luxurious it might be, could never provide the rich satisfactions of work well done.

Perhaps this case lacked the high drama of a Perry Mason courtroom scene, but it had its own kind of drama and conflict. Watching almost breathlessly, Connie became aware that the evidence was being presented for the consideration of the twelve good men and true in the jury box. What counted in the long run was the way in which they would understand and interpret it. This was a job of enormous responsibility and importance; without it the whole system would break down.

She began to watch the jurymen eagerly. None of them, it seemed to her, were particularly interested in the testimony. In fact, one of them was frankly dozing half the time. He missed most of Emery's telling points. It was only the violent pounding on the table of the plaintiff's lawyer that woke him up, and he looked resentfully around him as though his slumber should not have been disturbed.

When the judge had issued his instructions and the jury had been led away, Emery stacked papers neatly and put them in his briefcase.

"Aren't you worried, wondering what they will decide?" Connie demanded eagerly, forgetting that she was there only to take notes.

He looked rather surprised. "I never waste energy on worry," he told her. "I have done the best I can. From now on it is up to the jury." He turned, rested his hand briefly on his client's shoulder, and said, "There is a man I want to see. Will you hold the fort, Miss Wyndham? If by any chance the jury arrives at a verdict within the next hour will you call me at this number, please?"

Thinking about her new idea of law and the rewards of doing one's job and doing it well, which she had not suspected up to now, Connie was unaware of the passage of time. She was startled when there was a stir, a whisper, and someone said, "Quick work. The jury is coming back."

Connie ran in search of a telephone, dialed the number Emery had given her. He would, he assured her, be there at once.

In a surprisingly short time he joined her, and a few minutes later his client appeared, looking more haggard, more anxious than ever, his hands twisting restlessly. The plaintiff and the opposing counsel sat at another table, a couple of reporters appeared. Then the jury filed in and the judge made his appearance.

Connie had been so completely convinced by Emery's arguments that she sat in stunned surprise while the jury foreman announced the verdict, awarding forty thousand dollars to the plaintiff.

The defendant looked at his lawyer with discouraged eyes, his tired shoulders slumped in despair. "How am I going to raise that money? He knew perfectly well the intent of my aunt's will."

"Hard luck," Emery agreed.

"You did your best. I know that."

The defendant went away and Connie closed her notebook with shaking hands.

Emery glanced at his watch. "Good heavens, I had no idea it was so late, and you haven't had any lunch. Won't you join me, Miss Wyndham, before you get back to the office?"

"Why — thank you."

Sitting across from him in a famous restaurant she was unaware of the curious eyes that watched their table. Emery was a familiar figure there but he was not often seen with a woman, certainly not with one as young and beautiful as this.

"Perhaps," the lawyer said at last, "you would prefer to order something else if you don't like that."

Connie realized then that she had been pushing her food around her plate without eating it. "If that group of men," she burst out, so carried away by indignation that she forgot to be afraid of the senior partner, "men who look reasonably intelligent, could listen to that evidence and then decide against your client, I don't think much of your renowned jury system."

Ever since the meal began he had been studying her, the exquisite but unstressed grooming, the face that held intelligence and character as well as unusual beauty, the warm generosity that now flushed her face with indignation, the clear, steady eyes.

"There's nothing the matter with the jury system, Miss Wyndham," he said in his quiet voice. "What it needs is better material. To the best of my belief there was not a man on that jury who was capable of weighing the evidence."

"Then why weren't there some of that type, Mr. Emery?" Connie asked hotly. "This country has plenty of intelligent people who want the law to be administered well. Millions and millions of them. Why weren't they there?"

He smiled and she realized that when he relaxed he did not look so severe. "That is a good question. The trouble is that when they are called for jury duty, they ask to be excused."

"But why?" she insisted.

"Chiefly, I think, because they have never sat, as you have just done, and seen justice perverted because of ineptitude and indifference. They, the people who try to escape jury duty, prefer to leave the job to someone else, though it is one of their most important duties as citizens. Their real reason for this is simply that they don't care. The excuses they make are something else."

"What do you mean?"

"Well, for instance, they claim that their business will fail or they will suffer from some great financial disaster;

they cite ill health when they probably intend to play golf; they imply they are so essential to their jobs that they are irreplaceable, though, as we all learn in time, no one is irreplaceable.

"And yet, Miss Wyndham, they are the very people who cry the loudest for good men on the jury when they themselves have legal difficulties. No, you must not blame the law or the courts for what is, to some degree, the fault of most of the people I know and probably of those you know. There are few of them, men or women, who won't dodge jury duty when they can." For the first time a touch of the desperate urgency he felt was betrayed by his voice. "If only they could be made to realize that they can't afford *not* to serve."

While she studied the dessert menu he abruptly changed the subject. Connie was surprised to find that she was no longer afraid of the senior partner. He had become more human. She found herself answering his questions about her college education, her life at Stony Brook. For some reason she made no reference to those four years she had spent in the luxurious surroundings provided by the Kents.

"My father," she told him proudly, "was a guide in the Maine woods. He was the finest man I have ever known. He" — she swallowed — "I lost him only a few months ago."

"So you came to New York to build a career."

She looked up to find him smiling. She smiled back. "Well, it sounds more impressive, put that way. Actually, it was just a question of getting a job, of earning a living."

"I hope you'll be happy at Emery & Emery," he said.

"Everyone has been very kind," she assured him.

"And now I suppose the next step is marriage," he said.

She remembered Colin and felt the blood burning in her cheeks. Did Emery think she was interested in his younger brother?

"I am fancy-free," she said lightly.

Emery's face revealed nothing of his thoughts. He held her coat for her and took her back to the office without saying more than a few words.

As she sat down at her desk Miss Ellis turned to look from her to Stephen Emery who was entering his own office. Her lips pinched hard together. Connie smothered a giggle. Did the silly woman imagine that she and the austere senior partner were carrying on an office flirtation?

For the rest of the afternoon she typed her notes. She was still working when the rest of the office staff left. It was nearly five-thirty when she heard a chair scrape back in the office of the junior partner. A few moments later he stopped at her desk.

"Hello!" he said in pleased surprise. "You are working late."

"I've practically finished."

"That's the Brewer case, isn't it? Well, don't let Steve overwork you."

Connie thought of Stephen Emery giving the best he had in the cause of justice, of Colin the playboy doing as little work as possible.

"He expects a lot but I don't think that's so unreasonable. After all, he works hard, too."

"You just give overtime for the good of the cause, is that it?"

Anger bubbled over. "Look here, Junior—" She caught back the word but it was too late. Why, oh why, she wondered in dismay, couldn't she learn to control her unruly tongue?

The change in his face almost frightened her. "Is that your name for me?"

"It's everyone's name for you," she retorted. "It's the first thing I learned about you."

For once his careless amusement was gone. He looked deflated, almost defeated. Then he lifted his head arrogantly, and for the first time Connie really studied his face, a face that would have been exceptionally good-looking if it had not lost its capacity to fight. It occurred to the girl that, much as she admired Stephen Emery, it must be hard to be his younger brother, continually dominated by the inexorable force of the senior partner.

In a moment of contrition she said frankly, "I'm sorry. That was unkind. I shouldn't have said it. But things just slip out, somehow."

The gentleness in her voice made him drop his defensive arrogance, made him look at her as though he were seeing something more than just a pretty girl who was fair game. There was a curious expression on his face.

"All right. I get the message. You just don't like playboys. Isn't that it?"

"I don't think you like them either," she said unexpectedly. "It's just your way of getting back at your brother." The moment she said it she knew that it was true.

He grinned. "Like that character in *Alice in Wonderland:* 'He only does it to annoy, because he knows it teases.' "

"Something like that," she admitted. "But I begin to think there's more to you than that."

"Maybe," he told her, half joking, half in earnest, "I need someone to reform me. Would you care to take on the job?"

She laughed and shook her head. "I'm not that young. I know that if you can't do it yourself, no one can do it for you. Good night."

"Good night — Junior?"

She turned back from the door to smile at him. "Good night, Colin."

EIGHT

SNOW WAS falling heavily when Connie emerged from the overheated lobby onto Forty-second Street. Lights from the windows of the tall buildings vanished in a white curtain of snow; taxis snarled and twisted their way around the crowded corner of Vanderbilt Avenue, along Forty-second Street, down Park Avenue South. Buses halted with a hissing of brakes.

Almost blinded by snow, Connie waited for a green light and then started to cross the street toward Grand Central Station and the subway. As her foot touched the curb, someone jostled against her and she slipped, falling against a man who grunted at the impact and then steadied her.

"Nick!" she cried in surprise.

"Connie! How long have you been in New York?"

"Nearly three months."

"Why didn't you tell me?"

"How could I?" she asked in exasperation. "You didn't send me your new address. I had no idea where you were."

"Where are you going now?" He raised his voice above the racing of motors, the sounding of horns, braced himself as the commuting mob dashed past him into the station.

"Home."

"I'll give you a lift. Taxi!"

As Nick never did anything unless he expected to gain by it, Connie hung back. His insistent hand on her elbow propelled her into the cab. He gave the Kents' Park Avenue address.

"No," Connie called, and gave the driver the correct one.

"Where are you going?" Nick asked in surprise.

"I don't live with the Kents any more, Nick. I'm sharing an apartment with another working girl."

"*Another* working girl." Nick was silent for a moment. Then he asked rather anxiously, "You haven't quarreled with the Kents, have you?"

"Of course not." She was indignant.

"Hey, where are we?" he demanded in surprise as the taxi stopped.

"This is where I live."

"Here!" He looked horrified. Then he helped her out and paid the driver.

"Don't you want to keep the taxi?" Connie asked. "It is difficult to get around here."

He looked up and down the dingy street disparagingly. "I'll bet it is. But I want to talk to you for a while, Connie. I'm in a jam."

She fitted her key into the lock. "You always are, Nick," she said in resignation, and when the door opened she led the way down the dark, narrow hallway to the apartment, where she switched on lights and hung up Nick's snowy overcoat.

"Quite a comedown for you," he said, looking around. "Compared with the Kents' place this is practically a slum, isn't it?"

"It's all I can afford. Look here, Nick," she said crisply, "if you have anything private to say to me you had better do it now. My roommate will be home any time."

They stood facing each other in the little living room.

Something had changed in Connie, Nick thought. She had acquired an air of assurance; she moved like a person who was accustomed to standing on her own feet, to depending on herself.

Something had changed in Nick, Connie thought. Surely he had never been like this before, his eyelids twitching, his hands betraying a tremor.

"Connie," he said at last, "I'm in real trouble."

Her heart thudded. "Is it — that man — the one at the airport?"

"It's —" He broke off as though at a loss to know what to say. "I was never as glad to see anyone in my life as I was to see you this afternoon. Thing is that I have to have two thousand dollars within ten days. Or else."

"Or else what?"

"Or else your brother is going to jail," he said bluntly.

"Nick!" She sat down as though her knees had buckled under her. "What have you done this time?"

His weak mouth twisted with resentment. "That's right. Take for granted that the fault is all mine. Are you going to help me or are you going to see Dad's name dragged in the mud?" He watched her closely, saw the shadow fall over her face. "You can't let me down, Connie," he said, pressing his advantage. "You just can't. And it's the last time I'll ask you."

"It's always the last time," she said wearily. "Anyhow, I can't do it."

"You mean you won't." His expression was ugly.

"I mean I can't. There is less than two hundred dollars in my savings account. I have nothing but my salary, and, as this is my first job, there's just enough to keep me. What happened, Nick?"

He brushed aside her question. "Two hundred. That

wouldn't even stall them off. What about Stony Brook? Didn't you sell it?"

She shook her head. "How could I? The estate was not settled until a week ago."

"So that's out. You couldn't do it in time now. What —"

He broke off as Lil came in, a brown paper bag of groceries in one arm, cheeks flushed from the cold, snowflakes powdering the perky hat on her blatantly blond hair. She looked in surprise from Connie to Nick.

"This is my half brother, Nicholas Wyndham," Connie said. "Lillian Debaney, who is sharing her apartment with me."

She smothered a giggle as Nick, with an admiring look at Lil, gallantly took the bag of groceries into the kitchen for her, saying that if he had known Connie was hiding anyone as attractive as this he'd have been around long ago. Lil watched him with the grave attention of a child but there was no trace of her big, warm smile. Then she said that she had a date and she left abruptly.

Connie was aware that Lil rarely had dates in midweek because a model has to keep early hours if her looks are not to show the effect of lack of rest. She had deliberately left them alone for the evening.

"She is quite a dish, but not your usual style, is she?" Nick commented.

Connie was angered by Nick's swift change from exaggerated gallantry to unconcealed contempt. "Lil is one of the nicest and kindest girls I've ever known," she defended her roommate warmly. "She has gone out on this awful night just so that we can talk in private. Do you want to have dinner with me here?"

"Why not? What I feel like is a nice thick steak."

"Can you pay for it? If not you'll eat hamburg."

While Connie busied herself in the kitchen Nick asked about her job. He laughed when she described it.

"Well, what do you expect me to do?" she retorted. "I have to earn my living and I haven't any other training."

"With your Kent connections you could have hooked a rich man by now. You could have married someone who would keep you in the style to which you've been accustomed."

Without comment Connie set the table. Bright spots of color burned on her cheekbones.

Nick glanced at her as he lounged in the doorway to the kitchenette. "I had an idea Jeff Gray had fallen for you in a big way. What does he think of you working in an office?"

"He doesn't know anything about it. And you are quite wrong. Jeff is not interested in me; he is interested in Sandra Kent."

Nick was instantly alert, but her voice warned him not to continue the subject, though he made a mental note of it. "Do the Kents know about your job?"

"I haven't even told them I'm in New York."

"What's this all about? There's something darned queer about the way you are acting. What are you doing, anyhow? Hiding out?"

"Sit down," she said, and he pulled up a chair at the table.

For a few minutes he ate in silence. Then he looked at her. "What's happened between you and the Kents? You and Sandra used to be inseparable. Kent treated you as though you were his own daughter. You lived on the fat of the land." His mouth twisted in an ugly way. "That was probably Dad's influence. You were always his favorite. I notice Kent didn't offer me a college education."

"You were twenty-one at the time, you had refused to work for a scholarship, you told Dad you didn't want any more education. In fact, as I remember, you told him you didn't *need* any more education."

"All right. All right. No need to get hot and bothered. But I'm naturally interested in the big breakup of a beautiful friendship. What happened?"

"Not a thing. Believe me, Nick, not a thing. But Mr. Kent has done so much for me that I couldn't possibly expect anything more of him. He paid that imaginary debt to Dad a thousand times over. As for Sandra — well, our lives have different patterns now. There would just be strain and awkwardness if we tried to pick up where we left off. From now on she takes her place in society and I'm a working girl. So," she concluded with an attempt at lightness, "that's that. No hiding. No mystery. No quarrel. Just — life, I guess."

His eyes watched her face intently. "You're holding out on me, Connie. I can feel it. There is something you are keeping back."

That from Nick, she raged silently to herself. Nick who refuses to tell me anything, where he lives, how he lives, how he manages to support himself. She passed a plate of muffins without comment.

Unexpectedly Nick's fist crashed down on the table and she jumped at the sudden noise, spilling the muffins.

"Nick, what's wrong with you? You scared me half to death."

"I'll give it to you straight," he said between his teeth. "I've been working with — some guys." He hesitated and then smiled oddly. "You might call it a form of insurance. Part of my job was — uh — making collections. Well, anyhow, I got a tip about a sure thing at the races and I didn't report on the collections."

After a long time Connie said incredulously, though it wasn't a question, just a statement of fact, "You stole the money."

"You needn't put it that way," he said sullenly.

"How else?"

"Look," he said desperately, "these guys I've been working with play for keeps. They've laid it on the line. I've got to have that money, Connie. Got to."

There was a long silence. Connie got up to clear the table, her face white and set. Nick watched her.

"Well?" he said at last.

"It isn't going to jail that frightens you, is it, Nick? I don't know what you are mixed up in but you are not working with the kind of people who settle their problems through the law. It's the man at the airport you are afraid of."

"It's the man at the airport," Nick admitted at last, as though he were half relieved at having to tell the truth about it.

"Why didn't you let Jeff call the police that night?" Still no reply. "Oh," she said at last, "you are afraid of the police, too, aren't you?"

"Connie, listen to me. I know I've made mistakes. I know I — disappointed Dad. But I'm sorry now. Sorrier than you can ever imagine. I'd give my right arm to think he could have had some respect for me before he died. But I swear this to you. I swear it by anything you like. If you will help me out of this jam — and the danger is very real, very urgent, you can believe that — I'll stick to the straight and narrow from now on. Give me this one chance. Please."

Never before had there been so much earnestness in his voice. His eyes met hers steadily, pleadingly.

"I need your help terribly, Connie. You're the only one who can save me."

She came back to sit facing him, balancing uneasily on the chair with the broken springs. "Nick, I'd do anything I could but —" She flung out her hands helplessly.

"Can't you do *anything?*"

At last she said reluctantly, "I'll talk to Mr. Kent. I'll ask him to lend you the money. I'm sure he would do that if he knew I would repay him as soon as possible. Then I'll put Stony Brook on the market at once. I'm bound to sell it within a few months, six months at the most. People used to want to buy it."

"That's good, Connie. I knew you wouldn't fail me. Why, in a way, it would have been like failing Dad. To have his fine name disgraced by me when you could help me out —"

He lighted a cigarette, lounging back on the couch, eying her warily. "Look, do you have to tell Kent that you are borrowing the money for me?"

"But, Nick, I can't possibly ask anything for myself! Not possibly! You are asking rather a lot, aren't you?"

Nick hesitated, then his eyes met hers. "It's not just for me. It's for you, too."

"For me!"

"That's the awful thing about it," he said earnestly. "I could take anything for myself. But these guys know how I feel about you, my own sister, my sole family, and they've threatened, if I don't come across with the money, that something bad will happen to you."

"Nick!" She broke off to answer the door. The superintendent handed her a package.

"This came for you this afternoon, Miss Wyndham, by registered mail."

"Thank you." She came back to put the package on the table, to look at the return address with a puzzled frown. Then her face cleared. "Oh, those must be Dad's stamps. The executor wrote that he was sending them."

"Connie!" Nick's eyes brightened. "I know a guy who would buy them from me tomorrow and jump at the chance. This is wonderful."

"They don't belong to me. Dad left them to Mr. Kent."

"But —"

"I wrote and mailed the letter, which Dad signed, saying that they were to be sent to him, as a friendly message that could reach him across the Great Barrier. That's the way Dad put it. For some reason it mattered to him, Nick. I'll have to carry out his wishes."

"So that's that." His shoulders drooped in discouragement. Then he smiled at her. "All right, do whatever you think best." He started toward the door, putting on his overcoat. "What really went wrong between you and Sandra Kent? Friendships like that don't break up over nothing."

"I told you it hadn't broken up, but we live in separate worlds now."

"And which world is Jefferson Gray in?" Seeing her expression he gave a low laugh of triumph. "So that's it."

"Nick!" She clutched his arm. "Nick, Sandra loves Jeff."

He opened the door.

"Nick, please."

"I'll keep in touch."

When the door had closed behind him, Connie started toward the kitchen to do the dishes. There was a metallic sound outside and she went swiftly across the room, threw open the door. Nick was getting up from his knees.

"Dropped my fountain pen," he said. "Is it always this dark out here?"

"Always. Here, let me help you."

"Don't bother, it wasn't worth much anyway," Nick said, and he went down the hall.

As Connie turned, light from the living room floor lamp revealed something on the hall carpet. She bent over to pick it up. Nick's fountain pen. She turned it over, her fingers moved, a light flashed on.

"Nick!" she called. But Nick had already gone.

She went back slowly. What had Nick been doing with a flashlight?

When she had switched out the light in her room Connie lay for a long time staring up blindly at the ceiling. Nick a thief! Nick involved with criminals. She was glad with all her heart that her father could not know. And yet — and yet Nick had seemed to be in earnest when he said that if she helped him once more, just once more, he would reform. He would become the kind of man his father had wanted him to be.

For a moment she thought about his implied threat that if she did not come to the rescue his friends would punish her. She dismissed it. Things like that did not happen.

She would have to get in touch with John Kent, ask to borrow money until she could sell Stony Brook. It pinched her heart to think of the lodge going to strangers. That would be the end of her dream.

Her cheeks burned at having to ask Kent for money. She hadn't wanted the Kents to know she was in New York.

More than that, she hadn't wanted Jeff to know. She had been afraid to see him again, afraid that her precarious courage would fail her, afraid she would betray her love for him, afraid he would turn from Sandra to her and so spoil his life — and Sandra's.

Well, the time had come when she would have to get in touch with the Kents, pocket her pride, borrow money. She writhed with shame.

Sleet pattered against the window. Connie pulled blankets higher around her shoulders against the bitter winter night. Her tired thoughts were in a jumble. Somewhere Nick was out in the night but she did not know where he was going, where he lived. From Nick to Kent. Perhaps she could get in touch with him without Jeff knowing about her.

"Jeff," she whispered in the darkness. "Oh, Jeff!" The pillow was wet with her tears.

NINE

NEXT morning, Colin Emery passed Connie's desk with a gay greeting but he did not as usual ask her to have lunch with him. In his own office he buckled down to work, making a valiant effort to catch up with the cases he had been neglecting. When he was not interviewing clients or dictating, dealing with arrears of paper work, he was in the law library looking up references.

"What's happened to Junior?" Jane demanded over the lunch table in the cafeteria. "I'll bet the boss clamped down on him. He's a changed man. He has given me about twice as much work as he ever did before and no 'come hither' look about him either. He's all business. Though I must say, try as hard as he can, he'll never make the kind of lawyer the boss does. A round peg in a square hole, if I ever saw one."

"Then why did he become a lawyer?" Connie asked.

"For four generations the Emerys have been lawyers. You've seen those musty old portraits in Mr. Emery's office."

"Didn't it matter whether they were interested in the law or not?"

Jane shrugged. "Family tradition is hard to ignore, especially when the boss is there to remind you of it. All Junior was interested in was — you'd never guess — having a dairy farm! He spent a summer on one once when he was in college and fell for the rural life. He wanted to put his money into cattle and the boss hit the roof. So Junior —"

"Don't keep calling him that," Connie said. "He hates it. It just underlines what everyone thinks, that he's a kid brother being led firmly along in the right direction. It's humiliating."

Jane's eyebrows rose in an astonished arc. "Do my ears deceive me or have you fallen for our pet wolf?"

"I haven't fallen for him," Connie said crisply. "I'm just sorry for him."

"Sorry for him! For a professional playboy who thinks all girls are fair game? A man who's practically never done a real day's work in his life?"

"I think he's been forced into a profession that is all wrong for him and he doesn't know how to fight it except by, well, by goading his brother with his playboy ways. I don't believe that is the kind of person he really wants to be."

Jane leaned back in her chair and softly whistled the wedding march.

Connie flushed and then laughed. "I'll never fall in love with Colin Emery."

"The lady doth protest too much, methinks." There was an amused grin on Jane's face.

Connie shook her head firmly. "No, I'll never — it isn't —" She broke off in confusion, feeling hot color stain her cheeks.

After a startled look at that telltale blush, Jane tactfully changed the subject, describing in great detail a television program she had watched the night before.

As employees were not encouraged to use the office telephone for their private calls, Connie had to wait for evening to get in touch with John Kent. All day the prospect hung over her like a dark cloud. The humiliation of having to borrow money was bad enough; the fact that Sandra and Jeff would know she was in New York was intolerable. She could hardly avoid meeting them. And what would happen then?

When dinner was over that evening, the telephone rang and it was Lil, as usual, who answered it. After all, the calls were generally for her. She held out the telephone to Connie.

"For you," she said.

Connie's heart sank. It would be Nick, of course, and she would have to put him off. Instead, it was Sandra's voice, familiar and yet oddly different.

"Connie! Why on earth didn't you let me know you were in New York?"

"Well —" Caught unprepared, she was at a loss for an answer. "How did you learn where I was?"

"Mary told me weeks ago she had seen you but she didn't know where you were staying or how long you planned to be here. Then today I ran into Nick, of all people. He said that you are working here in New York."

"That's right. And it's great fun."

"I must see you, Connie. Have dinner with us tomorrow evening. . . . No, I simply won't let you off. There's no telling when I'll have another free evening, not for at least ten days, and I want to hear all about what you have been doing." Sandra laughed, and again there was that odd sound in her voice. "No more hiding away. Tomorrow at eight. Promise?"

"I promise," Connie said reluctantly.

Next morning she was haunted by her promise to have dinner with the Kents. She would have to ask Kent to lend her money. She would have to find some plausible explanation for not having informed Sandra that she was in New York. There had been something strange about Sandra. She had seemed to want to see Connie, and yet — and yet —

Connie jerked away from her wandering thoughts to realize that she had not heard a word of what Stephen Emery was dictating in his quiet, precise manner.

"I'm terribly sorry, Mr. Emery. I just let my mind wander." And if there was ever a lame excuse, she thought, that was it.

"So I observed."

"I'm sorry," she said inadequately.

"Where were you?" he asked in amusement. "It seemed to be far away."

"In a cloud, I guess. It won't happen again."

As she was gathering up notebook and pencils he commented casually, "I shouldn't worry too much about a slight lapse of attention. We are very glad to have you here at Emery & Emery. Very fortunate."

Connie's eyes opened wide in astonishment. Never before had the senior partner been known to pay anyone a compliment.

"You seem to have a good influence on my brother," he added. "He is really working for a change. I have an impression that the credit belongs to you."

Connie was horrified to hear herself say impulsively, "I think he's the one who deserves the credit, Mr. Emery. It's fun to buckle down to work that you love but it's sheer drudgery to do work that's not congenial. There doesn't seem to be any reward in it for its own sake."

Why did I say that? she wondered when she got back to

her desk. She had been impertinent, inexcusable. In any case, Colin Emery was old enough to fight his own battles. They were no concern of hers.

She tackled her notes, typing briskly. She was relieved that Stephen Emery was not in his office when she went in to leave the letters for his signature.

By the time Lil got home that night Connie had finished her bath. "Don't cook for me, Lil," she called. "I'm going out to dinner."

"Oh, swell!" Then Lil joined in Connie's laughter. "You know what I mean. I'm so glad you're going out for a change. Who is it — a new boy friend?"

"No, a girl I knew in college," Connie said evasively.

"Oh." Lil's disappointment was evident in her voice but when Connie came into the living room the other girl stared at her. "Connie! You're simply dazzling. That jade green satin is perfect with your hair, and that style, with one shoulder bare — Céleste has made a specialty of it this season. People love it. You look — I never saw you look like that before."

Connie smiled, touched by Lil's honestly expressed admiration that was completely without envy. It helped to restore the confidence that had been badly shaken by the knowledge that tonight she must face Sandra in a different relationship from any they had had before.

Connie found that she was oddly breathless, that her heart was beating hard and fast when the doorman at the Kents' Park Avenue building opened the taxi door and greeted her.

He beamed at her. "Miss Wyndham!"

She smiled. "Horrid night, isn't it, Brixton?"

"Not when you come home," he declared.

When you come home. But she wasn't coming home, Connie remembered as she went up in the familiar elevator, when she was greeted by the familiar parlor maid, when she entered the familiar long drawing room with the draperies of the many windows drawn against the night, the vases massed with flowers.

Then Sandra came running into the room to greet her warmly, Sandra in a stunning white evening dress, exquisitely groomed, but still with that queerly withdrawn, half-alive look she had worn so often in the past, a look that made her almost plain.

What was I afraid of? Connie wondered. Everything is the same. Everything is all right. There is nothing to be afraid of.

"You look wonderful," she said. "I've missed you so much, Sandra."

Sandra stood with her hands on Connie's shoulders, looking at her with searching eyes. "You look wonderful, too," she said and, though she smiled, the smile did not reach her eyes, did not warm her sober voice. To her own surprise, Connie found herself thinking of Lil's warm smile. She wondered whether Sandra had always been so remote. She hadn't said a word about missing her.

A moment later John Kent, short, stout, ruddy-faced, came in with his deliberate walk that just escaped being a strut, and shook hands with her.

"Well, Constance, this is pleasant. I hope we'll have some opportunity to discuss your plans."

She looked at him uncertainly.

"Specifically, what do you want to do about Stony Brook? Your father asked me to keep an eye on your affairs, you know."

"Father, Connie won't want to discuss her problems the very minute she gets here," Sandra protested.

My problems? Connie wondered. There was something here she did not understand.

"But I thought that was the whole point. The fact that you canceled all your appointments for tonight — oh, well, later then," Kent said, somewhat surprised. "But it is a mistake to let these things drift. I've made reservations at the Wiltown." He ushered the girls out and down to his waiting car.

The Wiltown, although it had opened only a few weeks earlier, was already one of the most fashionable Manhattan restaurants. Kent's table was beside the dance floor and the members of the band were just returning to their places after a brief rest when the headwaiter led the way to the table. There was always, Connie remembered now, a certain amount of bustle when John Kent entered a restaurant. The days when this spotlight effect had been a commonplace seemed like part of another life. Looking around her, seeing the people in evening dress, the hovering waiters, the violinist softly touching his strings, Connie thought of the noisy cafeteria at which she usually ate, and she grinned to herself.

The grin helped to relax the strained tension around her mouth that had been there ever since Kent had made clear, though inadvertently, that Sandra had deliberately lied. She had not called Connie because she had a free evening. She had rearranged her plans in order to see Connie. For a moment she had looked chagrined when Kent made the revelation but she had not attempted to explain.

As Connie sat down she glanced at the nearby tables. They provided a cross-section of this world of luxury: a famous senator, a Broadway producer, a well-known sportsman, industrialists, people from the Social Register. Her eyes rested on a table where, to her surprise, Stephen Emery sat with a group of friends. There was no reason, of course, why Emery should not frequent fashionable restaurants, but somehow she imagined him always in his own library, surrounded by law books, when he was not in his office.

Emery recognized her with equal surprise, he bowed and then his eyes moved on to Kent whom he obviously recognized, passed to Sandra where they lingered, and finally were raised to someone who was joining the Kent table.

Connie's eyes raised, too. A tingling along her nerves had given her a second's warning.

"Hello, Jeff," she said coolly.

"Connie!" For a moment his face lighted, warmed with delight. Then, his voice as colorless as her own, he said, "Sorry to be late, Sandra. Good evening, sir."

Connie looked up straight into Sandra's eyes, and her heart was cold at what she read there. Something had roused Sandra's suspicion and she was watching every move, every expression, alert to every word spoken by either Connie or Jeff, for any glance exchanged between them.

This, Connie knew in a flash, was Nick's doing. His meeting with Sandra had been no accident. He had deliberately planted a seed of distrust in her mind. But what had he hoped to gain?

The dinner, outwardly pleasant, was a long punishment to Connie. Over her hung the realization that, before the evening was over, she would have to borrow money from Kent. And there was another factor, one she had not foreseen. When she had made her sacrifice, and made it freely, without bitterness, she had not imagined what it would be like to be in the company of Jeff and Sandra. The pain seemed to be more than she could bear.

As the meal progressed, she was aware that she need not have worried about Jeff. The past appeared to be entirely forgotten. After that first moment of spontaneous delight he had paid her no attention beyond the requirements of good manners. For a short time Kent threatened to engross all his attention, discussing business until Sandra insisted, with a half-annoyed laugh, that he let it go for the evening.

"Jeff is yours during the daytime," she declared, "but this evening he belongs to me." There was a faint challenge in the smiling look she gave Connie, who smiled back gaily.

When Jeff asked Sandra to dance, Connie made up her mind not to watch them, but in spite of her determination she could not look away as they circled the room. Obviously they had danced together many times. They talked little but when they did it was with an easy camaraderie. There seemed to be no indications of a deep attachment between them. She scolded herself when she was aware of a secret feeling of relief.

She turned her head to find Kent watching her with a curious expression. Then he, too, looked at the dancing couple, a sudden question in his eyes, which lingered even after Jeff and Sandra returned to the table.

He suspects, too, Connie thought in alarm. What could Nick have said? Or else I must wear love like a banner. I was off-guard. I should have known that he sees everything.

"Well, Constance," he said, "I understand you are earning your living. Very sensible of you. What are you doing?"

When she had explained he said, "A stenographic pool? With the education you have been given surely you could do better than that."

It was the first time he had ever reminded her of what he had done for her. Connie felt herself flushing.

"It may not be glamorous as jobs go," she said defensively, "but I like it better every day. I had never realized before that our whole civilization depends on the kind of law we have and on the way it is administered. Stephen Emery says —"

Sandra began to laugh. "I simply can't picture you in a law office, drawing up deeds, or whatever they do."

"Don't," Jeff said with a half-laughing grimace, "mention the law at this moment. Today I had a terrific struggle to get excused from jury duty."

"Why didn't you simply refer the matter to me?" Kent asked. "You are indispensable to the business."

"Stephen Emery says that no one is indispensable."

"Your friend isn't infallible," Kent remarked in the tone that usually ended any dicussion. He was not accustomed to having his remarks questioned.

"After all, Connie," Jeff said, attempting to justify himself in answer to her implied criticism, "there are men who need the extra money they earn on jury duty. They are the ones who should be in the jury box, as a matter of justice."

"Whether they are competent or not? A lot you care for justice!" Oh, when, Connie wondered in dismay, will I learn to curb my tongue? Nevertheless, carried away by her conviction, she went on, "If people like you really cared about justice you wouldn't get excused from jury duty and leave it to incompetents to decide the course of American justice. If that's all you can do for it, then God save America from her own irresponsible citizens."

"You've changed," Jeff said quietly.

"Stephen Emery says that the men who think they can't afford to spend time sitting on a jury are the very men who can't afford not to. Stephen Emery says —"

"You seem to have a high opinion of this guy," Jeff said, stung into anger.

"I have."

"Miss Wyndham, will you dance with me?"

Connie turned to see Stephen Emery standing beside the table. "With pleasure," she said, and introduced him to her friends.

Emery danced as precisely, efficiently, and impersonally as he did everything else. He spoke with an edge of amusement on his voice. "I must thank you for that glowing testimonial you gave me."

Connie laughed. "Well," she admitted, "they were talking about getting off jury duty and it annoyed me and —"

To her amazement the austere Emery chuckled. "I don't imagine Kent is accustomed to being lectured."

Connie smothered a laugh. "He isn't. It was awful of me. Especially —"

"Your friend is his daughter?"

"Sandra? Yes."

"Sandra?"

"Well, Alexandra, really. But no one except her father ever calls her that."

"Alexandra. A regal name for a regal person. One doesn't often see a young woman with such a splendid carriage, such poise and dignity."

Connie gave him a quick, surprised look. He sounded, she thought, as though he had been completely bowled over by Sandra Kent.

"She's an unusual person." Connie added impulsively, "Why don't you ask her to dance, Mr. Emery, and find out for yourself?"

Emery looked somewhat taken aback but he did not seem to be annoyed. Indeed, when they finished the dance, Connie watched as he led Sandra out onto the floor. To her amazement she saw that the unapproachable senior partner was unbending, was talking, was listening intently to Sandra, his face alight with interest.

"Sandra seems to have made a conquest," she said with a laugh.

"The great Mr. Emery appears to be irresistible," Jeff remarked tartly. "Dance, Connie?"

There was, after all, no possible excuse for not dancing. She moved away in his arms. After the first moment she was aware that dancing had never been like this before. They moved as one person.

"This is the first time I've ever danced with you," Jeff said abruptly, breaking the silence.

"And probably the last." Connie was aware of the hardness, the hostility in her own voice but she dared not, for so much as a second, let down the barrier or she would melt into his arms as she longed to do.

"Why?" When she made no comment Jeff held her away, searching her face. "Why?"

"Because I don't belong in this world any more, Jeff. I'm a working girl now."

"Why didn't you tell me you were in New York?"

She made herself smile at him while she evaded a direct

answer. "Where else would I be?" she asked challengingly.

"Of course. You love New York."

"Of course."

His eyes held hers. She looked at the face she so dearly loved, tried to look away, but his eyes refused to release her, still searching for the answer to some question.

"Are you happy, Connie?"

"Are you?" she countered.

"Let's not quibble," he said impatiently. "You're in some kind of trouble, aren't you?"

"I?" In her astonishment she stood stock-still and a couple behind bumped into her. Jeff's arm tightened as he swept her out of the way.

"Sandra told me. She said that you needed money; that was the reason you came tonight."

For a moment Connie was so shaken by anger that she could not speak. She had left Jeff free for Sandra and now Sandra had deliberately humiliated her. How could she have done it?

She laughed. "Sandra is mistaken. I'm doing very well."

"But surely you know that if you need anything — anything at all — any time at all —"

The band had stopped and there was one of those momentary and unpredictable hushes in which his voice rose clearly. They had come to a halt beside Kent's table. The older man got to his feet as Jeff pulled out Connie's chair and his expression frightened her. Then he turned with frowning eyes to watch his daughter and Emery who had paused across the room. Connie realized that the two girls whom she had met the morning she arrived in New York had been right in saying that Kent's heart was set on Sandra marrying Jefferson Gray. Kent was in a bad temper because both Connie and Emery were daring to interfere with his plans. He turned to Connie.

"By the way, Constance, let's arrange an appointment so that we can discuss the disposal of Stony Brook."

Connie forgot even Nick and his need for money, Nick and his danger. She remembered only, with a stab of pain, the last time she had discussed Stony Brook with Jeff, when he had wanted to live there with her. From his quick look she knew that he, too, remembered.

"According to Alexandra, you are in urgent need of money," Kent said, and color stung her face and then drained out of it. Never before had he spoken to her like that. "And since Stony Brook is the only source on which you have to draw, you would be wise to sell it at the earliest possible time."

He was making clear that she could expect no help from him. It was fair enough, of course, as he owed her nothing. She thought a little grimly that Nick had defeated his own ends by whatever he had said to Sandra.

"I'd like to sell it as soon as I can," she said lightly. "It's better to forget the past and start fresh."

"Good. Good." Kent moved restlessly. "It's getting late. As a working girl you'll have to be up early. Why did Alexandra consent to dance a second time with that fellow?"

Sandra and Emery were returning to the table, laughing and animated. Sandra held out her hand. "On the seventeenth, then, at seven-thirty. Good night, Mr. Emery."

He bowed to them and returned to his own party.

"What's that about the seventeenth?" Kent demanded.

"Mr. Emery is taking me to see the Royal Ballet."

"Really, Alexandra, what got into you? You know nothing about the man except that he is Constance's employer. And he is old enough to be your father."

"But he's not at all like a father, is he?" she said sweetly. "Or would you know about that — Father?"

TEN

AT THE Park Avenue address the long car slid in to the curb. Kent helped Sandra out, though Jeff remained with Connie.

"By the way," Kent said casually before the car moved away to take her home, "I suppose you'll send me the stamps Bill wrote me about?"

"I'll see that you get them," Connie promised.

His cold eyes studied her. "Good. I'll be expecting them."

"Good night, Connie," Sandra said. "It was nice to see you again. Remember, you can always call on me if you need anything. Give me a ring sometime."

Sometime. The polite word that means no time. That means never.

Connie wanted to cry out, "Sandra, doesn't all our past friendship and affection and trust mean anything? Is it all over?" But she knew the answer.

While the car moved smoothly and silently through the city streets with their sordid display of blackened snow, Jeff and Connie sat staring out wordlessly. Even Jeff's nearness could not abolish the consternation in her mind. The stamps! Kent had virtually demanded them, and his implication that she had come to dinner only to ask for money made it evident that she could not borrow money from him. There was nothing left except Stony Brook and months might pass before a buyer could be found. And Nick had so little time left by the ultimatum of the man with whom he had become involved. What on earth was she going to do? What would happen to Nick? And the men who had threatened her? Surely they would not really harm her.

"Winter is ugly in New York," Jeff said, breaking the uneasy silence between them. "Maine must be magnificent now, clean and white, unsmirched by man and all his machinery and his noise and dirt."

She managed a laugh. "It would be wonderful if you didn't mind traveling on snowshoes."

"Snowshoes are fun." Jeff helped her out at Lil's apartment, looked quickly at the building but made no comment.

"Good night, Jeff. Nice to see you again."

"Connie, is everything all right?"

"Of course," she said promptly, smiling as brightly as she could.

There was no answering smile on his face. "Something is wrong," he said doggedly.

She chanted softly from Gilbert & Sullivan:

And I'm all right
And you're all right
And everything is quite all right.

"Good night, Jeff," she repeated, and left him standing beside the car.

She went swiftly down the ill-lighted hall to Lil's apartment, put the key in the lock, and the door swung open on darkness. She reached for the light switch and removed her key, frowning. That was odd. She was positive she had closed the door firmly behind her when she left. Oh, of course, Lil had a date, too, and she had left the apartment after Connie had gone. Still, it wasn't like Lil to be careless, and Connie was sure the door had been ajar when she started to unlock it.

She stood hesitating, not frightened, but uneasy. Then she went swiftly through the apartment: living room, the two bedrooms, bath, kitchenette. Feeling rather absurd, she went back to open the closet doors cautiously and to peek under the beds.

Of course, there was no intruder, but perhaps someone had come and gone. There had, after all, been a whole evening in which the apartment had been unoccupied. Someone watching outside would have known that both girls had left. Suppose a burglar had robbed the place. This time she looked not for a person who might be hiding there but for objects that might be missing.

The first indication she had that someone had really been in the apartment was a cigarette in an ashtray. Neither she nor Lil smoked and Lil's date for the evening had given up cigarettes weeks ago.

In her tiny bedroom Connie picked up the big handbag she carried to work. That noon she had cashed a check for thirty dollars. There was no money in the billfold now. So far as she could determine, nothing else was missing.

Slowly she undressed, pulled on a warm quilted robe, slid her feet into lined slippers, and went back to the living room to wait for Lil, to tell her what had happened, to learn whether Lil, too, had been robbed.

At first she lay on the couch, but realizing that this made her sleepy, she sat erect, kicking her heels idly. There was something — different. She kicked again. She had hastily shoved the stamp album under the edge of the couch until she could send it to Mr. Kent — it would be as safe there as anywhere for a day or two. She had noticed then that when she sat her heels struck against the package. Now, her slippers swung back under the slipcover with nothing to stop them.

Frantically she jumped off the couch, lifted the slipcover. The stamp albums were gone. She sat back on her heels, staring incredulously at the empty space under the couch. The stamps! It was all her fault. She should have taken them with her this evening, seen that Mr. Kent got them at once. But the package had been cumbersome and, anyhow, expecting to borrow money it would have been too embarrassing to precede her request by presenting the stamps. She had been so sure they would be safe for a day or two. No one had ever before stolen anything from her. Unless she had rented a safety-deposit box — but that had seemed extravagant for so few hours.

At first she was too stunned to think. Then, little by little, she became aware of the extent of the disaster. John Kent would never believe the stamps had been stolen. He would assume that she had sold them for her own profit.

She was still crouching on the floor, tearless, white-faced, when Lil came home.

"Connie! What's wrong, honey?"

With an effort Connie tried to control her shaking. Lil put her on the couch, drew a quilt over her, heated milk in the kitchen and made Connie take the glass. Until she had drunk all of it, Lil refused to let her speak.

Then she said, "What happened to you, Connie? Did something go wrong on your date?"

"We've had a burglar. The door was ajar when I came home." She described her search, finding the cigarette in the ashtray, discovering that the money she had withdrawn from the bank that day was gone, and her realization that the stamps had been stolen.

Lil, with her sturdy common sense, was aware that there was nothing in all this to have such a shattering effect on her roommate, who was not inclined to be hysterical. To gain time she made a search of her own room and returned to say cheerfully that nothing of hers was missing.

She sat in the chair facing the couch, her legs curled up under her, making her usual complaint about the broken springs.

"Stamps," she said thoughtfully. "Now who would bother with anything like that? If it had been jewelry or something valuable, that would make sense."

"But they were valuable, Lil. They were supposed to be worth a lot. I don't know how much."

Lil gaped at her. There was something here she didn't understand, but she wasn't the kind of person to force confidences. The most pressing need at the moment was to help Connie, to take away the look of horror that had widened her eyes.

"What did the police have to say?" she asked casually.

"Police! Why — I didn't call them."

This time Lil sat bolt upright. "Connie! You should have reported this the minute you found out you'd been robbed. That's what the police are for. Working in a law office you ought to know that better than I do."

Connie made no reply, but she had begun to shake again. She started to throw off the quilt, to get up.

"Never mind," Lil said quickly, "you stay there and

keep warm; you've had a shock. I'll call them myself." She forced herself to laugh cheerfully. "I've always wanted to do that; wanted to say, 'Get me a policeman.' "

"No!" Connie cried out in sharp protest as Lil lifted the telephone.

For an endless moment the two girls looked at each other and then Lil replaced the telephone.

"So that's the way it is," she said slowly.

"I don't know what you mean." Connie was desperate.

Lil's big warm smile was missing. She looked gravely at Connie. "Let's not fool each other, honey. Did your half brother know you had the stamps and how much they were worth?"

Connie could not make herself lie to Lil. Instead, she burst into heartbroken, racking sobs. With the deep human understanding that characterized her, Lil remained quiet until the relief of tears had left Connie exhausted. Then, gently, she helped her off the couch and persuaded her to go to bed.

"I know you don't want to talk about it," she said after she had opened the window a bare inch against the bitter night and had switched out Connie's light. In the dark it was easier to speak. "I won't ever mention it again, but I have to say this now. You are a fine and honest person, Connie, but what you are doing now is wrong."

"Nick is my half brother."

"And you are helping to convince him, if he still needs any convincing, that the law doesn't apply to him. I saw the kind of person he was as soon as I laid eyes on him. He wasn't your kind of person at all. Good night, Connie." The door closed behind her.

It was nearly daylight when Connie finally fell into an

exhausted sleep. All that long night she stared into the darkness. The day that had begun long hours ago had been the most disastrous of her life. She had lost Sandra's friendship; Kent had made clear that he had withdrawn all support and assistance from her because, she realized, he suspected her — how unfairly! — of attempting to take Jeff from Sandra. She had seen Jeff changed, different, cynical, the past forgotten. By agreeing to its sale, she had lost Stony Brook. Now she could not keep her promise to send the stamps to Kent and she knew he would brand her with the stigma of dishonesty.

Worst of all, Nick was a thief. He had taken advantage of that evening when the apartment was empty to steal the stamps. Never, from the moment when she had realized that they were missing, had she had a moment's hope that Nick was not guilty. She remembered finding him on his knees outside the door where he had lost the flashlight, which he had said was a fountain pen. He must have been tampering with the lock in some way.

When she finally fell asleep she dreamed of that shadowy figure at the airport, the man who had been waiting, gun in hand, for Nick to appear. He had been afraid at the time; he had been more afraid when he had come to the apartment, asking for help.

Then she remembered that he had promised, if she would help him once more, that he would go straight, he would become the sort of person his father had wanted him to be. Surely, surely, he had not been lying then. Perhaps, after all, she was wrong. Perhaps Lil had been right and she should have reported the theft to the police.

Next morning Connie sat late over a leisurely breakfast, alone in the apartment, because Lil was working that Saturday. In spite of herself she was relieved by Lil's absence, though she knew that her roommate would be true to her word, that she would never again make the slightest reference to the robbery unless Connie herself introduced the subject.

When the knock came at the door about noon, Connie's heart leaped. It was Nick! Now everything would be all right. He would restore the stamps. She ran to fling open the door, stood staring.

"Hello, there," Jeff said pleasantly. "I hoped I might find you at home."

Her hand crept to her throat. "Jeff!" she whispered.

"Aren't you going to ask me in?" he said teasingly.

"Why—of course." She stood aside so he could enter.

He tossed hat, overcoat, and gloves on a bench against the wall and came to sit facing her, his expression friendly but impersonal. Only his eyes, not impersonal at all, were watching her, watching the nervousness she could not conceal, the drawn expression of her face, the droop of her lips.

"Pleasant place, the Wiltown," he commented when the silence had lasted too long, a silence she was unable to break.

"Very pleasant," she agreed. "And didn't Sandra look lovely?"

He gave her a quick look through the long narrow eyes that were one of his chief charms. "Very nice. But, of course, Sandra is a very nice person." He grinned. "Your paragon or superman or whatever he is, Emery, seemed to think so, too."

"He's not mine." Connie was stung into reply. "And he's

neither a paragon nor a superman. But he is a fine lawyer with exceptional ability."

"So I gathered." Jeff's tone was rather dry. It occurred to Connie that he was jealous because of Emery's obvious admiration for Sandra. "It must be quite a load to carry so much perfection."

"He's not perfect." Eager to stick to an impersonal subject, Connie found herself telling Jeff about Emery's blind spot in regard to his younger brother. "Because he loves the law and feels his family traditionally belongs to the law, he is trying to make Colin over. Sooner or later, unless Colin fights back, he is going to be destroyed, and with the very best intentions."

"They say the road to hell is paved with good intentions," Jeff said lazily. "It isn't what we mean to achieve that counts; it's what we do achieve. And certainly it's a risk to tell anyone else how to live his life."

Connie looked up to find Jeff's eyes fixed on her in a quizzical look.

"Take Kent, for instance," he went on. "He would be the first to tell you how good his intentions are, how well he means. But, though he probably thinks he is a wonderful father because he has provided Sandra with every possible luxury, he is an egoist using her for his own ends. If you told him that, he'd blow up. He'd say it's all for her own good."

He grinned. "I think Sandra is beginning to get wise to her father. Did you notice that crack of hers last night?" He broke off. "Connie, I'm starving. Come out and let's have lunch somewhere." His tone was so casual, the past so deeply buried, that she could not refuse without ungraciousness.

Luncheon at the Plaza was gay and impersonal. Connie found herself laughing more than she had since her father's death. Afterwards they sauntered toward Central Park and he hailed a hansom cab.

"Will you be warm enough?" he asked.

They moved forward at a slow walk, the cloppety-clop of horses' hooves drowned out most of the time by taxis, by a riveter somewhere on Central Park South. Here in the park the snow was clean and sparkling under a clear cold sky.

Jeff seemed content to prolong the moment without speech but Connie was made uneasy by the silence in which she could hear so many unspoken words.

"Jeff," she said abruptly, "I don't need to ask how your job is going. You're making the success I thought you would. I could tell by Mr. Kent's manner."

"You could, couldn't you?"

Disturbed by something in his voice she said anxiously, "You like it, don't you?"

"I'm making money. That's the main thing. That's what you wanted me to do, isn't it?"

She bit back the words she wanted to speak. She did not know this new Jeff. Seeing him hard and without illusions it was difficult to remember the eager man with whom she had driven through a snowstorm in Maine.

"Speaking of money," Jeff said, "something was all wrong last night. Sandra told me you were hard up. Kent implied as much. Look here, Connie, if you want to sell Stony Brook I'll take it off your hands now. You'd be doing me a favor and I know how you hate the place." If there was a momentary bitterness in his voice, it disappeared completely. Perhaps she had only imagined it.

"And what would you do with Stony Brook?" she managed to say. "You have no time now for vacations in the woods."

"But I could always look forward to them. People need something to look forward to."

He wasn't serious, of course. His future was all mapped out. Within a few years he would be taking Kent's place and the world would be his oyster. He was simply trying to be kind to her. As Sandra had pointed out, he was extraordinarily kind and people were apt to take advantage of that kindness.

"Thanks, Jeff, but I don't know where Sandra and her father got the idea that I was in any sort of trouble."

His gloved hand took her chin, turned her face toward him. "Look at me. That's better. You can't look at me and lie. Forget the past, Connie, and that foolish dream I had. Remember that before I — spoiled things — we were friends. Real friends. Remember how I felt about your father. Now tell me the truth. I know you so well; right now you are trying to carry a burden that is too heavy for you. Share it with me. You can trust me, you know."

"I know," she said huskily. And she knew that she could. Whatever impassable barriers might exist between them, she could rely on him for his understanding and his support, his assistance in carrying a burden that was too heavy for her.

The horse plodded on through the park. The huge buildings that lined Fifth Avenue and Central Park West seemed far away. There was only the moment — and the truth.

She told him the story, holding back nothing. He was silent for so long that she said, as though defending herself, "Nick is Dad's son. I couldn't call the police. Could I?"

"Connie, how serious do you think Nick's trouble is?"

"Really serious," she said promptly. "He's scared out of his wits."

"I knew at the airport that the man meant business and I tried to make Nick believe that. I wish now I'd gone after the fellow, but I had knocked you down to keep you out of his range and you seemed — more important. Anyhow, Nick didn't want the man caught. Tell me exactly what Nick said."

He listened intently as Connie repeated the story. "A kind of insurance? You're sure he said that? And he makes collections. Good lord, it sounds as though he had got himself involved in the protection racket!"

"What's that?"

Jeff took a long breath. "There's no easy way of telling you this, darling." He seemed unaware of his use of the endearment, though she looked up at him quickly through long, silky eyelashes. He was intent on his thoughts, almost unaware of her. "The protection racket has flourished in New York for decades. Briefly, it consists of gangs who threaten small businesses — that is, they usually find small businesses their easiest prey — that their store or factory or showroom or whatever it is will be robbed or burned out or bombed — oh, yes, that has happened, too — if they are not paid a certain amount of money every week as 'protection.'"

"Oh, no!" Connie cried in protest. "How could Nick conceivably let himself be involved in anything as vile as that?"

Jeff shrugged. "Frankly, I am not worried about Nick. So far as 'letting' himself be involved, I'd find it just as easy to believe he organized the thing. No, what I am worried about is you."

"Me?"

"That thing Nick said, that you could be involved, that they might hurt you. I don't like the sound of this business at all."

"But that's not possible," she whispered, wide-eyed. "I haven't done anything to them."

His arm went around her suddenly, holding her against him. "Don't look like that, darling. Please, don't. I won't let anything happen to you."

"But why should it?"

"You are Nick's sister, a way of using pressure on him."

"Then what ought I to do?"

"Leave it to me," Jeff told her. His voice became businesslike and impersonal. "Now let's be sensible and practical about this and see what can be done. First, how can I get in touch with Nick?"

"I don't know. He has never given me his address."

"Then we'll start with the stamps. We've got to find Nick, Connie. That's the most important thing. We've got to make him see reason and, if necessary, I'll give him enough money to get out of the city, away from those hoods. But I'm not going to make it too easy for him. I'm going to force him to understand that there's no place in society for men who refuse to carry their own weight honestly."

"But how are you going to do it?"

"I collected stamps as a kid and I still know something about them, know some of the good dealers. Perhaps we can trace the stamps and that will give us a start toward finding Nick."

"He has a friend who's a stamp dealer," Connie exclaimed. "That's how he learned about the Nuñoz collection. It was written up somewhere."

"Good. That will give me a lead. I can find out something about the stamps that are missing. What can you tell me about them?"

"I don't know a thing about Dad's own stamps. I never saw them. That one morning after I reached Stony Brook he talked to me about Señor Nuñoz's collection and he told me a little about them, showed me a few things."

Her brows wrinkled as she tried to remember. "Oh, yes, I can recall some of them: Guatemalan quetzal birds, red, yellow and green. They were printed wrong so the poor birds stood on their heads. Actually, Jeff, it seems to me that most of those stamps had what they call inverted centers. Do you know what those are?"

Jeff nodded, smiling.

"Well, there were some from Persia, and a United States airmail stamp with the plane upside down."

Jeff grinned encouragingly at her worried expression. "I'll bet I can get a line on them if they should come into the market. Anyhow, I'm going to do my darnedest."

He hesitated, cleared his throat. "Another thing, Connie, there was something wrong in the atmosphere last night, something had changed the Kents' attitude toward you. Suppose I explain to them that —"

"No!" She cried out violently. "Never. I won't permit it, Jeff. If you ever betray my confidence, I'll never forgive you, not so long as I live."

He was startled by her overwrought condition. "Okay, Connie, I won't say a word. And stop worrying, please. You aren't alone in this any more. If you hear from Nick, let me know at once and try to find where he is, though the chances are that if he took the stamps, as we both believe, he'll sell them. That would get him out of his dangerous spot, and so it's more than likely that he won't get in touch with you at all. Meanwhile, I'll run down those stamps if it's the last thing I ever do."

"Oh, Jeff," she cried impulsively in her heartfelt gratitude, "I don't know what I would do without you."

There was a long pause. Then Jeff said, his voice cold and strange again, "You seem to be managing."

ELEVEN

WHEN Jeff had left Connie at her apartment he stood hesitating for a moment on the sidewalk and then turned rather aimlessly to walk toward the East River. New York, as he was constantly rediscovering, was made up of thousands of neighborhoods, each leading its separate life, with its own stores, its own churches, its own schools, its own small community interests. Small towns. Villages. Separate yet a part of the whole complex civilization of the great city.

Within a block of the shabby neighborhood where Connie lived he found himself on a block of huge, luxurious apartment buildings. Here trees were planted, canopies protected the tenants from the weather while they waited for taxis or entered their own cars. A doorman in uniform was in attendance. All you had to do, Jeff thought, was to cross the avenue with its heavy stream of traffic and, presto, you had moved from one world to another, as separate and distinct as night and day.

To make the transition on foot, as he was doing, was easy. To make it, as Connie had made it, as a way of life, was a tremendous change, one she had deliberately chosen for herself. But why? Why? The thought kept pace with his footsteps. Why? He could still remember the scorn and contempt in her voice when she had lashed at him for wanting to cast his lot in the quiet, untroubled world of the Maine woods. She had made clear that what she valued was success, money, power, influence, the glamour and excitement of New York.

And yet she was living in a shabby, rundown building; she was working in a minor clerical position. There was something he did not understand about Connie; something that it was desperately important to understand.

On one point he had no doubts at all. With her exceptional beauty and charm, with the electric quality of her personality, Connie could marry any man she wanted, one who would be able to give her the things she seemed to want. If she had not yet attained them it was because she had made the choice herself. He came back to his unanswered question. *Why?*

He had reached the river now and he stared down, fascinated as always by the water traffic, by the soaring bridges with their endless lines of cars, by a jet leaping through space toward some unknown destination, by Long Island spread out across the river.

Connie. It seemed to him that she had never been out of his thoughts since he had left her in Maine, his heart sore from her rebuff. And yet he had forgotten how beautiful she was, how lovely, how lovable.

In the weeks since he had left Maine he had doggedly tried to suppress the dream he had had, the dream of living in the Maine woods with Connie, of building a life like Bill Wyndham's, of having a family of laughing, healthy children growing up around him, of Connie beside him, comfort and delight and reward.

Well, that was out. That was over. What Connie wanted was New York and glamour, excitement and success. He would give them to her if he could. But there were two huge obstacles to that dream, to the dream that was almost good enough, the dream that was second best. The first, the overwhelming obstacle, was that Connie had rejected him because she found a life of wealth and ease more important than a simple one. If she were to accept him only because he was wealthy and successful, would they ever be happy?

The second obstacle loomed larger from day to day. From the beginning he had realized that John Kent had displayed a great deal of interest in him; that he had encouraged him, helped him to advance more quickly than other men. More than once the older man had implied, without being definite about it, that he had Jefferson Gray in mind for his successor. Until he met Bill Wyndham, Jeff had been dazzled by his good luck; it seemed to him that life offered nothing he could not obtain in time. Even now he was profoundly grateful to Kent.

He did not know when he had first become aware that Kent was deliberately throwing him and Sandra together. In the beginning he had paid little attention. Then Kent began to drop hints. The man who succeeded him would require more than salary. He would need the support of a solid fortune behind him. Sandra was to be his sole heir and she would have a fortune in her hands, one that would, of course, be available to her husband.

More than once Jeff had planned what he must say to Kent, some tactful way of explaining that no one could decide for him whom he was going to marry. He was held back partly out of a real regard for Sandra, partly because he knew that she was no more in love with him than he was with her. When and if the time came, she herself would make clear to her father that she intended to be the mistress of her own fate.

Lately, however, there had been a change. Sandra

seemed to take for granted that he would invariably be her escort, that he would be on hand when she wanted him, that he would fill in at dinner parties, that he would be a dancing partner. Then, last night, when they had been dancing at the Wiltown, she had spoken of the opera.

"Pick me up tomorrow about a quarter of eight," she said.

He had looked at her in surprise. "Sorry, Sandra, I have other plans for tomorrow evening."

"You'll have to change them," she told him, a touch of sharpness, a touch even of command, in her voice. "Father helps support the opera, as you know. He doesn't like having his box unoccupied and he can't go himself. He would be rather — annoyed if you couldn't make it."

"I — see," Jeff remarked thoughtfully, and at that moment he began to see a great deal.

Sandra smiled slightly. "I thought you would." After a few moments she added, "Oh, by the way, Jeff, do be nice to Connie tonight, won't you?"

"Why shouldn't I?" he asked in surprise.

"The poor girl has finally got in touch with us to borrow money and it must embarrass her when Father has already done so much for her. I knew when she called that she would want something. She always does."

Jeff stared unseeingly down into the East River, remembering that conversation. For a bleak moment he wondered whether Sandra and her father were right. Was Connie simply after money, after what she could get from her friends? She had practically told him herself in Maine that money was what mattered, what she respected. He recalled her quoting her father, who didn't want her to be a sacrifice like her mother.

For a long time he stood there. Suppose she really were a

gold digger. Suppose she didn't, couldn't love him. Suppose — what did it matter, after all? Whatever she was, he loved her. And she — was it Colin Emery she loved, the lawyer whom she had defended so warmly, whose brother she had praised so lavishly? The brother who had obviously fallen with a loud thud for Sandra.

What would happen, he wondered in some amusement, if Stephen Emery and Sandra Kent should become serious about each other? They were alike, he suspected, in many qualities: an exceptional regard for appearances, a deep respect for business and professional success, a need to be a leading part of the social fabric of their world.

What would Kent do in that case? Jeff found himself wishing that it would happen. As things were, he felt like a fly in a spiderweb, caught up in Kent's ambitions rather than his own. One thing was sure: Kent would not accept lightly having his arrangements changed, his plans upset. He was not a man accustomed to having his wishes disregarded.

The stamps! Jeff's dreaming mood dissolved and he was once again back in the practical world. Nick had undoubtedly stolen the stamps to get money to repay the sum he had pocketed instead of turning over to his — well, gang was probably the right word. Nick was in real trouble, in real danger.

In a way he deserved it, of course. If it weren't for Connie, Jeff would not dream of helping him. But Connie had been threatened not only by the gangsters but by Nick himself. Jeff had no faith in Nick's promised reformation. He remembered Nick's warning his sister that unless she divided any money she got with him she would be one very, very sorry girl.

He recalled his fight with the man at the airport. The

fellow had meant business. And he had dared to threaten Connie. Connie in danger!

How in heaven's name had Nick become involved with a gang, got into the protection racket? Probably he had thought it would be easier than earning an honest living. Well, Jeff thought grimly, he has learned now just how easy it is to live outside the law, to be in the clutches of men whose only code is one of violence.

He still had the revolver which he had taken from the armed man and he had placed it in his safe-deposit box. Now, however, he must get it out, try to discover the identity of the owner. Until Monday, however, he would be unable to get at the box. At least he could attempt to find the missing stamps.

He turned back, walking with more decision, entered a drugstore, and checked a telephone directory. He dialed the number with little hope. Weekends were bad times for reaching businessmen. But a brisk voice answered.

"Morton speaking."

"Oh, good. This is Jefferson Gray. I don't know whether you remember me but —"

"Gray? No, don't tell me. Let me think. Gray — uh — U.S. stamps."

Jeff laughed. "That's right. You're a marvel with that memory of yours. By any chance, can you give me some time this afternoon?"

"Come along now, if you like. I won't be closing for another hour. I'm at the same address and I'll be glad to see you."

Jeff got out of the subway at Fourteenth Street. The stamp dealer had a small, dusty shop on the second floor of a dilapidated old walk-up on lower Fourth Avenue, on a block made up chiefly of secondhand bookshops. There was no one but the owner in the shop when Jeff went in. Morton was a stout, elderly man with thick glasses who got up to hold out his hand as Jeff appeared.

"You haven't changed a bit," he declared. "Good to see you again. What are you collecting now?"

"This is rather a queer deal," Jeff told him. "I've got to withhold names. You'll see why in a minute." He told about the theft of the stamp collection. "What I want to find out is how to go about getting them back. Naturally I'll be happy to pay for your time and expenses, whatever may be involved."

Morton listened, his eyes studying Jeff's face thoughtfully. Not often you saw such a well-set-up young fellow; not often you saw a face with that much character and determination.

"There are crooked dealers in stamps just as there are crooks in every field," he said at last. "The thief would probably know one of them before taking the stamps. Unless, of course, he had a private collector waiting for them."

"Can you help me?"

"Not unless you trust me a good deal more than you have so far," Morton said bluntly. "I've got to know what those stamps were. How else —"

"Yes, of course. I see that. This is confidential?"

"Naturally."

"The most valuable part of the collection belonged to a Mexican, a man named Tomas Nuñoz."

Morton's eyes were alert. He held up a pudgy hand. "Just a minute," he said. He got up to rummage through a stack of dog-eared magazines devoted to stamps, riffled through pages, gave a grunt of satisfaction as he came back to his desk. "I thought so. There was an article about them a few months ago. He left the whole collection to —" Pages turned. "Yes, here it is. To William Wyndham."

"That's it," Jeff said. "Wyndham was a great and valued friend of mine. He died last October, leaving his stamps to an old acquaintance. Not long after Wyndham's death the stamps were stolen. We've simply got to find them, Morton."

"Just what is involved?" Morton asked slowly.

After a pause Jeff said, "What is involved is not only my desire to see that Wyndham's wishes are carried out, but to make sure that the integrity of his daughter, who had the stamps in her possession, is not questioned and that the — the man who inherited the stamps will not find himself in a position where he can cause Miss Wyndham any awkwardness, any unpleasantness."

Morton, his eyes still on the article, nodded his comprehension without looking up. Young Gray's voice had betrayed him. He seemed to be deeply involved in the welfare of Wyndham's daughter. Morton found himself hoping that the girl deserved Gray's assistance. He would hate to see this fine young man wasted on a girl who was not worthy of him.

"Well, what can we do?" Jeff asked impatiently.

"There's a pretty exhaustive description of the Nuñoz collection here. At least we know what we are looking for."

"Then you'll help me?" Jeff said eagerly.

"Sure I'll help you. I'll start making some inquiries. I know most of the reputable dealers and some," Morton chuckled, "who aren't. But they have to be handled differently, of course. They wouldn't tell me anything for free, even if they knew. I spend too much time trying to expose them, to keep the business clean."

"Then how can we go about it?"

"Look here," Morton suggested. "Let's draft an ad for some of the more valuable stamps in that collection — no mention of Nuñoz, of course — and see what happens. A phony dealer would steer clear of me but you could do it yourself under another name, and if you flush any game we'll figure out the next step."

Together the two men wrote an ad asking for the twenty-four-cent airmail stamp with the inverted center. They decided to sign it Winterson, using Morton's home telephone number. Morton agreed to get in touch with Jeff as soon as he had a lead.

Jeff was feeling more light-hearted when he left Morton's shop and went back to his apartment to have a hasty meal and dress for the opera. As he stood before his mirror adjusting his white tie, he wondered what he was going to do about Sandra. The night before, she had revealed qualities that had disconcerted him because they were so like her father's. She had practically reminded him that he was not a free agent, that he was expected to act as her escort whenever he was required to do so. And yet the perplexing factor was that Sandra was not in love with him. He could not be mistaken about that.

I'm not going to be a tame lapdog, he thought grimly. Not for any amount of money. Not for any degree of business success. If my position with Kent depends on my attitude toward Sandra, then I'll have to give up the position.

He was fully aware of what was involved. Never again, by any possible chance, would he be able to hold a comparable position, one with the same high salary, certainly not one with the same dazzling future. It wasn't the kind of position a man could afford to throw away lightly. And without it he would have no possible chance with Connie.

He adjusted a white silk evening scarf around his neck, slipped into his overcoat. Connie represented everything he wanted in life. No, he realized suddenly, she didn't. His own integrity mattered more. It would be an empty life without her, but at least he would be able to face himself.

Again he found himself worrying about Connie. Something had changed the attitude of the Kents toward the girl he loved. Was it some awareness on their part of his love for her or was it something about Connie herself? He remembered again the violence with which she had refused to let him explain to them about her difficulties with Nick. And again he found himself faced with the puzzle of Connie who refused to marry a man without suitable ambition and yet had chosen the obscure, almost impoverished, life she was now leading.

Sandra was waiting in the long drawing room for Jeff when he arrived. Tonight she glittered like a Christmas tree in one of the new jeweled evening dresses cut on the lines of a sari that had become so sensationally popular.

His brows rose a trifle as he looked at her. "That's gorgeous raiment you've got on," he said lightly.

"It's not my usual style," she admitted. For a moment her really beautiful blue eyes rested wistfully on his face. "Céleste talked me into it. Was it a mistake, Jeff?"

"Not if you like it."

Her mouth twisted wryly and then she said, with a touch of her father's impatience, "What are we waiting for? Shall we go?"

At first it seemed as though the trip to the opera would be a silent one. At last Sandra broke the silence with an amused laugh in which there was something artificial.

"Connie seems to have gone off the deep end about that man she is working for. The way she pitched into you and father over evading jury duty!"

"She was right, I suppose," Jeff said. "I hadn't given it much thought before. She made me feel like a bit of a shirker so far as my civic duties are concerned. After all, I owe something to my country."

"Oh." Sandra was silent again.

"He seemed to be a pleasant sort of man," Jeff remarked. "That is, if you like stuffed shirts."

"Mr. Emery isn't a stuffed shirt," Sandra said quickly, and Jeff grinned to himself in the darkness of the car. "Mature men are always more interesting, but I shouldn't think he would attract Connie. Or that she would attract him, for that matter. She's so frivolous. Always was. All she has ever cared about is having fun."

"A stenographic pool in a law firm doesn't strike me as a riotously frivolous way of life," Jeff said mildly.

Sandra touched his arm with a gloved hand. "Jeff, my dear, you respond to everyone who appeals to your pity and your chivalry. You simply must not let people make use of you."

"I don't intend to, Sandra," he said, his voice unexpectedly hard. He held out his hand as she stepped from the car to face the usual battery of cameras. Then they were in the lighted lobby.

A few minutes later, in Kent's box, he slipped off her evening coat, held her chair, and then sat beside her. The orchestra was already making muted sounds as the violinists tuned their instruments. Ushers were moving swiftly up and down the aisles. Just before the lights dimmed and a wave of applause greeted the entrance of the conductor, Jeff turned to scan the row of boxes. He caught his breath.

Connie was sitting beside a handsome man in evening clothes, a man who was leaning toward her attentively. No wonder, he thought. He had never seen her look so breath-takingly beautiful.

Across the opera house Connie's eyes met his, moved on to Sandra. She nodded coolly and then flashed a brilliant smile at the man beside her.

TWELVE

WHEN Connie had left Jeff at the door that afternoon and returned to the apartment, she had found Lil, who had come back after her morning's work. Lil met her with her usual warm smile.

"Surprise," she called gaily. "I've got an unbirthday present for you."

"What have you been up to?" Connie was aware that Lil had worried about her comment regarding Nick the night before, that she was anxious to make amends, in case she had hurt her.

"Look," Lil said eagerly. She opened a suitbox, removed tissue paper, held up a blue and white evening dress. "Did you ever see anything lovelier?"

"It's exquisite," Connie breathed, enraptured.

"Madame had it returned today. The woman who bought it has to go into mourning. It's never been worn, and it's your size, so —"

"For me!" Connie squealed in delight.

"I could hardly wait for you to come home," Lil said, her face glowing. "With that hair of yours and your coloring it will be simply perfect. Come on, let's see how it looks when you try it on."

"But, Lil," Connie expostulated, "where can I wear anything like this? It's for formal occasions and I never have dates."

"Why not?" Lil asked bluntly. "You're the most beautiful girl I've ever seen. You've got everything you need to attract simply scores of men and yet you spend all your evenings alone. I can't figure you out, Connie."

"There's no mystery."

"Once you said you were a one-man woman. I'd like to lay my hands on that one man, that's all I have to say."

Connie threw back her head, laughing helplessly. Then, unexpectedly, her eyes filled with tears.

"I'm sorry," Lil said. "But, you know, I wonder if you're right, Connie. You think you'd spoil the life of the man you love and the girl who is your best friend. I wonder, aren't you kind of deciding for them what's the best way of leading their lives? I mean — well, people should work it out for themselves. That is," she stumbled on, "if your one man loves you it would be no good trying to turn him over to someone else. I mean —"

As the telephone rang, Lil picked it up, her brows arched, and she handed it to Connie.

"Miss Wyndham, this is Stephen Emery. I've just discovered that my box at the opera is not going to be used tonight. If I send you a ticket do you think you could make use of it? Joan Sutherland is singing *Lucia di Lammermoor.*"

"I'd love it," Connie said in delight.

"Good. I'll send a messenger with your ticket at once. I hope you enjoy the evening, Miss Wyndham." The telephone was shut off.

"Lil! My boss is sending me a ticket for the opera tonight, just in time to wear your exquisite dress!"

Lil glowed with pleasure. Then her smile faded. "Just *one* ticket," she said gloomily.

Connie laughed. "That doesn't matter. It's the opera that counts, not the company."

"Maybe." Lil didn't sound convinced.

"What are you doing tonight?"

"Nothing." When Connie looked surprised, Lil explained, "I was going out again with Robert but he's getting serious and so I thought I'd better break it off now. I don't like girls who cheat and lead a man on just because they want someone to take them places. He'd be better off with a girl who liked him more. Not that he's not a nice boy but — I don't know — I just won't settle for him and that's that."

"More power to you," Connie said.

When she had put on the blue and white dress, cut as only a master can cut, she and Lil looked at each other in mutual congratulation.

"It's perfect," Lil declared. "I've always said you could wear clothes better than anyone I ever saw."

"Anyone would look fine in this," Connie exclaimed. "It's the most beautiful dress I've ever worn."

At Lil's insistence she took a taxi to protect the new dress and her satin slippers from the winter streets. On the short drive she found herself thinking of Lil's comments. Queer that, after she had been objecting to the way John Kent tried to guide Sandra's life and Stephen Emery tried to guide Colin's life, Lil should accuse her of doing the same thing. Interfering with Jeff and Sandra. Absurd, of course.

The door of the box at the Metropolitan was opened for her and she went in, removed her coat and sat toward the back, as it was empty. For a few minutes she looked around the rapidly filling house, at the brilliant lights, listened to the soft tuning of strings, heard a light ripple as a hand brushed over the harp that would later introduce Lucia, glanced along the boxes, at the women's gleaming shoulders and sparkling jewels, the men's white shirt-fronts. This was the last time she would ever sit in the Metropolitan Opera House. Next year, the historic old building would be just another of New York's discards. Her imagination filled the stage with the famous singers of the past, Caruso, Geraldine Farrar, Melba, Tetrazzini; filled the boxes with the glittering figures of old New York society.

There was a faint movement behind her as the door of the box was opened and someone came in.

"Well," a man said, startled, amused, delighted. "The Snow Queen."

She turned in astonishment to see Colin Emery, in formal evening clothes, smiling down at her. His eyes missed nothing from the burnished hair to the heightened color in her cheeks as she caught sight of him, to the exquisite evening dress that fell in graceful folds to the satin-slippered feet.

He tossed his overcoat and hat on a chair at the back of the box, drew up chairs in the front and made her sit there beside him.

"A jewel like you should not be hidden. You are definitely for display," he declared. He added, still with that note of amusement in his voice, "There are times when I find Steve's efforts to lead my life for me rather tiresome, but this is definitely a chalk-up for him."

Of course, Connie realized, he was quite right. Emery had deliberately planned this meeting between them. It amused her to know that he had done so after seeing her with the Kents. Apparently he felt that her social connections were suitable. She was aware of a pang of anger and then, meeting Colin's eyes, seeing his amusement, she leaned back in her chair and laughed.

"The joke is on us, Mr. Emery," she admitted.

"I'm not sure." His smile faded. "After all, no man can be wrong all the time, though Steve does his best. But perhaps for once I underestimated my brother."

He leaned toward her with the familiar expression on his face, the look of the successful bachelor on the prowl. "Mr. Emery?" he said reproachfully. "Last time it was Colin."

Connie, looking across the theater to escape his demanding eyes, saw the Kent box, saw Sandra speaking earnestly to Jeff, met Jeff's eyes. She nodded in greeting and then turned with a brilliant smile to her companion.

"Colin it is," she agreed, and then leaned back in silence as the conductor lifted his baton.

After several attempts to speak to her, Colin realized that she was listening intently to the music so he did not attempt to disturb her again. Actually Connie heard nothing of the first half of the act. Across the room were Jeff and Sandra, engrossed in each other, living in a world in which she no longer had a place.

Then Joan Sutherland's voice soared and rippled, trilled and rang out through the theater in its incomparable loveliness, and for a little while beauty was enough.

But when the end of the first act came, Connie could no longer escape into the magic of music. Nor would she let her eyes roam again toward the box where Jeff sat with Sandra. Instead, she turned to Colin with an impish smile.

"Well?" she asked challengingly.

"Steve planned this, of course," he said, answering her implied question. "He practically used a bludgeon on me to get me here tonight. He not only approves of you but this, my dear," and he chuckled, "means that he thinks you are good for me."

Connie laughed, too. "Heaven forbid!" Then she sobered. "Colin," she said impulsively, "if you weren't a —"

"A playboy?"

"No, a lawyer — what would you like to be?"

"I'd like to be a dairy farmer," he said promptly. "Go ahead and laugh."

"I'm not laughing."

"What! The young beauty in the ravishing dress, the smart sophisticate, the New Yorker to her bones? You think it's not funny to have a dairy farm?"

"This New Yorker to her bones," Connie told him, "was brought up in the Maine woods. If things had gone right, this smart sophisticate would be living there today, helping to turn a private lodge into a paying camp for vacationers and hunters and tourists."

His jaw dropped in sheer astonishment. "Are you, by any remote chance, serious?"

"Completely serious," Connie assured him, and he looked into the steady eyes and nodded.

"And you can't do it?"

"No," she said briefly. "That's out. Forever." She forestalled his next question. "But why don't you follow your own dream? What prevents you?"

"Well, I —" He was somewhat taken aback. "Things just didn't work out that way," he said lamely.

"Did you try to make them work out that way?" Before he could reply she said, "Forgive me. I shouldn't have said that. I've been haunted all my life by an unruly tongue that speaks before I can stop it."

And that's not the worst of it, she told herself. Jeepers, maybe Lil is right and I am trying to tell people how to live their own lives. What's got into me lately? I can see what's wrong with other people but not what's wrong with myself.

The dimming of the house lights ended the conversation. This time Colin made no attempt to distract her attention from the music, but she was aware that he was studying her, a perplexed frown on his good-looking face.

During the second intermission she found herself, in spite of her resolution, glancing toward the Kent box. Sandra was surrounded by a group of friends. There was no sign of Jeff. Then the door of the Emery box opened and she looked around to find him smiling down at her.

"Jeff! Isn't Sutherland wonderful tonight? I want you to know each other. Mr. Gray, Mr. Emery. You met his brother last night, Jeff, at the Wiltown."

"So that's it," Colin said, enlightened.

"That's it," Connie agreed with a sidelong smile. She found Jeff watching her gravely.

"I won't keep you, Connie." His manner was rather stiff, unexpectedly formal. "I just wanted you to know that I saw that friend of mine this afternoon; he was interested — and hopeful."

"Oh, good! Thank you so much." She could not keep the fervor out of her voice, and for a moment Jeff's face warmed.

"I'll let you know as soon as I hear anything. Good night, Mr. Emery. Connie."

When he had gone Colin said, "Now I get it. The plot is coming clear. Steve saw you at the Wiltown last night so now you are good enough for — Junior." He smiled at her outraged expression. "But please don't underrate me. I know Junior isn't good enough for — what did your handsome friend call you? — Connie."

"I'll tell you one thing, Colin Emery," Connie snapped. "If you are weak enough to let your brother lead your life for you, you deserve just what you get!"

Oops, she thought, there I go again. The curtain rose on the last act and she forgot her companion in the torrent of song that filled the theater as Sutherland did the famous Mad Scene.

Cheers, applause, calls, the curtain swirling open and shut, the red-haired prima donna bowing, waving. Then the house lights went up and Colin lifted her coat over her bare shoulders.

"Not tonight, but thank you," she said when he suggested a supper club.

When the taxi drew up before the shabby apartment building Colin helped her out, asked the driver to wait, and took her door-key.

"I'm glad my roommate is home," Connie confessed.

Colin smiled down at her. "Afraid I'm going to put on my wolf's clothing?"

"Oh, no, it's just — well, last night there was a burglar while we were both out and somehow I wouldn't like to go into an empty apartment."

"A burglar!"

As they walked down the narrow dark hallway she explained briefly that the apartment had been entered and some money taken from her handbag. As she reached for the doorknob he checked her, knelt in front of the lock and flicked his lighter. When he stood up he was frowning.

"That lock looks scratched to me," he said, "though it's hard to tell in this light. Someone may possibly have made an impression and had a key cut. If I were you I'd get a new lock right away."

"I will," she said fervently and then opened the door.

Lil, wearing her exotic lounging pajamas, was on her knees beside the chair with the broken springs. She had turned it upside down and she was poking futilely at the spring. She turned in surprise as Connie came in followed by Colin.

"Lil, this is Mr. Emery. My roommate, Lillian Debaney."

Lil gave Colin a quick look and then her face lighted with its heartwarming smile. "Welcome to the palace, Mr. Emery. Sorry to upset things, Connie, but I finally decided to stop lamenting about this chair and do something about it. The only trouble is that I don't know what to do."

Colin tossed his coat and hat on the bench by the wall and bent over the chair. "Here," he said briskly, "you'll never fix the thing that way. We need some heavy twine to tie those broken springs and some burlap. Do you have any?"

Lil chuckled. "Why, of course. We are fully prepared for all emergencies at all times."

"Tell you what," Colin said, ignoring this frivolity, "I've got all sorts of stuff in my workroom at home. Suppose I drop around tomorrow morning and see what I can do."

"Fine!" Lil said enthusiastically before Connie could speak.

Colin picked up his coat and hat. "See you about eleven, then." He was gone before Connie had a chance to say good night.

For a long time there was silence in the room. Then Lil said, "For a girl who set out with only one ticket, you seem to have done all right."

Connie laughed. "I think my boss is trying to make a match for his brother."

"Oh." Lil's voice was curiously flat. As Connie started toward her own room she said, "He's terribly good-looking, isn't he?"

"Who? Colin?" Connie said absently. "Why, yes, I suppose so."

When she was half undressed she heard Lil call from the other room, "I suppose he's fallen in love with you."

"Who? Colin?" Connie called back, still absently.

"Of course, Colin! Who else were we talking about? He could hardly help it, looking the way you do tonight."

"Uh-uh," Connie said. "If I were as beautiful as Queen Nefertiti he'd never be in love with me. It's human nature to rebel when someone tries to force you to fall in love, or at least to plan a marriage for you."

"Oh."

Connie switched out the light and got into bed. Some time later she heard Lil moving around her room. "Anything wrong?" she called sleepily.

"No, I'm just trying something with my hair. I didn't mean to disturb you."

ii

Connie awakened at her usual time next morning and then, remembering that it was Sunday, turned over to sleep again. There was a sound of bustle in the kitchenette and she called, "For heaven's sake, what are you doing up so early?"

"Just mixing a batch of cinnamon buns," Lil replied. "Go back to sleep."

When she finally got up, Connie took her bath, a long leisurely one on Sunday with plenty of bath salts, in contrast with the swift shower of week days, and dressed in a leaf-green wool with a cowl neck. When she went into the living room she stopped short. Lil, instead of her usual exotic lounging pajamas, wore a deep red wool skirt and matching sweater. When she looked up, Connie barely recognized her. The false eyelashes were gone, and so were the extravagant makeup and the teased hairdo. Curiously enough, her eyes seemed bigger, brighter, softer without the makeup. Her face looked younger and sweeter.

She watched Connie steadily with something anxious in her expression. "Well?" she asked at length, with a new shyness.

"Lil, I've never seen you look so nice."

The anxious expression faded. Lil jumped to her feet and Connie noticed that, instead of spike heels, she was wearing loafers, which made her seem much smaller.

"Why you're just a little girl," she exclaimed in surprise.

"I hope Madame won't mind," Lil said with a worried look.

"What caused this transformation?"

Lil was silent for so long that Connie looked at her in surprise.

"I've got your breakfast ready," Lil said hastily and went into the kitchenette. In a few minutes she returned, set up a folding table before Connie who was watching the color coming and going in the other girl's face.

"Lil," she said sternly, "look at me!" When Lil did so she went on in her stern manner, "Prisoner at the bar, confess!"

"I've got to watch those cinnamon buns," Lil mumbled.

"You'll stay right here and I don't want you to evade questions. Is it — is it Colin?"

"You aren't in love with him, are you, Connie?"

"Not a bit," Connie assured her.

"It doesn't make a scrap of sense," Lil said, still flushed, letting her coffee get cold, ignoring the orange juice, the bowl of cereal. "He's not my kind at all. I'm not his. I never could be. I knew that when I saw him, so handsome and impressive in evening clothes. You know that's the first time I ever saw a man in white tie and tails, except on television or in the movies. No, not a bit my kind. Only I took one look at him and I knew he was the one for me. That's why —"

"Why you spent half the night washing the rinse out of your hair," Connie prompted, laughter sparkling in her eyes.

Lil nodded, her face sober. "He saw me like that, you know, sort of flashy, and I could tell he was ready to flirt any time. Only — I don't want it that way. It was important he should see me just the way I really am. If he doesn't like that then — well, the sooner you know for sure, the better off you are. Only I didn't want any deception, anything dishonest."

Connie jumped up and hugged her. "Good for you," she exclaimed, but her heart was twisted with pity. Never in the world would Stephen Emery agree to accept a sister-in-law like Lillian Debaney. Never could she, with every effort, be able to fit into the Emery social life. Worst of all, it was difficult to imagine the sophisticated Colin having any genuine interest in the simple, unpretentious housewife who was the real Lil.

Well, she thought, Lil is probably right. You can't build anything lasting on pretense. The sooner the truth is known the better.

When the knock came at the door, promptly at eleven, she opened it. "Good morning, Colin." She began to laugh. "Good heavens, what have you got there?"

"Chair-mending service, madam," Colin said briskly. He was as unlike the Colin of the night before as possible. He wore baggy slacks and a turtleneck sweater, and he was loaded down with balls of twine, rolls of burlap, a tool chest. He set them on the floor and rubbed his hands with satisfaction. Then he sniffed.

"Coffee?" he asked hopefully.

"A good workman," Connie informed him, "expects to do his job before he is paid for it."

"Very poor policy," Colin told her.

Lil came in, carrying a tray with coffee and a plate of piping-hot cinnamon buns.

"We thought you might like a cup of coffee," she said.

Colin looked at her in surprise, taking in the full extent of the metamorphosis. Then he reached enthusiastically for the tray. "Food first, work later," he decided. "And you, Connie, could learn a great deal from your roommate. That's the way a man likes to be treated."

"It's things like this that are ruining labor today," Connie grumbled.

While she busied herself in her own room, getting clothes ready for the coming week, paying bills and writing letters, she could hear the buzz of conversation from the living room, punctuated by constant outbursts of laughter. Now and then she came in to see how they were getting along. Colin seemed to have strewn every spare inch of space with burlap, twine, tools, and the dismantled springs of the chair.

No one from Emery & Emery, Connie thought in amusement, would ever recognize Junior, the dapper bachelor, in the man with the tousled hair who was sitting cross-legged on the floor, tying the broken springs.

"Here, give me that," Connie heard him say. "You'll break your nails. So you're a model? Now that must be a glamorous job."

"Glamour, ha! You walk up and down, smirking, for six or seven hours a day. Of course, the shop is glamorous, but not for the people who work there."

"Where would you like to work?"

"In my own house," Lil said defiantly.

Colin looked up quickly, finished tying the springs and sat back to admire his handiwork. "Now all I hope is that I haven't any parts left over. Imagine my embarrassment! Let me call your attention to a magnificent piece of work."

"Don't," Connie warned Lil, "give him any praise, for heaven's sake. He's vain enough as it is."

"I don't know," Lil said thoughtfully. "That's not bad at all, considering he's only a lawyer."

"Just for that," Colin threatened her, "I'm not going to take you into partnership when I set up as an upholsterer."

Lil smothered fictitious sobs. "All my dreams destroyed," she wailed.

"You've already had more than your share," Colin said severely. "I usually charge extra when people watch me work."

"Ha," Lil scoffed, "I'll bet you never get a chance to collect on that."

"She doesn't like me," Colin complained to Connie, "and I want to be liked. Here I am, working my fingers to the bone —"

"And eating us out of house and home at the same time," Connie reminded him. "That's the fifth cinnamon bun you've had."

"Great Scot, she even keeps count of every bite I eat. You are the two most disagreeable, unpleasant females I've ever met. Hey, Lil, roll that burlap toward me, won't you? I can't get up."

"Another cinnamon bun and you'll need a derrick," Connie told him unkindly.

Next time she returned to the living room the chances of ever finishing work on the chair seemed remote. Lil and Colin were still sitting cross-legged beside it on the floor but they weren't working.

". . . dry as dust," Colin was saying gloomily.

"Well," Lil remarked, "if you think law is dry as dust why don't you do what you want to do, for heaven's sake?"

"Just walk out and buy a dairy farm, I suppose."

"Exactly."

"Lady, you don't know my brother Steve. He'd think I was out of my mind. All that work — and manual work at that —"

"But you like manual work," Lil pointed out. She looked questioningly at the neglected chair. "At least I guess so."

Colin laughed and set to work again. "So you think being a dairy farmer makes sense," he said.

"What makes sense is living your own life, not letting someone live it for you. Do you want Steve's approval or your own? That's what it really boils down to. And it looks as though you'll have to make the choice."

"I thought I had made the choice," Colin said slowly. "It's queer, but in a way I'm not so sure now."

It was midafternoon when he gathered up the debris and looked at the finished chair. "Let me come back, won't you?" he said, a curious humility in his voice. "It's fun being here. And I'm a good handyman. Please let me come." He grinned mischievously. "Steve will be delighted if he thinks I'm coming to see Connie."

There was a long, awkward silence and then Lil said, her voice curiously flat, the big smile gone from her sober mouth, "No, Colin, if you are ashamed of me, I don't want you to come back."

THIRTEEN

CONNIE was typing rapidly when Colin came in the next morning. He stopped at her desk.

"Look here, Connie, I want to explain about that stupid thing I said, that Steve would be delighted if he thought I was coming to see you. I wouldn't have hurt Lil for the world. She's a little darling. I just want you to know —"

"Miss Wyndham?" Stephen Emery said from the doorway and, with a muttered comment, Colin went on to his own office.

Connie gathered up notebook and pencils. Then the telephone on her desk rang. She looked with apology at Emery and lifted the telephone. Uncharacteristically, the senior partner, instead of moving away, approached until he was almost beside her desk, obviously listening.

"Miss Wyndham speaking."

"Constance, this is John Kent. I've just had an offer through a broker for Stony Brook. Twenty-two thousand five hundred. It's an excellent offer and I don't think you could do better. I suggest you accept it."

"Thank you, Mr. Kent. Of course I'll take your advice."

"Then I'll put it through right away. It's a cash deal so you'll have the money very shortly. I understand it won't be unwelcome."

"Money is never unwelcome, is it?" Connie said lightly.

"Thank you again." She put down the telephone, feeling strangely empty, bereft, forlorn. Stony Brook no longer belonged to her. She would never see it again.

When she was seated beside Emery's big desk she opened her notebook and looked up, waiting for dictation. Instead, the senior partner was leaning back in his chair watching her thoughtfully.

"The Kents are great friends of yours, aren't they?" he observed.

"Mr. Kent and my father were great friends. And Mr. Kent put me through college because my father once saved his life. For four years I practically lived with them when Sandra and I weren't sharing a room at college. Yes, we were friends for a long time."

"Were?" Emery said alertly.

Connie was aware of a faint tingle of anger along her veins. Her relationship with the Kents did not concern Stephen Emery. She met his eyes squarely, smiling without making any answer. She had been willing, almost eager, to make clear that she claimed no social equality with them; she did not want him misled about her position. Beyond that she had no intention of confiding in him.

After a moment, when he realized that she was not going to speak, not going to satisfy his curiosity, he said, "Did you enjoy the opera?"

"Very much." Connie's lips twitched in an amused smile. "And the company you provided."

Some inflection in her voice made him say quickly, "You aren't angry, are you? I simply meant you to have a pleasant evening."

"I did have a pleasant evening, Mr. Emery. Very pleasant. I have always loved that opera and I like Colin."

There was a faint, pleased smile on his lips at her use of

his brother's first name. "But? I gather you have some reservations in your mind."

She leaned forward, bronze hair swinging softly around her face, her eyes level and direct. Magnificent eyes the girl had, Emery thought. A truly beautiful creature. She would make a most effective hostess for Colin; and, with her loveliness and her charm, she would keep him interested; in time she would make him settle down.

"I suppose people don't like being treated as though they were puppets, Mr. Emery," she surprised him by saying.

"What do you mean by that?" There was no smile on his face now. It was cold, remote, hostile, but Connie found that she was no longer afraid of him.

"I mean that you deliberately manipulated Colin and me to serve your own ends when you arranged for us to meet in your box at the opera."

"My own ends?" he said stiffly.

She nodded. "You think Colin is just a playboy, wasting his life, and you want him to settle down with a suitable wife, don't you?"

"Certainly, Miss Wyndham, you can't think, if I had any such idea in mind, that there was any conceivable want of regard for you! It seems to me that any young woman could regard it as a compliment. The highest kind of compliment to her appearance, her manner, her character, her —"

"Her friends," Connie flashed. "After you saw me with the Kents you had this idea, didn't you?"

She had stung him into anger, but he struggled for control. "Naturally I find background important. Colin must not marry a girl who cannot be a suitable hostess for him."

"Poor Colin," Connie said.

Emery got up to walk to the window, to look unseeingly out at the great curved Pan-Am building, at the moving traffic so far below, looking like a child's toys, stopping, starting, as though pulled by an invisible giant's strings. Like puppets, he thought. The girl believed he had been trying to manipulate her and Colin as though they were puppets.

Her reaction baffled him. He had fully expected that she would be flattered by finding Colin in the opera box, that the whole situation would delight her, and she would use all her woman's wit to bring about a proposal. Instead she had been offended.

When he came back he leaned against the desk, holding her eyes with his own. "You could save him, Miss Wyndham. That is a solemn charge."

She shook her head without reply.

"You mean you aren't interested in my brother. Is that it?"

"I mean that the only person who can save Colin is Colin himself. You have tried, and I know you thought it was for the best, to decide what kind of life he should live, what kind of person he should be. Only it doesn't work, Mr. Emery. It has never worked. No one can make basic decisions for other people. A man can be a whole man, a good man, only if he is himself, the kind of person his own nature meant him to be. And Colin isn't like you. He has really tried, I think, but he never satisfied you because he wasn't as good a lawyer as you are. And you always let him see you thought he was a failure. That's why he became a playboy. It was a kind of retaliation, a way of saying, 'You'll be sorry.' "

"You don't understand." In spite of himself Emery revealed a momentary irritation.

"Wait," she said eagerly. "Please let me explain, because this is important, Mr. Emery, and it's something you won't ever see for yourself."

His lips tightened and she thought, oh dear, here I go again.

"You won't find it in the law books. It's part of the wisdom of the human heart. To you law is a mission; to Colin it's dry as dust. You can't make him over; you can only distort him, shackle him, thwart him, make him less than the person he should be. The other day I read the wisest statement. Logan Pearsall Smith said: 'The test of a vocation is when you love the drudgery that goes with it.' You love that drudgery; Colin is bored by it. The vocation is wrong for him."

"And he would do better as a dairy farmer, I suppose."

"If that's what he wants. Yes, by all means. You see, I think it's better for a man to be the very best dairy farmer there is than to be a poor lawyer."

"I see." Emery's fingers drummed on the edge of the desk. "You take it for granted, young and inexperienced as you are, that my theories won't work. Has it occurred to you that you may have failed to understand my objective?"

"I think," Connie said, "I understand your real objective even better than you do yourself. As for your theories, I have seen them tried before. In fact, during the past four years I have watched Mr. Kent try to force Sandra into the pattern he has set for her."

The expression on Emery's face changed. She had caught his attention. He was listening alertly.

"Mr. Kent believes he's a perfect father, that whatever he decides is for Sandra's own good. But only as long as it is what he wants himself. It was never enough for her to be

Sandra; she has to take the place of the son he wanted. She'll have to marry a man who is able to succeed him in the business."

Stephen's expression altered. His mouth tightened.

"For her own good, of course," Connie said with a little smile. "As a result, Sandra has never had a chance to find her own kind of happiness; she has never had confidence in herself because being herself wasn't good enough for her father. She has never known the happiness that comes with having someone like her as she is. Just for herself. Someone to have faith in her, to value her, as Sandra, not as Alexandra Kent, her father's puppet."

Emery was silent.

"No, Mr. Emery, it doesn't work. There's no real magnanimity in trying to make people live your way. It's just vain and conceited and selfish and — and stupid."

A vein was beating hard in Emery's temple and Connie, in reaction against her outburst, found herself shaking. "I'm — sorry. Truly sorry. I just tried to make you understand, but I guess it's no use."

"What it boils down to," Emery said in his coldest, most impersonal voice, "is that you and Colin aren't interested in each other."

"Colin might have been interested in me if you had kept your hands off," Connie said honestly. "In fact, he was interested. But no man likes being forced to fall in love, to have his wife picked out for him. As for me, I like him immensely — and you would, too, if you ever let yourself know him as he really is — but I'm not in love with him."

"You may be mistaken about the effect of your charms," Emery said, watching her. "Colin told me last night he had spent most of the day at your apartment, repairing some furniture, I believe. The domestic touch. He enjoyed himself immensely. That was genuine and I was quite competent to understand it."

"It wasn't I who made the day so pleasant for him," Connie retorted. "It was my roommate, a girl you didn't arrange for him to meet."

"Your roommate! And who is she?"

"Her name is Lillian Debaney, she comes from a Middle-Western farm, and she models for Céleste."

"A model!" Emery's face was dark red. "So that's your revenge for what you term my interference. Some cheap little model."

Connie's notebook tumbled off her lap as she sprang to her feet, spots of angry color burning in her cheeks. "You've insulted me by assuming that I'm not a person, just a puppet. You've insulted Colin by refusing to respect his own qualities, his own personality, his own integrity. But Lil — she has more kindness and understanding and — yes, wisdom — than you've ever suspected existed, Mr. Emery; more wisdom than you'll ever have. I'm — I'll tell Tommy I am resigning as of now."

ii

She slid her tray onto a table in the basement cafeteria and turned as Jane Clark set a tray across from her.

"Connie! Is it really true? Have you quit?"

Connie nodded. Up to now she had been too angry to stop to consider her situation, but now the reaction had set in.

"I cleared out my desk and told Tommy I was leaving. I won't be back this afternoon, Jane."

The sandy-haired girl looked at her, looked away as she began to eat her lunch.

"I suppose it was on account of Junior," she said in resignation. "I warned you that he would cause trouble."

"It wasn't Colin's fault," Connie said. "I had a fight with Mr. Emery." It was impossible, of course, to explain that Emery was trying to get Connie to marry his brother. Things were difficult enough for Colin without that.

"I can't understand it," Jane admitted. "Everyone likes you," she laughed, "except poor Miss Ellis, who is eaten up by jealousy, and your work is good. Mr. Emery was pleased with the way you handled that job in court for him on the Brewer case. I heard him tell Tommy so. 'Efficient, intelligent, competent.' And he doesn't usually give anyone much credit. Are you sure you don't want to change your mind?"

"I'm quite sure."

"What are you going to do now?"

"I don't know," Connie admitted blankly. "Go back to the employment agency, I suppose. I — surely Mr. Emery won't be resentful enough to refuse to give me a recommendation. He's a hard man but he is fair."

Jane looked past Connie. "I see your steady admirer is watching you again."

"My admirer?" Connie repeated in astonishment.

"Haven't you noticed him? That red-headed man with the broken front tooth. Last three times we've lunched together I've seen him come in after we did and sit where he could keep an eye on you. In fact, the last time he even followed you to the elevator and got off at your floor to see where you went."

"Oh, nonsense," Connie said lightly. "You must be mistaken. He probably works on the same floor."

But when she stood up she let her eyes roam casually around the cafeteria, saw the red-headed man, saw the small eyes watching her. She turned away with a curious shiver of distaste.

"Let me know what you do," Jane said. "Don't lose touch with me. All good luck, Connie!" She laughed. "And may the future be free of wolves."

When she reached the street, Connie stood uncertainly. It was a strange feeling, having no destination, no work to do on a week day. She should go back to the employment agency and apply for another job. She was perfectly aware of that. Her backlog of savings would not support her long. But the novelty of being free, of having a whole afternoon at her disposal, was a temptation she could not resist.

The air was cold and a stiff wind was blowing, but though the sky was leaden there was no snow and the sidewalks, for the first time in days, were dry and clear. She began to walk aimlessly, enjoying the crowds, the endless variety of the streets, the sound of countless foreign tongues, the talk of peoples of all races and backgrounds.

At Madison Avenue she turned north, still walking slowly, pausing to look in shop windows. It was in one of these that she saw the reflection of the red-headed man who had stopped close behind her. She was aware of a queer uneasiness and tried to dismiss it. After all, there was no reason why the man should not be walking in this direction. Or perhaps it wasn't the same man. Perhaps he wasn't aware of her. Just a coincidence brought to her attention by Jane's comment.

She moved on again, stopped again. Once more the man was behind her, staring into a window, apparently absorbed. As it was filled with women's hosiery, his attention was a little extreme.

A block farther on she began to distinguish those following footsteps from others on the street. The man walked heavily, bearing down on his heels. She glanced toward the curb. The wise thing would be to take a cab, to get away from him, but she recalled that she had only a little change in her handbag, that Nick had taken the thirty dollars she allowed herself for incidentals. She found herself hurrying.

At the corner people were waiting for the light to turn. All of a sudden she had to get away. She could not stand there with the man waiting behind her. Lurking. She turned and walked swiftly east, passed a window that bore the small, unobtrusive plaque CÉLESTE, and without pausing to think, she turned back, opened the door, and went in.

A smart-looking woman in a beautifully made black dress, unadorned except for a small gold broach, black hair drawn back severely from a narrow, clever face, came forward in a leisurely manner, observant eyes summing Connie up from head to foot.

"Madame, may I help you?"

"I — " Connie came to a full stop. She could not say she had come in to escape being followed. It sounded too melodramatic. She could not pretend she had come to look for clothes. On her budget it would be absurd, and it would be unfair to take up the woman's time.

"I'm sorry —" she began. Stopped again.

The front door opened and she turned in a flash, her heart pounding. But it was not the red-headed man; it was Lil Debaney who was returning from lunch.

"Connie!" she cried in delight. "Madame, this is my roommate, Constance Wyndham, the one I told you about."

The discreet look of welcome vanished from Céleste's

face. Once more she studied Connie, this time shrewdly, appraisingly. "Will you walk for me, please? Take off the coat first."

"But —"

"Oh, please do," Lil begged her.

After a moment's hesitation, Connie removed her coat and walked slowly the length of the room.

"Stop there," Madame said. "Now turn. Just a half turn first, please. Smile a little. Now walk toward me. Raise your arm. So. Lillian, have her try the heather tweed first and then the Gray Mist." She looked at Connie. "The tweed, you understand, requires merely a good carriage and a fine figure, which you have. The Gray Mist is subtle; the lines must be understood to be displayed properly." She looked back at Lil, who was beaming with pleasure. "If your friend is satisfactory, she can model the wedding trousseau for Miss Abbott when she comes in this afternoon."

A few minutes later, half bewildered, half dazed, Connie found herself swept into the back of the shop, past the dressmakers with their busy sewing machines, past the cutting table, past a desk covered with designs and samples of material, toward the three small dressing rooms used by the models.

Lil hugged Connie. "I knew you'd be fabulous," she said. "I stick pretty much to young styles and Madge does the high fashion. But she's home now with a sinus attack. You can't model when you are sneezing and have a red nose."

Too excited and occupied to wonder why Connie had unexpectedly arrived and, apparently, applied for a job, Lil helped her into the tweed suit.

A moment later Connie walked slowly into the shop,

paused for a moment, half turned to reveal the back of the suit, and then walked down the room. By an instinct she had not known she possessed, her body moved as though she were walking freely along a country lane; her hatless head was held as though she breathed pine-scented air; there was almost an illusion of wind stirring the shining hair.

Céleste's nostrils flared but she said only, "Very nice, thank you. Now the Gray Mist. Lillian will find you some evening slippers."

The Gray Mist wasn't, Connie thought, a dress at all. It was a soft cloud of smoke that left shoulders and arms bare, that swirled like mist around her.

Connie walked more slowly, with a shorter step, pausing for a moment to lean against a pillar, head slightly turned to one side as though she dreamed, one arm raised to show the superb lines of the bodice, then moving with a slight twist that set the billowing skirt in motion around her.

"The trousseau," Céleste said. "Lillian will show you. And," as Lil led Connie toward the dressing rooms, "if you can interest any of my customers in the dresses on the rack at the left in back, which I have been unsuccessful in selling, you will, of course, receive a commission." For a moment she looked at Connie, frowning.

"I have seen you somewhere before. You have an unforgettable face, mademoiselle. The bone-deep beauty. Perhaps in magazines? For whom have you modeled?"

"I have never modeled before."

"Then you have the flair. Just the same I have seen you."

"Perhaps in your shop, Madame."

"You have been a customer of mine? Odd. I should think I would have remembered."

"No, a friend of mine is one of your customers. I have come here with her."

"Who is that?"

Connie hesitated and then followed Lil out of the room while Céleste stared after her. The girl had come in looking panic-stricken, as though she had been running away from something. She had been completely taken aback by the little Lillian's suggestion that she become a model. What had the little Lillian said about her some weeks before? Beautiful face and figure and carriage.

Roommates. Madame's eyebrows drew together again. Strange roommates, the little country girl who had so greatly improved when she simplified her hairstyle, and this lovely creature with her distinction.

Friend of a customer? Hmm. Madame shrugged her shoulders. If that were true, sooner or later she would remember. She always did.

FOURTEEN

THE AFTERNOON passed like a dream. Lil and Connie changed from dress to dress, retouching makeup, rearranging their hair, changing shoes to fit the suits and dresses, the negligees and sports clothes.

Then out of the stuffy back rooms with their bare floors into the salon with its wall-to-wall carpet, its discreet perfume, the customers sitting on the gray satin couches, commenting, exclaiming, sometimes bored or critical, and always Madame, serene, dignified, making no extravagant claims, merely introducing each garment and pointing out its unique qualities.

When she made her first appearance before customers Connie had to brace herself, take a long breath, and force herself to open the swinging doors at the back, to encounter the inquisitive eyes. After the third or fourth hasty change, her mind occupied with the garment she was to display and the best way of presenting it, she began to forget herself. She realized, little by little, that, after the first glance, the women forgot her as a person, that they thought of her only as a clothes horse, an animated dummy that walked and turned and backed and smiled, always that same fixed, dreamy smile.

It was only when the climax of the afternoon was reached, with the modeling of the wedding gown, that Connie became aware that she was more than a figurine, she was a woman, romantic, passionate, ardent, making a pretense of the ceremony that was dearest to a woman's heart. As Lil adjusted the filmy white veil, Connie looked at the tall, slim figure in its bridal satin, at the face seen like a dream through the veil, at the train that Lil and the dressmaker were carefully adjusting.

She paced slowly into the salon, walking with slow, measured steps, eyes down, as though on her way to the altar, and then at the end of the room she turned, paced back, made another turn, and the swinging doors closed behind her.

Then at last the customers were gone, the dressmakers were folding up material, getting out coats and hats, and Connie was slipping into her own coat. That afternoon Madame had, during a lull, told her what salary she might expect. To Connie's pleased surprise, it was twenty-five per cent more than she had earned at Emery & Emery. *Had* earned. Already the law office seemed light years away.

As she and Lil left Céleste's for the night, Connie drew a long breath. "Well!" she said.

Lil squeezed her arm. "I knew you'd be a natural. Didn't I tell you so? Didn't I? Let's buy a steak for dinner to celebrate."

When they reached home they set down their bags of groceries on the kitchen table and then Connie flopped on the couch, kicked off her shoes and moaned. She looked down at her feet.

"Well," she said in surprise, "they are still there. I thought I'd worn them off clear up to the ankle."

"You'll get used to it," Lil assured her. "Now you just keep your feet up and rest."

"You've been modeling, too," Connie reminded her.

"But it's not my first day. I never was so surprised as

when I walked in after lunch and there you were." For the first time it occurred to Lil to wonder how it had happened. "Connie, what about your other job?"

"I quit," Connie said briefly.

Lil busied herself in the kitchen. After a while there came the sizzling sound of broiling steak. Connie turned to see Lil standing in the doorway, swathed in a big apron, looking at her.

"Was it something to do with Colin?"

"I had a quarrel with Mr. Emery, his older brother," Connie told her. "He seems to think that he not only runs Emery & Emery but that he runs me, too. So I blew up. And I resigned." She began to laugh. "I'll bet that man never heard so many home truths in his whole life."

"He wants you to marry Colin, doesn't he?"

"I told him I wasn't interested in Colin and that Colin wasn't interested in me."

Lil still waited, knowing that her roommate was holding something back. Connie liked her too much to lie to her. To change the subject she said, "But I never told you the real reason why I went darting into Céleste's." She explained then about the red-headed man and was relieved to see that the incident caught Lil's interest, distracting it from the quarrel with Stephen Emery.

"You say this man had been watching you in the cafeteria, followed you to see where your office was, and then today he trailed you until you ducked into Céleste's, where he could hardly follow. I don't understand it, Connie. He didn't try to speak to you?"

Connie shook her head. Now that she was home, that she had Lil's comforting and fortifying presence, she did not understand why she had been so frightened.

"What did he look like?"

"Like a rat," Connie said. "He was rather shabby and flashy; in the cafeteria I saw he had a broken front tooth; he walks hard, coming down on his heels; he has red hair."

"How old?"

"Perhaps forty-five."

"Well, he didn't bother you, after all. He didn't try to speak to you. He didn't make any attempt to snatch your handbag. He could hardly be a kidnaper. What do you suppose he wanted?"

Without waiting for a reply Lil went back to serve the dinner and the two girls ate ravenously. When the dishes had been cleared up, Lil settled down in the now mended armchair.

"What's it all about, Connie? You've thought of something, haven't you? I can tell by your expression."

"Nick," Connie said. She told Lil about the armed man at the Maine airport, about Nick's job described as a "form of insurance," about the danger he had been in, about his saying that she might be in danger herself if he could not raise the money.

Lil listened round-eyed.

"I thought," Connie said helplessly, "that if he had really taken the stamps they would bring in enough money to clear him and that things would be all right for him."

"But, after all, you don't know that this red-headed man has anything to do with your half brother."

"No, I don't, but why else would anyone follow me like that? Why should this man care to know where I work? I don't like it, Lil. I'm — frightened."

They were still talking about it when the bell rang and Lil, after a startled look at Connie, got up to release the catch on the outer door. She held the apartment door ajar.

"Who is it?"

"Colin Emery."

It wasn't the careless young man about town who entered the apartment and greeted the two surprised girls. It was a very angry young man. He stood glowering down at Connie.

"What's this I hear about you resigning today?"

"I got a better job," she said quickly. "I'm working for Céleste, where Lil is. And a lot more money, Colin."

"Don't stall. Just how much did Steve had to do with you quitting your job, Connie? I want to know the truth. Everyone in the place knows you had a long talk in his office. Did he try to bring any pressure to bear?"

He mustn't quarrel with his brother, Connie thought. That would only widen the breach between them, stiffen Steve's determination to make Colin live according to his plans. She made herself laugh gaily.

"You'd be surprised," she said. "We spent most of the time talking about an old friend of mine, a girl with whom I suspect your brother has fallen in love."

Colin's jaw dropped. "Steve? Iron-man Steve?"

Connie gave a soft ripple of laughter. "You see," she confided, "I told him Sandra was having a pretty unpleasant time because her father runs her life for her, wants to decide whom she can marry, all that."

Colin's angry expression relaxed and he began to laugh. "Well, I'll be darned. If you aren't the one with the wily tricks."

"Then," Connie went on rapidly, trying to get over a dangerous subject as quickly, as lightly, as possible, "I swept haughtily out and—" As dramatically as possible she described her pursuit by the red-headed man. To Colin, of course, she made no reference to Nick, the stolen stamps, and Nick's association with men who were probably gangsters.

"You say this guy followed you? That's all?" Somewhat to the surprise of the two girls, Colin refused to take it seriously. "Heavens, gal, don't you ever look in the mirror? He probably kept looking just to make sure his eyes hadn't deceived him in the first place."

Colin dismissed the red-headed man and began, loudly and fulsomely, to admire his own handiwork on the chair. "What you two girls need is a man about the house," he declared.

"All talk and no work," Lil muttered. "The hot-water faucet in the kitchen is dripping away, driving us crazy. And what with the water shortage, it's practically a crime as well as a nuisance."

"Got an extra washer?" Colin took off his coat and a few moments later he was happily busy.

"Found an old catalog last night," he remarked casually, "from one of those real estate agencies that specialize in farms. Some amazing bargains. Of course, this one was out of date but you can still pick up some nice property in Connecticut and New Jersey for a few thousand dollars."

"It's not the land," Lil pointed out. "It's buying good stock that takes the real money. And the way to do that —"

Lying back on the couch, Connie listened vaguely to their voices, their arguments, their laughter. Colin hadn't taken the red-headed man seriously. She would try to forget the incident. There wasn't, after all, anything the man could do to her. Nothing to be afraid of. Nothing at all.

When the faucet had been repaired, Colin looked at

Connie, noticed the dark smudges under her eyes, and reached for his coat and hat.

"I'll be on my way and let you rest. Sure there's nothing wrong about this new job of yours?"

Connie smiled reassuringly at him. "Not a thing," she declared. "It's going to be fabulous."

While Lil accompanied Colin to the door, Connie went into her own room. She was brushing her hair, wearing a quilted satin robe of leaf green, her favorite color, when Lil stopped to say good night. The outside bell rang, three short rings, and the two girls exchanged startled glances.

"I'll go," Lil said. She released the catch at the outer door but did not unlock the apartment door. "Who is it?" she called.

"Colin."

She opened the door, looked at him in surprise. He was panting as though he had been running.

"What's wrong?"

"Connie's red-headed man," he said. "He was waiting outside the building when I went out. I recognized him from her description. So I tackled him."

"You what!"

"Oh, I just said, 'What are you doing here? If I find you within ten blocks of this place again I'll knock your head off.' "

Connie had come to the door of her bedroom now, clutching her robe around her, white-faced.

"Colin!"

"He took off like a jet plane. I chased him for half a block until he reached the subway stairs, and he shot down them as though someone had fired him out of a gun. I don't think he'll be back. Just the same, I shouldn't have brushed off Connie's story so lightly. I don't like this, girls. In the morning I'll be around with a new lock for your door and a safety chain. It can't do any harm. Well, good night."

Colin hesitated. "Look, this sounds melodramatic and all that, but watch your step, will you? Don't let people in unless you know who they are. Don't go off on dark streets by yourself. And don't," he grinned, "get led astray by any fake telephone calls."

"Fake telephone calls?" Connie repeated in surprise.

"You know the kind. 'A friend is in the hospital. Come quick.' Or, 'This is your long-lost uncle. Meet me at the Astor.' Or, 'This is Lawyer Jones. I have something of interest to tell you.' "

Connie began to laugh. "It sounds like a soap opera."

Colin grinned. "Okay, but it might not be so hilariously funny. All I'm saying is, just make sure you know the setup is legitimate."

He waved his hand and was gone. Lil shoved home the bolt. She turned soberly to Connie. "Now I begin to understand how you felt. I— guess I'm frightened, too."

"Nothing is going to happen," Connie said. "Why should it? We have no enemies. Nothing is going to happen."

FIFTEEN

AS A RULE Jeff was an avid newspaper reader, but that morning he ignored headlines, war scares and politics, looking eagerly to see whether his advertisement had been printed. Copies of it had been sent to all New York dailies and to the stamp magazines.

There was no time to look at the rest of the paper. He had waited for his bank to open in order to retrieve the revolver from his safety-deposit box so that he could check the number and find out in whose name it was registered. So it was after eleven when he finally reached his office.

"Mr. Kent has called you several times," his secretary told him, looking worried. "He sounded rather impatient. He asked me to inform him as soon as you came in."

"Go ahead," Jeff grinned at her. "And don't look so alarmed. He won't bite you."

"That's what you think," she said darkly.

Jeff laughed, closed the door of his private office behind him, and began to look over his mail.

In a few minutes Kent came in, walking in the ponderous way that was so nearly a strut. It was customary for people to go to Kent. He had not entered Jeff's office half a dozen times in as many years and Jeff was fully aware that the situation was unusual.

Kent waved Jeff back as he started to rise, and settled himself in the most comfortable chair.

"Tried to get you a couple of times."

"I was late this morning. I wanted to get to the bank as soon as it opened."

"Not running short of money, I hope."

"You say you wanted me?" The question was gently put, but Jeff made clear that there was a no-trespassing sign on his private affairs.

"The Wilmot deal," Kent said. "Haven't you been sitting on your hands on that? Now is the time to put it over. We've got Wilmot in a bind. Put on the pressure now and he'll sell out — he'll have to — and at our price."

Jeff found himself thinking that Kent's approach was not so unlike that of gangsters. He had never thought that way before.

"I've got a lot of other jobs on my hands," he began.

Kent nodded. "It occurred to me," his voice was casual, "that you might have something on your mind, something worrying you."

When Jeff made no reply, Kent went on with an attempt to be jovial that was out of character, "I can't afford to have my most promising man slipping."

"Have I been slipping lately?" Jeff's tone was blunt. Kent must know how much work he had been handling. He had done the job of three men and they were equally aware of the fact.

Kent took his time lighting a cigar. "No, you are doing a fine job. On the whole." When Jeff made no comment he went on, "Of course, you've had arrears of work to catch up on since you came back from Maine."

"Everything is up to date now."

"Yes, I know. I've wondered if — since you came back — there's been something different about you. Not the same old zest."

Kent waited again and finally said, "Alexandra has noticed it, too. She's been worrying about you, Jeff."

"That's very nice of her, but quite unnecessary."

"She's afraid that Constance Wyndham may have asked you to shoulder some of her problems. That's rather a habit with her, I understand from my daughter."

Under the desk Jeff's hand doubled into a fist but he managed to say evenly, "Is it? I have never noticed it myself. So far as I know, she has tried to carry her own weight very gallantly, and without any help, certainly with none from me."

"Glad to hear it," Kent said heartily. "Bill Wyndham was a fine man — not practical, but as honest as they come. And yet his children are — well, they are good people to stay away from."

The telephone on Jeff's desk rang and for once he welcomed that noisy interruption. All his control was needed not to lash out at Kent for his comments, his ugly insinuations about Connie.

"Mr. Gray? This is Morton." The stamp dealer chuckled. "I think we've flushed your game for you. Before I left home this morning I had a telephone call for a Mr. Winterson. Fella says he has that twenty-four-cent airmail stamp and maybe he can lay hands on some other inverted centers. He'll meet you at a bar on Third Avenue. Just a minute, I took down the address. Here it is."

Jeff reached for a pencil and jotted the address on his engagement pad. "That was quick work, Morton. But how am I supposed to recognize him?"

"He'll be carrying a rolled up *Daily News* in the left-hand pocket of his overcoat and he'll be sitting at the back of the bar. Twelve o'clock, he said. Doesn't give you much time. I tried to reach you earlier."

Jeff looked at his watch. "I'll just be able to make it. Thanks a lot, Morton." He set down the telephone and turned to Kent. "Sorry, sir, but I have an urgent appointment."

Kent settled himself more firmly in his chair. "Not in any trouble, are you, Jeff? After all, I have a right to ask. I've given you a lot of responsibility here and I can't afford any scandal attached to your name. This business — I couldn't help overhearing — meeting an unknown man in a shady neighborhood — that's not the way the Kent Enterprises do business."

"This has nothing whatever to do with the Kent Enterprises."

"Like that visit to your bank this morning?"

"Like that visit to my bank."

"Jeff, I want a straight answer to a straight question. Were you getting out some money for Constance?"

Jeff's jaw dropped in sheer astonishment. "I was not. And there's no conceivable reason for believing that, whatever her need, she would accept financial assistance from me."

"And yet I overheard you offering to help in any way, at any time. Very fervent about it."

"I went to the bank," Jeff said at length, "to check on the number of a revolver which I managed to get away from a gangster. I want to find out who bought it, to trace it, if possible."

"You've been tangling with gangsters?" The veins over Kent's cheekbones were purple.

"Well, I tangled with one, at any rate." Jeff's voice was still even. "That's hardly a crime, sir. In fact, the citizen who stands back and does not try to prevent the shooting of another person is rather a peculiar sort of man, isn't he?"

"I don't like this business, Jeff. I don't like it at all."

Unexpectedly Jeff laughed. "Neither do I. These people aren't exactly the kind of company I care to know. But —"

"But?"

"I'll have to follow it through now. And, I repeat, it has nothing to do with Kent Enterprises."

Kent drummed his thick fingers on the desk. "Can you give me your word that this extremely nasty situation in which you seem determined to involve yourself has nothing to do with the Wyndhams?"

Jeff's silence was answer enough.

For a long moment Kent studied the narrow eyes which looked steadily back at him. From the beginning he had had a high regard for Jefferson Gray. He had recognized the young man's exceptional qualities, the potentialities that could be developed. He had begun slowly to build his plans for the future around him. And he was not accustomed to having anyone or anything interfere with his plans.

"No wonder Alexandra is worried about you," he said. "Constance seems to have her claws in you rather deeply."

"What I can do for Connie is a privilege," Jeff said steadily. "And I fail to see, sir, why this should concern Sandra in the least, though I appreciate her —" he hesitated, "her anxiety on my behalf."

"Perhaps I can help you see. Alexandra is my only child. Her welfare and happiness are important to me. Anything that threatened them would not be — tolerated. The Wyndhams have received all they will ever have at my hands. I have fully discharged my obligation to Bill Wyndham. Any attempt on the part of his children to interfere with my plans would be unfortunate for them. Most unfortunate. I might say disastrous. Is that clear now?"

"Very clear." Jeff stood up. "And now, if you will excuse me, sir, I have an important appointment."

His thoughts were whirling as he caught a down elevator and went through a revolving door onto the street. He hailed a cab and gave the address of the Third Avenue bar.

Kent had pulled off the velvet gloves and revealed the iron hand. Unless Jeff stayed away from Connie not only his own job and his future would be jeopardized, but Kent would quite deliberately set out to make life difficult for Connie. Remembering the ruthless position he had taken in regard to Wilmot, Jeff knew that Connie could expect no mercy from him. In the past Kent had, more than once, used his widespread influence to prevent men who had challenged him in some way from holding jobs. He had wiped out several rivals by stock manipulation.

What could he do, Jeff wondered, to protect Connie not only from the gangsters who threatened her but from this new and possibly even more serious threat?

"Cut out the panic," he told himself. "One thing at a time. First, I'll have to get back the stamps. Then, well, as a last resort I can have a frank talk with Sandra. It will be awkward but, after all, it's not as though she cares anything about me. She is following her father's wishes — or orders. Her happiness isn't involved. I'm sure I can make her understand."

The Third Avenue bar was dingy and dark. Only half a dozen men were there, talking idly. Jeff walked back toward the far end of the bar where he saw a man sitting alone. A thick-set man with red hair. His overcoat hung open and in the left-hand pocket there was a rolled up copy of the *Daily News*.

Jeff slid onto the next stool. He did not glance at the man beside him, though he was aware that the latter was studying him closely.

"Winterson?" the red-headed man said at last, his voice cautiously low.

If Jeff had any lingering doubts that the "stamp dealer" was legitimate, they were dispelled by this furtive approach. For a moment he did not move and then he swung around.

"That's right." He looked the other man over carefully. He had a face like a rat. He smiled wolfishly, revealing a broken tooth.

"Got something to show you." He pulled out an envelope and drew from it a card on which was mounted the airmail stamp with the inverted center. "Nice, isn't it?"

Jeff examined it as well as he could, because the other man held on to it firmly as though fearing that it might be snatched out of his grasp.

"Very nice. How much do you want for it?"

"You can have this little item for nine thousand dollars. Cash. The list price is a lot higher, so this is a real bargain."

"Cash?"

The red-headed man nodded. "No checks." He had a strong lisp when he spoke, probably a result of the broken tooth. "Just nice folding money. Well?"

"I don't carry that much cash around with me," Jeff said.

"Who does? How long would it take you to get it?"

"This afternoon. No, I'm booked with appointments until after four. Too late for the bank. Tomorrow. Say twelve o'clock. Here?"

The red-headed man slid off the stool. "Okay."

"Do you have any more inverted centers?"

"May have a few. Some Persian items. Some Latin-American stuff."

Jeff schooled his face not to betray his jubilation. This man had the Nuñoz collection. He was sure of it.

"I'd like to take a look at them. I might be in the market, if the price is right."

"Always glad to make a sale. But cash, remember. Nothing but cash. See? You come alone tomorrow."

Jeff smiled. "What makes you think I was alone today?"

Again the wolfish grin. "Had a friend outside. If there had been anyone with you he would have given me the high sign."

The smile faded from Jeff's lips. These boys were taking no chances.

The red-headed man saw that he had made his point, nodded, tossed the *Daily News* on the bar, and went out.

Jeff waited until the door had closed behind him and then he moved rapidly. By the time he got outside, the red-headed man was across the street, talking to a thin young man in a green overcoat. They separated, the younger man going into a drugstore while the red-headed man turned the corner.

To Jeff's exasperation he had to wait for a light before he could cross the street. Just as he reached the far curb the man he was trailing turned into an areaway. By the time

Jeff reached the building, a rundown old apartment that was little more than a tenement, there was no sign of him. For a moment he hesitated. He didn't know what prevented him from going down the area steps. He waited without quite knowing what he was waiting for.

In a few minutes there were heavy footsteps and he ducked into the doorway of a small cleaning establishment. The red-headed man had come up the steps and was heading back toward Third Avenue. When he was out of sight Jeff went quietly down the steps, paused for a moment to peer through a grimy window into the basement apartment. Someone was there, a man sitting at a table with a stamp album open before him. There was no mistaking that profile.

Softly Jeff entered the basement. There were two doors. He approached the one on the left noiselessly, turned the knob gently so there would be no telltale click, and then flung open the door.

Nick Wyndham leaped to his feet, his chair falling over with a crash as he turned around. When he recognized Jeff his lips drew back from his teeth in a snarl.

"So Holt double-crossed me!"

"No, I followed him here."

"Why?"

"I was looking for you."

As Nick started to bluster, Jeff said coolly, "No point in trying to bluff it out, Nick. I know you stole the stamps."

Nick dropped the useless pretense. "So what? Kent has no right to them. I have more right than he has. They belonged to my own father."

"Let's get the picture clear. If those stamps aren't turned over to John Kent, he is quite capable of causing you more trouble than the hoods you are working with. Hand them over, Nick."

"Try to make me."

"That," Jeff declared, "will be a pleasure." He lunged for Nick, grabbed him by his necktie, gave him a short jab to the jaw that sent him staggering backward. He followed up with a second blow and then a third. Nick pitched over and dropped on the rug. Jeff jerked him to his feet.

"Had enough?"

Nick nodded, gasping.

"Sorry to do it but violence seems to be the only language you understand. Now give me those stamps."

Nick stood swaying. He indicated the album on the table. "Go ahead and take them," he said sullenly, "but I can tell you now what will happen. Those stamps were all I had to clear myself with those goons."

"So?"

"Take them away and the boys will kill me. I'm not joking, Jeff. You'll sign my death warrant if you take those stamps."

"I'll give you enough money to get out of town," Jeff told him, "and to keep you until you can find yourself a job. But I mean an honest job. The day I find out you've gone back to the protection racket you'll deserve everything that goes with it. Is that clear?"

"How did you guess about the protection racket?" Nick was startled.

"I didn't guess. You practically gave Connie a blueprint of what you were doing."

"Why should you help me?" Nick was suspicious.

"I liked your father."

"And you like my sister," Nick said softly.

"Let's keep Connie out of this!" Jeff was sharp.

"If it can be done. If it can be done."

"What do you mean by that?"

"I leave it to you," Nick said. "If you know so much about the setup you can guess the rest. If you're so anxious about Connie I'll leave her to your tender care." The sneer on his face changed to a mocking grin. "The way the two of you try to protect each other! It's right touching."

"Protect each other?"

Nick's voice rose to a falsetto which he apparently thought was an imitation of Connie's voice. " 'Don't hurt Jeff. He loves Sandra.' Or words to that effect." He saw Jeff's expression and laughed. "Didn't you know? Well, that's my Boy Scout deed for the day. Okay, if I'm getting out of here with a whole skin it had better be fast. When they come back —"

"Pack your things and come along." Jeff scooped up the stamp album. In a few minutes Nick had tossed some clothes into a suitcase and closed it with shaking hands. He was really afraid.

Out on the street he looked cautiously up and down the block before he dared venture into sight. Once more Jeff went to his bank, this time to draw out enough cash to keep Nick going for a time. Nick's eyes opened wide as he riffled quickly through the bills before putting them into his wallet.

"That's all there is," Jeff warned him. "You'd better make it last. I'm not going to fork over one more thin dime."

"Okay, okay," Nick said carelessly.

"Where are you going?"

Nick hesitated for a moment. "Penn Station," he decided. "Trains going everywhere from there all the time. I'll take the first one that goes a long, long way."

"Keep in touch."

Nick smiled, an unpleasant smile. "I'll do that little thing," he said.

SIXTEEN

JEFF stood outside the bank, watching Nick push his way rapidly through the lunchtime crowds on the street. However much he might lie, one thing was true. The man was scared to death.

Jeff glanced at his watch and tried to remember the appointments he had made for the afternoon. Then, on impulse, he found a telephone booth and called his secretary, asking her to cancel everything. He would be unavoidably detained. Kent would be angry if he found out, and Jeff was sure that he would find out. But Jeff had set out on his own course and he was determined to follow it.

He felt, he acknowledged to himself with a grin, like a small boy playing hooky from school. Well, if he was going to make this a holiday, even a stolen one, he might as well enjoy it. And for the first time since Connie had refused to marry him, he had something to enjoy. Unreliable as Nick was, he had not, Jeff thought, been lying when he made his mocking comment about the way Connie and Jeff protected each other. If it were true, if Connie had rejected him out of loyalty to Sandra, his life could take on more meaning.

He went to the Princeton Club for lunch, met a couple of old friends, and sat around the table chatting idly for an hour and a half. Then he retrieved the stamp albums from the Club safe, got his coat and hat, and walked the few blocks to the building where Emery & Emery had its offices.

The receptionist looked at him approvingly. It wasn't often she saw a man who had so much charm and yet did nothing to exploit it.

"Miss Wyndham," she repeated. "I am sorry. Miss Wyndham is no longer with Emery & Emery."

Feeling rather like a man who had put his foot up for a step and comes down hard because there is none there, Jeff turned blankly away. What did that mean? Had Connie been fired? Unlikely, to say the least. Stephen Emery, the man who had danced with her at the Wiltown, had seemed to approve of her. How could he help it? And his younger brother, the good-looking Colin, had certainly appeared to be enamoured when Jeff had seen them together in the Emery box at the opera.

At a loss to know how to fill in his unexpected holiday, but with a dogged determination not to return to the office, Jeff went in search of an old college friend who was now with the FBI. He gave him the number of the revolver he had wrested from the gangster and told him the story of Nick's activities as Connie had told it to him.

"Do you think you can trace the ownership of the gun?" he asked.

His friend grinned and reached for a telephone. A surprisingly short time later he reported, "The buyer was Thomas Styles of Newley, Connecticut. A year ago he had a robbery in his house and this was among the missing items."

His grin faded. "Look here, Gray, I don't like this story. Your friend could find herself in a spot. It's a favorite line with these hoods, learning who the nearest relation is and putting pressure on."

"I'll look out for her."

But when he reached the street Jeff wondered rather bleakly how he was going to do it. Connie had left her job for some unknown reason and he did not even know where to find her.

At half-past five that afternoon he rang the bell at Connie's apartment. When she opened the door she looked at him almost as though he were a stranger.

For a moment he waited for her to ask him in. Then, abruptly, he thrust the stamp album into her arms. "I got this for you today," he said. "And I've sent Nick out of town. He'll be safe there."

"Oh, Jeff!" For a moment her cold face warmed as he drew her toward him, and then he saw the man in shirt-sleeves who was busy retying the cords on the venetian blinds at the window. A man who seemed very much at home. Colin Emery.

He stepped back. "It's all right, Connie. Good afternoon."

"Wait, Jeff! Please wait." Connie held out the albums to him. "I have one thing more to ask of you. One last thing. Please, please, give these to Mr. Kent."

"Okay." The door closed behind him. He stood in the winter dusk thinking bitterly, "So Nick lied again."

ii

Earlier that afternoon Connie had been resting in one of the fitting rooms at Céleste's shop. The morning had been hectic because of several important customers from Chicago who had wanted to replenish their wardrobes.

Between one and three there was generally a lull while the regular clientele enjoyed leisurely lunches. Unexpectedly Céleste came into the fitting room. There was something odd in her expression as she looked at Connie.

"Will you show the Blue Moon, Constance?" There was a little smile quirking her lips. "I think it will suit your friend."

"My friend?" Connie was startled.

"I remember now with whom you came to my shop before. It was Miss Kent. And perhaps, if she is interested, you might model that April Night. It is not quite her type, of course, but it is striking. Lately she has been choosing a more exotic line."

Lil was still at lunch. With the help of one of the dressmakers Connie mechanically put on the blue dress, a velvet sheath, adjusted her hair and her makeup. Her face seemed to have frozen. Of all eventualities this was the one she would most have wanted to avoid. For a moment her feet seemed to be rooted to the ground.

I can't, she thought, I can't do it. Then she took a long breath and, with her head held high, she walked slowly into the shop, eyes fixed on an imaginary horizon, a smile on her lips.

She heard Sandra's gasp, a smothered cry. She forced herself to look at her friend's face. For a moment the eyes of the two girls met. What would Sandra do? Surely she would not cut her!

At last Sandra said, her voice crisp and cool, "Will you have the model turn once more? I'd like to study the lines of the back."

Connie felt her hands clenching and forced them to relax. She revolved slowly.

Then Sandra smiled. "Ah, Miss Wyndham! What do you think? Is it me?"

"I think," Connie said slowly, expressionlessly, "it would suit you very well, Miss Kent."

Sandra nodded. "I always rely on your flair for style.

Very well, send it to me, Céleste. And, by the way, do let Miss Wyndham have a little time off. I'd like to discuss my wardrobe with her."

In case Céleste remembers that I was with her, Connie thought, Sandra has made clear that we did not come here as friends.

"Of course, Miss Kent," Céleste said smoothly. "The rest of the afternoon, Constance, if Miss Kent wishes."

While Connie was removing the Blue Moon dress Lil came back from lunch. "That's Alexandra Kent, the heiress, out there," she whispered excitedly. "Did you see her? Connie, what's wrong? You look as though you were on the verge of collapse."

"Nothing's wrong," Connie said thickly. "I just feel a little faint."

"You'd better sit down for a while," Lil said in alarm.

"I can't. That is, it's all right, Lil. Madame is giving me the rest of the afternoon off."

When Connie went into the shop Sandra had already left. She was waiting outside in her car. Connie got in beside her.

"Just drive anywhere," Sandra directed the chauffeur. For a few moments they rode in silence, toward Park Avenue, north, west, and finally through Central Park.

"So that's where you went when you left Emery & Emery," Sandra said at last.

Connie looked at her in surprise.

"This afternoon I went there to see you," Sandra told her in a voice Connie had never heard before.

"Why on earth —" Connie began.

"I thought we ought to have things clear between us," Sandra said. "They should have been clear a long time ago, four years ago, to be exact. You've always known my situation. You knew I had to marry to suit father. The only possible man was Jefferson Gray. You knew he was the only one with whom I could have found a bearable life. But, though you've lived on Kent charity for four years, though you've taken every admirer I ever had, everything I ever wanted, you weren't satisfied, were you? You wanted Jeff, too."

"Sandra! Sandra, please stop. You don't know what you are saying. The terrible thing about words spoken in anger is that they — exist. They are always there. They can't be wiped out after you have forgotten them, when you don't mean them any more."

"I don't want these words wiped out, Connie. I went to Emery & Emery today to tell you to stay away from Jefferson Gray."

"But I haven't —"

"Don't lie to me. You've been seeing him. As I got out of the elevator I saw him leaving the Emery & Emery office."

"But I wasn't even there."

"I discovered that. An elderly woman was at the reception desk when I went in. She said you had had to leave; that there had been some trouble about the junior partner."

"Miss Ellis," Connie said. "That could only be Miss Ellis. And it isn't true. I wasn't fired, Sandra. I left of my own free will."

"That doesn't seem to be the general impression. But about Jeff —"

"I haven't tried to take Jeff from you. I never would, not if my life depended on it. But you don't love him, Sandra. You're just fitting into your father's pattern. And trying to fit Jeff in. We'll never meet again, you and I, but if there were any way I could repay my huge debt to the Kents it would be by making you believe that you have a right to be Sandra, her own self, not just her father's daughter. Will you please stop the car? I'd like to get out."

Sandra might have been deaf. After a long time she said, "Nick told me you were planning to marry Jeff not because you loved him but because you needed his money."

"So that's why you asked me to dinner. To have your father sell Stony Brook for me, to give me money in order to free Jeff."

"That's why."

The car stopped for a light. Quickly Connie opened the door and got out. The light changed and the car moved on, across the street, out of sight.

Connie blinked tears from her eyes and looked around. She was on Central Park West almost at the north end of the park. She took a path through the park, crossed Fifth Avenue, and started east. She was surprised to discover that her tears were still falling and she brushed them away impatiently.

Before going home she stopped at a luncheonette for coffee and freshened her makeup. She did not want to encounter Lil's anxious eyes, Lil's friendly questions.

But when she opened the door she found Lil engaged in banter with Colin Emery, who was complaining about the operation of a venetian blind and was bent on repairing it.

"Not now," Lil wailed. "You mess up everything in the place and I have to get dinner."

"I'll take you two girls out to dinner."

Grateful that Lil had been too preoccupied to notice her, Connie escaped to her own room. She had a bad headache, she told Colin, so she'd have to ask for a raincheck on the dinner. The headache was true enough, she thought, as she lay on her bed.

The ring at the bell came while Lil was busy so Connie went to answer it. It was Jeff! *Stay away from Jeff,* Sandra had said. *You've always taken everything I wanted.*

Then the stamp albums were, unbelievably, in her hands; Nick was safe. It was all Jeff's doing.

He looked over her shoulder, saw Colin working on the venetian blind, and his eyes shut her out, they were the eyes of a stranger.

I'll never see him again, Connie thought, numb with pain. Never again. She jumped nervously as the telephone rang.

"Please take it, Connie," Lil called from the kitchen.

"Connie?" It was Nick's voice. "Have you heard from Jeff?"

"Yes, he was just here. He left the — the —"

"Okay, I know. You don't have to spell it out. I have a few minutes before train time so —"

"Where are you going, Nick?"

"What you don't know you can't tell."

"But, Nick, I wouldn't say a word."

"They have — ways. That's why I called, Connie. I just wanted to say — look out for yourself."

"Nick," her voice rose, "just one thing. Please! Does — one of them — have red hair?"

She heard Nick gasp. "Yeah. Why?"

"He's been following me. Who is he, Nick? What does he want?"

"His name is Guy Holt."

"Guy Holt?"

"He's bad medicine, Connie. Very bad medicine. So long." She heard the telephone click at the other end.

She stared unbelievingly at the phone and then set it down. Then she saw that Colin had stopped working, that he was watching her without a trace of his usual light-heartedness. Before he could question her she went hastily into her room and closed the door. She sagged against it.

SEVENTEEN

IT WAS one of those wickedly expensive French restaurants with simple decorations, no music or entertainment, but truly superlative food and service. The tables were widely spaced so that there was plenty of privacy for each, no necessity for people to crowd past, no likelihood of overhearing conversations or having one's own overheard.

At a table for two Sandra Kent sat facing Stephen Emery. The waiter had helped them to compose a meal that, he assured them, would be like a poem.

When he had gone Sandra looked across the table to find Emery's eyes on her face. No man had ever looked at her in that way before, as though everything he saw gave him great pleasure, and Sandra, who was usually self-possessed, found herself blushing.

Three or four times she had seen him, ruthlessly breaking previous engagements to be with him: the Royal ballet, a play, a concert, and tonight dinner at the quiet French restaurant. Usually reserved, Sandra discovered that she talked more with this man than with anyone except Connie. Connie who had been her closest, most intimate friend. Connie who was now her enemy.

She tried to put aside her memory of the afternoon, her attack on Connie, Connie's unexpected reply. Was there any possibility that Connie had been telling her the truth?

"And what exciting things have you been up to?" Emery asked.

Sandra smiled at him. "You'd never guess. This afternoon I paid a visit to your office."

"My office! Why didn't you let me know that you were there?"

"I wouldn't have dreamed of disturbing you."

"You wouldn't have disturbed me." For a moment his eyes held hers and then he smiled. "Or perhaps you would. Yes, you would undoubtedly have been disturbing. But I think you have already guessed, Alexandra, that I like being disturbed by you."

He was telling her the simple truth. He really meant it. This distinguished, aloof man, Stephen Emery, admired her as no other man ever had. She was unaware of the change caused by that genuine masculine admiration. Her face glowed, came alive, achieved a kind of beauty.

"In any case," she said rather hastily, "my reason in going there was to see a — a friend of mine."

"Miss Wyndham, of course. Remember I met you through her." For a moment the self-contained Emery seemed rather at a loss. "Yes. Well, as you were probably told, she has resigned. We were — ah — sorry to lose her. I hope she has found a position that suits her better."

"She has become a model for Céleste." Sandra said tartly. "I found her there by sheer accident. I do a considerable amount of buying from Céleste."

"A model!" He was startled. "I can't understand it."

Sandra, sipping clear soup, said, "To be frank with you, Stephen, I can't understand it either. Connie is a strange girl. I begin to think that I have never really known her. As to why she left her job with you I've heard two very different versions. Your receptionist, an elderly woman, said that she had been forced to leave because of some trouble with your younger brother."

"An elderly woman? That must be Miss Ellis. Now and then she relieves the regular receptionist. I've been told by Colin that she was rather unpleasant to Miss Wyndham. The jealousy of a plain woman for a beautiful one."

Sandra was aware that she, too, was jealous. The way Stephen spoke of Connie's beauty reawakened the anger that had driven her earlier in the day and that had faded into discomfort, almost into a feeling of guilt, after Connie had left her.

He was speaking again. "But, in a sense, what the woman said was true. There was some trouble about my brother but it was not of Miss Wyndham's making. It was my own. I did something that seemed justifiable to me at the time but that I have been thinking since might have been a profound mistake. My brother — do you mind my discussing these personal matters with you, Alexandra? I'd like to have you understand. That's why I was so insistent about you dining with me tonight. And I haven't thanked you properly yet, have I, for breaking another engagement for me."

Sandra's fingers touched the corsage at her shoulder. "Surely these exquisite gardenias are adequate thanks. Anyhow —"

"Anyhow?" he prompted her.

"I'd like to have you tell me these personal things."

"Good. I hoped you might. Well, the thing is that I probably took my responsibility toward my younger brother too seriously, or rather, as Miss Wyndham believes, I misunderstood what that responsibility really was. We're a family of lawyers and I thought Colin should follow the family tradition. In fact, I insisted on it. Result is that, in rebellion, he has simply turned into a playboy who shirks his job as much as he can. Then when I began to observe Miss Wyndham, the beauty and charm and that fine sense of integrity she has, I thought that if Colin were to marry her she would probably be the one girl who could make him settle down."

For a few minutes he devoted himself to *coq au vin*. "So Miss Wyndham challenged me with treating her and Colin as though they were puppets, of failing to respect my brother as a person and leaving him free to live his own life. Then she resigned and left the office."

Again there was a small silence at the table. Again it was the usually taciturn Stephen who broke it.

"She is an unusually fine person. Obviously she has to earn her living but she isn't mercenary or she would have jumped at the chance to marry Colin. And she has the courage of her convictions. She threw away her job in her attempt to help my brother, though she obviously has no personal interest in him."

While the waiter removed plates, substituted others, they spoke of casual matters. When they were alone again he asked abruptly, "Was I wrong, Alexandra?"

"Wrong in what way?"

"Wrong in trying to make Colin a successful lawyer, in trying to help him find a suitable wife.

Sandra was silent, her fingers crumbling a roll. She was filled with a wave of self-disgust. What had she done to Connie? How could she have been so cruel, so unfair?

"Alexandra?" Emery said.

"Yes, I think perhaps you were wrong," she said slowly. "It's hard to tell what is best, isn't it? For other people, I mean."

"I asked because I thought you'd have a special understanding. Miss Wyndham believes that you, too, have been a victim of well-meaning interference; that your father has attempted to manage your life for you." He smiled more deeply. "She said you had never had an opportunity to find yourself, to be yourself, to discover happiness in your own way. She was most indignant about it."

Tears suddenly blinded Sandra. She blinked them away. I wish, she thought, I hadn't spoken to Connie as I did. And I can't wipe them out. Words, she said, are always there once they have been spoken. They will always be there. Bitter, angry words. Unjust words.

"I think we all make bad mistakes in judgment, Stephen, and perhaps the one I've made in regard to Connie is worse than the one you've made in regard to your brother. What hurts me most is realizing that it is Connie, really, who is paying for all these mistakes."

"I hope not," Stephen said, but without a great deal of interest. The girl beside him was so much more absorbing. "She's a nice girl. I hope not. Still that is not what interests me most. What seems most important to me is that you should not pay for the mistakes of anyone else. I'd like to think that you were completely free to make your own choice, your own decision."

But that, of course, was impossible, Sandra thought. She could not conceivably marry a man who could not be a son to her father, the son who could replace him eventually at Kent Enterprises. And yet it would be wonderful to marry a man who looked at her not with Jeff's cool detached friendship but with warmth, with admiration, with something deeper, more thrilling than either, something for which she was not ready to find a name.

Before she could speak there was an outburst of delighted laughter. Stephen turned his head and said in surprise, "Good lord, there's Colin. I wonder who the girl is?"

ii

"It looks awfully fashionable and expensive," Lil said, hanging back.

Colin's hand tightened on her arm as he steered her into the French restaurant. "This is my party. I want to show you off and there will be no back talk from you, young lady."

"Yes, sir," she said with mock humility. "Yes, master. Okay, boss."

But when she noticed that there were no prices listed on the menu she balked again. "Colin! It must cost the earth. I'm scared to order. Let's go somewhere else."

He grinned at her. "Why didn't I meet you sooner? Most of the gals I know like spending money, especially mine."

"But you can't afford it."

"Hey, I'm not on relief yet."

"But if you're going to stock your farm with really fine cattle, besides all the equipment and machinery you will need —"

"Hey," he protested again. "I haven't got that farm yet."

"But you will," she said confidently. "And I was thinking last night that one of my uncles works for a company that manufactures farm machinery and he could maybe get you a discount."

Then he laughed. "You know what? I'm always happy when I'm with you. So we'll count off the dinner against the money I'll save on farm machinery. You busy next Saturday? I thought you might drive out with me to look at a couple of places that are on the market."

"I'd love to."

He was delighted by the glow in her face. "That's the way girls usually talk about nightclubs or jewelry or mink. Instead, you get all excited about looking at dairy farms."

"They are more important than jewelry," she said calmly, "and lots more interesting."

His eyes twinkled at her. "How would you like to be a milkmaid for the rest of your life?"

"You'll never make money by depending on hand labor,'" she said severely. "You should have electric —"

He leaned back with a shout of laughter that suddenly died on his lips.

"What's wrong?" Lil asked.

"My brother Steve. Across the room. With that girl with the brown hair and the white dress."

Lil turned casually. "That's Miss Kent, the heiress. She's one of Céleste's biggest customers."

After a while Colin said in concern, "You aren't eating. Don't you like the food?"

"It's out of this world but —"

"What's wrong, Lil?" The teasing was gone. "You can tell me, dear."

"Well, it's just — well, your brother wants you to — to like Connie and you were going to tell him it was really Connie you came to see and —"

"And," Colin said, his voice very quiet, very gentle, "you said you didn't want me to come back if I were ashamed of you. Do you think I'm ashamed, Lil? Lil, look at me! I can't even begin to believe my luck at having found a girl like you. And I don't intend to lose you if I can help it. What I'm setting out to do, as of now, is to try to be worthy of you, to deserve you. Then I'm going to bring up that question about the milkmaid again."

Lil's eyes were sparkling. "I told you before," she said with mock severity, "that it doesn't pay to do the milking by hand."

A little later Colin said, his voice serious, "Lil, what's all this about Connie? Did you hear that telephone call tonight? Nick — that's her half brother, isn't it? — he knows the red-headed man who has been following Connie."

"Did you see her face when she came in tonight, Colin? She had been crying."

"That man had been annoying her?"

Lil shook her head. "I don't think so. She was upset earlier this afternoon. Miss Kent came to the shop today and asked Céleste to have Connie get off. She wanted to talk to her. Connie looked — just awful. Half sick."

They were both thoughtful. Then Colin said, "That guy Gray —"

"Who?"

"The man who brought her some stamp albums this afternoon when I was fixing that venetian blind."

"Stamp albums!" Lil's face lighted up. "So she got them back. But how did you know the man's name?"

"Met him at the opera the night Steve," and he grinned, "set up a budding romance for Connie and me. A fine-looking fellow. He was sharing a box with Miss Kent, though I didn't know then who she was. He came around between acts to speak to Connie. Talked as though they were old friends."

"How odd," Lil said. "Connie has never mentioned him to me. I didn't even know she had any friends in New York except some girl who called and asked her to dinner. An old school friend, she said." Her mouth opened. "Jeepers! Do you suppose they are the ones?"

"I don't know what you are talking about."

"Well, once when I was asking why a girl like her didn't have dates she said she was a one-man woman, only the man she loved was going to marry her best friend and she couldn't spoil both their lives."

Colin frowned over her story. "Do you know this brother of hers?"

"I've met him," Lil said shortly, "and I didn't like him at all. He's — well, he's all the things Connie is not: sly and insinuating and filled with fake flattery and — dishonest. I wouldn't trust him a foot."

"Has he anything to do with the stamp albums she was so excited over getting tonight?"

"He has everything to do with them," Lil snapped. "We both think he stole them."

iii

"Sure they are gone?" the fat man asked.

"I've searched high and low," the thin one answered.

Guy Holt, the red-headed man, sat at the scarred table in the basement apartment. "If only I hadn't put that air-mail stamp back! We'd have had that at least. Winterson was ready to give me a cool nine thousand in cash. No haggling over price. No questions asked. He would probably have taken a lot more of them off our hands. But I didn't want to carry the thing around with me. We've always been careful not to have any hot stuff on us a moment longer than necessary."

"What it comes down to," the fat man said, "is that I counted on you fools having enough sense to keep an eye on Nick. He was always the weak link. When we found out his father had inherited that big stamp deal he tried every way to keep us from getting it. Then he held out on our collections. Now, when he has a chance to clear himself with us, he first turns over the stamps and then he takes them back. Though how he thinks he'll be able to dispose of them on his own I can't imagine. He doesn't know the right people."

"So what do we do?" snarled the thin man. "Sit back and let Nick get away with thousands of dollars' worth of stamps? There's no hope getting Winterson's money now."

"I've sent out word," the fat man said. "Nick'll be picked up. He hasn't got sense enough to hide. Anyhow, he's practically out of money. He can't get far."

"Unless someone gave him the money," the red-headed man suggested.

"We'll get him." The fat man was sure of that. So sure that the other two, tough as they were, shivered. They wouldn't want to be in Nick's shoes. "I always get them. Once word gets around that anyone has put anything over on me I — well, I can't afford it."

"Meantime he has the stamps," the thin man repeated.

The fat man ignored him. He turned to Holt. "Look here, your idea that someone has given him money — is that an educated guess or what?"

"He has friends," Holt said slowly. "Especially there is that good-looking sister of his. She's the best line we have on Nick."

"How much have you found out about her?"

"Quite a bit. She worked for Emery & Emery, a law firm —"

"Law," the fat man said thoughtfully. "Not so good. Not good at all."

"She quit a few days ago and I trailed her to a fancy dress shop. Céleste. She got a job there as a model."

"Any boy friends?"

Remembering the man who had threatened to knock his head off and had chased him to the subway, Holt decided to keep his mouth shut. He, too, was afraid of the fat man.

"What difference does it make?" the thin man protested. "She's no use to us."

"She's Nick's sister," the fat man pointed out. "We could always use her as a lever if he tries to get away with anything."

"Knowing Nick," the thin young man said, "I'd expect him not to care what happened to his sister. He's for Nick first. What we need is someone with money."

"And that," Holt said, "is just what we've got. This afternoon after I met Winterson, I dropped around to see what the sister was up to. She came out of the shop with a customer and got into a big Lincoln, uniformed chauffeur at the wheel. I checked on the license. Car belongs to John Kent. The girl was his daughter, heiress to thirty million. And, if you remember, Nick told us once his sister went to school with the Kent girl, lived with them like one of the family, and it was to Kent she intended to give those stamps."

"So?"

"So if they are such close friends as all that, how much money would the Kents put up to — well, to get the girl back?"

There was a long silence in the room. Then the fat man shook his head. "Nope."

"Why not?" Holt demanded.

"Kidnaping is as dangerous as shooting a policeman.

You'd better put a gun to your own head and pull the trigger. Nope."

"I wasn't thinking of kidnaping exactly. But this girl is devoted to her brother. If she thought he really had to have a big chunk of money — and I mean *had* to have it — she could ask the Kents herself. No risk in that, so far as I can see."

"But —"

"How you going to make her know that it's serious?" the thin man asked. "How you going to get her to believe you?"

"She'd believe me."

"What makes you so sure?"

"She was at the airport with Nick that time the boss sent me to get the stamps. She knew it was serious, all right. Some guy jumped me and took away the gun. I had all I could do to get away. He was on me like a prize fighter. Wouldn't be surprised if he was a judo expert, too."

The thin man chuckled rather maliciously. "You sure looked beat up when you came back."

Holt was eager to dismiss the subject. He hadn't shown up well in that business in Maine. He had made a mess of it and the fat man had told him so in no uncertain terms. The boss didn't make allowances for failures. That was why when Nick was found he would get it. Get it bad.

"My idea is to approach the girl," Holt said. "Tell her Nick's in a spot. Ask, say, a hundred thousand in cash to take the heat off him."

The thin young man drew in his breath sharply. "A hundred thousand!"

"Chicken-feed to the Kents," Holt said.

"But how could you arrange to get the money without leaving a trail straight to you?"

"I'll think of something. Lots of ways."

"And the girl? She'd be all right, wouldn't she?" the young man asked.

"All right? Oh, sure," Holt said heartily. "Sure. No harm to her at all." He winked at the fat man whose lips quirked upwards in a smile.

EIGHTEEN

INTO her dream came the insistent ringing of a bell. Connie groped sleepily for the alarm clock, then awakened enough to realize that it was the telephone. She stumbled out to the living room. Lil still had not returned from dinner with Colin.

"Hello?" There was the sound of heavy breathing at the other end of the line. "Hello!"

"Miss Wyndham?"

"Yes."

"This is New York Hospital. Is Nicholas Wyndham your brother?"

"Yes. Yes."

"He is asking for you. Emergency ward. Can you get here at once?"

"I'm on my way." Connie hung up, started toward her room at a run. Stopped.

Don't fall for any fake telephone calls, Colin had advised her, laughing. *Be sure you know they are legitimate.*

That voice at the other end of the line. There had been something oddly familiar, oddly disturbing, about it. Then she remembered. The man lisped. He lisped as the man at the airport in Maine had done.

With trembling fingers she searched the Manhattan telephone directory, dialed the number of the New York Hospital, got the emergency ward. A few minutes later she set down the telephone. No patient named Nicholas Wyndham had been admitted.

After a long time she dressed, her numbed fingers fumbling awkwardly with buttons and zippers. Cautiously she removed the chain from the door, peered into the hallway. For once she was grateful that it was kept so dark. She stole on tiptoe to the outer door, looked outside. The street was empty. There was not, as she had half expected, any lurking pedestrian. No cars passed.

Then she heard the low sound of an idling motor. Not far up the street a shabby Chevrolet had drawn in to the curb. It was parked, of all unlikely places, outside a small delicatessen that was closed for the night. She knew then that it was waiting for her.

She fled back to the apartment, put the chain on the door and once more checked the telephone directory. Graham . . . Grant . . . Gray, Jefferson. She dialed the number. It was late, how late she had no idea, but that didn't matter.

Jeff's voice was alert, wide awake. "Yes?" he said.

"Jeff! Oh, Jeff!"

"Connie! What's wrong?"

The words poured out in a jumble so that, between her haste and her panic, he could barely understand them.

"And he's outside now. Waiting for me," she concluded. "I'm terrified."

"Is your door locked?"

"Yes. Of course."

"Keep it that way. Don't unlock it for anyone. Anyone, do you understand? I'm on my way."

"Oh, Jeff!"

ii

"Come in, sir," Jeff said in surprise, standing back to let Kent enter his living room.

Kent looked around, summing the place up. A comfortable room with the unusual luxury in New York of a fireplace in which logs were blazing. A deep chair drawn up near the fire, with a table beside it holding his book, Wilkie Collins's *The Moonstone,* first and greatest of all English detective novels. A radio was tuned low, playing Scarlatti.

When Kent was seated, Jeff waited courteously for him to explain his unexpected call at — he glanced at his watch — ten o'clock.

"Our talk this morning was interrupted," Kent said, "so I thought we might finish it this evening. I hope you found that rather unconventional meeting at a bar satisfactory. I noticed that you didn't return to the office this afternoon. Postponed the Elton conference, didn't you?"

"The meeting was quite satisfactory." Jeff got up and went to his big desk. He came back to set a large package on the table between their chairs. "This, sir, is the stamp collection that Mr. Wyndham bequeathed to you. My meeting this noon was for the purpose of tracking down the man who had stolen it. Connie was desperately anxious that it should go to you as soon as possible, in fulfillment of her father's wishes."

"Stolen?" Kent looked at him skeptically. "What's all this about?"

"I think it's time you knew the whole story," Jeff said and told him everything from the time of the encounter between Nick and the gunman at the Maine airport to the moment when he had seen Nick walk away from him, headed for Pennsylvania Station and his escape from New York.

"And where did you get this extraordinary story?"

"Part of it from my own personal experience; the rest of it from Connie."

"And you believed her?"

"I believed her."

"What it boils down to," Kent said, "is that the Wyndhams discovered that the stamps were more valuable than they had supposed so they intended to hold on to them. When I inquired about them, they staged this business and made you pay, and pay heavily, to get them back."

"You are mistaken, sir." Jeff spoke as coolly as he could, trying not to betray his anger. "Nick was in fear of his life this afternoon when he left me."

"Well, Jeff, I confess I am disappointed. I had expected better things of you. What we must settle now, without further delay, is this. Are you going to keep the place I've made for you with Kent Enterprises or are you going to dangle after Constance Wyndham whenever she calls on you."

"I assume that I can't do both."

"You can't do both. There is no place in my plans for Constance Wyndham."

The telephone rang and Connie, her voice shrill with terror, was talking so fast he could hardly understand her.

He put down the telephone, shoved back his chair. Rapidly he summarized Connie's story. ". . . and the man is waiting outside her apartment now. Please call the police and give them her address. I'm on my way."

Kent stood up. "This is another Wyndham trick. I'm surprised at you for falling for it."

Jeff dialed the police himself and then pulled on his overcoat.

"Just a minute," Kent said, in a tone Jeff had never heard him use before. "If this is your answer to what I've been saying, I must ask you to hand in your resignation in the very near future. I want a man I can rely on."

"Very well, sir."

"Jeff! You can't do this. Your future depends on the choice you make now. Why are you so carelessly willing to throw it away?"

"Because I love her."

Jeff ran down the stairs, too impatient to waste time waiting for the elevator, hailed a cab, and sat on the edge of the seat until it turned into Connie's street. The drive seemed endless, though it had been made in record time.

"Oho," the driver said over his shoulder. "Looks like there's trouble here."

A prowl car, red light blinking, was drawn up outside Connie's apartment. The outer door was open and Jeff went in quickly without waiting to ring. There was a policeman in the dark hallway, and Connie's door was open. As Jeff started toward it, the man in the hall stopped him.

"It's all right," Jeff said. "Miss Wyndham telephoned me. I'm the one who put in the call for the police."

Connie appeared at the door with another policeman. "Jeff!" she cried and ran straight into his arms.

He held her tight. "You all right?" he asked.

She nodded.

"What happened after you called me?"

The policeman explained. "He got away. The Chevrolet took off as soon as we came up. We lost him." He turned to Connie. "That was smart of you, checking with the hospital before you went out. Watch yourself, young lady, and report at once if you see or hear anything more of this fellow."

"I will," she said fervently. "And thank you very much."

"That's what we're here for."

When the two policemen had gone Jeff followed Connie into the apartment. "Don't look so little and scared," he said unsteadily, and gathered her to him again. Her arms crept around his neck. She clung to him.

At length he held her away from him. "Now then, tell me all about it."

When she had done so he said, a chill in his voice, "So it was Colin Emery who suggested that you check on any strange telephone calls."

She nodded. "You see, he found the red-headed man outside the apartment and chased him away, so he knew I hadn't been imagining things."

"I take it this guy Colin is looking out for you." Before she could answer he said, "Get to bed now and sleep. You look exhausted. Good night."

He was gone before she could thank him for answering her panic-stricken call for help. It took all her self-control not to run after him. Then she realized belatedly the meaning of what he had said. He was jealous of Colin. He thought it was Colin she cared about. She was lighter-hearted when she went to bed.

iii

It was Lil's turn to sleep late next morning. She had a half-day off to compensate for the Saturday morning she had worked.

When she had come home the night before, the two girls had talked for hours about the fake telephone call, the man who had waited outside for Connie to swallow the bait, and the timely arrival of the police and Jefferson Gray.

There were dark shadows under Connie's eyes and she did her best with makeup to conceal them before she left for work. It wouldn't do for a model to look haggard and exhausted. She must appear fresh, rested, smiling, whatever turmoil her thoughts might be in.

She perched a tiny green hat on her russet hair, fastened her coat around her because the March winds were biting, and left the apartment.

Pedestrians were hastening down the street toward the subway, trucks and taxis and private cars moved almost bumper to bumper in the early rush hours. For once Connie took comfort in the heavy traffic. This was better, safer, than last night's deserted street.

Just before she reached the subway, she was engulfed in the usual mob milling around the newspaper stand, hurrying down the subway steps. A man brushed against her so that she lost her balance and fell toward the curb.

In an instant one arm was around her to prevent her falling, a hand covered her mouth to stifle any sound, and he was forcing her into the waiting car, a shabby Chevrolet.

Dazed by the suddenness of the attack, Connie looked wildly around. Someone must see and come to the rescue. The crowd steamed past. A bulky woman in a fur-collared coat saw the struggle, hesitated, and then scurried to the subway entrance.

Connie was flung into a corner of the rear seat. Before the door had closed the car was moving away.

The man beside her held out a knife with a long, ugly switchblade. "If you call out you'll get this," he said. "If you're good you won't be hurt. You're in no danger — if you do exactly as you are told."

She recognized the red hair, the ratlike face, the broken tooth, the lisp. This was Guy Holt, the man about whom Nick had warned her, the man who had watched her at the cafeteria, followed her along the street. Last night he had made that telephone call and he had waited for her to fall into his trap.

"But why? But what? But —"

The light reflected on the switchblade and she was silent. She sat with her shoulders rigid, her gloved hands holding each other tightly, heart hammering painfully against her side. Her lips were dry.

This can't be happening, she thought. Not in bright daylight. Not on a crowded street. All around her there were people and yet she could not call for help.

They had turned south, moving in bumper-to-bumper traffic. Then they were in the Holland Tunnel, deafened by the thunder of motors reverberating in the narrow space. At last there was daylight ahead but they had passed the toll booth almost before she realized it. She had not had a chance to call for help. Anyhow, she admitted to herself, with that switchblade against her side she was too afraid to utter a sound. A knife was so terribly swift. So final.

Now they were on the Jersey Turnpike headed south. Where were they taking her. Where?

The driver was a thin young man. The man beside her, Guy Holt, sat staring ahead but aware of every motion she made. Wild ideas crossed her mind of flinging open the door and plunging out into the moving traffic, of running down the window and screaming for help. She abandoned each in turn.

Jeff, she called silently in her mind. Jeff, come find me.

Don't let them hurt me. Jeff! Jeff! But there was no one to hear that silent cry.

It was midmorning when, after leaving the turnpike, the car moved more slowly along an abandoned dirt road. For some time Connie had been aware that they were following the Jersey shoreline, flat, uninteresting country. Now they were headed toward the beach and a dismal line of summer cottages that were closed for the winter.

It was before one of these that the car finally stopped and the red-headed man got out.

"Here we are," he said jovially. When Connie made no move he added, "Will you get out by yourself or shall I haul you out?"

She stumbled out, pulling her coat tight around her as the spray from the ocean cut into her face. She looked around in despair. How could anyone find her here? This was a place without landmarks, with almost no cottages, and such as there were looked like cheap summer cottages anywhere. Nothing to distinguish them. The only difference about the one before which they had stopped was that the windows were boarded up.

The thin man who had been driving pulled out a key and unlocked the door.

Inside as outside, it was typical of inexpensive summer resort cottages. There was a small living room, dark because of the boarded-up windows, a smaller bedroom, a kitchenette and bath. The place was damp and cold with a chill that struck deep into the bones.

Holt bent over to light a small gas fireplace, which provided the only heat. There was a hiss, a smell of gas, and then the artificial logs caught with a twinkling blue light.

The thin man went into the kitchenette carrying a paper bag of groceries he had taken from the car. "Coffee, bread, butter, canned soup, baked beans. Enough to keep her going two-three days."

Two-three days. Huddled close to the gas fire Connie moistened her lips.

"What do you want of me?" she asked.

"It's like this, sister," Holt told her. "You know your brother got himself in bad trouble?"

She nodded.

"Very bad trouble. Now he had a chance to clear himself, to get all right with the boss. He was going to give us some valuable stamps. Instead, he's gone off and taken the stamps with him."

"But—" she began.

"That makes two mistakes," Holt said. "The boss doesn't like mistakes. One is bad enough. Two is all there is. All there is," he repeated meaningfully.

She stared at him, her eyes immense, dark-shadowed, her lips white, her breath coming unevenly, shallowly.

"Nick hasn't got the stamps," she said. "A — a friend of mine took them away from him and sent Nick out of town to get him away from you. My — the friend gave them to — to the man they really belong to."

After a long time Holt said, "Well, what do you know? Now that's just too bad. There's only one way now to save Nick from what he's asked for."

"You mean he'll be killed?" It was a strained whisper.

"What do you think?"

She dropped into a wicker chair, staring unseeingly at the flickering gas fire.

"Now here is where you come in. There's one chance, just exactly one chance, to save him. That depends on you."

All the past was wiped out. Nothing remained except the

fact that Nick was her brother, that he was Bill Wyndham's son, that he was in danger.

"I'd do anything — anything —"

"Now that's the right spirit. Cooperative. I told the boys I was sure you'd be cooperative once you knew the score. Now what you're to do is to write a letter to your friend, Mr. John Kent, or, if you prefer, to his daughter — we don't care which, broadminded, that's us — and say that they've got to get a hundred thousand dollars together in small bills — unmarked — and be prepared to deliver them when they get the word. And no tricks. No police. Or — Nick gets it."

It was a long time before Connie spoke, and her voice was flat and dead. "I can't do it."

"You've got to do it."

"You don't understand. It wouldn't make any difference. They — Mr. Kent doesn't like Nick. He doesn't like me any more. He told me just the other day I could not expect to have anything more from him. Ever. He meant it."

"Look —" Holt began harshly.

She put out a shaking hand. "I was planning to borrow enough money from him to get Nick out of this — mess he is in. I found that I couldn't."

There was a small silence. Holt's small eyes never left her face. At last he turned to the thin young man who was waiting tensely in the background, eyes fixed on Connie's face in a bemused look.

"Go out and get the car warmed up, Max," he said. "I'll be with you in a minute."

"You won't — hurt her —"

The wolfish grin twisted Holt's lips. "I won't hurt her — unless I have to." As Max lingered, he growled, "Get out! Do I have to tell you everything twice?"

Max went out with a frightened look at Connie. Holt waited until he heard the motor turn over.

"So Kent won't pay up — even to save you."

"I know he won't. Believe me, I'd do anything for Nick but this just wouldn't work."

The truth in her tone was inescapable. For a long bleak moment Holt stared at the picture of his own failure, at its effect on the boss who did not excuse failures.

He glanced toward the door but Max was at the wheel of the car. "We'll give you twenty-four hours to think it over." He looked around. "But no sense in making this too homelike for you." He chuckled. "You might not want to leave it."

He went outside, she heard him moving around the cottage. Then the flame in the gas fireplace flickered, died down, went out. He had shut off the gas.

A few minutes later she heard him lock the door. The car rolled away.

Before the sound of the motor had faded, Connie was out of her chair, trying the doorknob, beating on the solid oak door. What else? The windows! She forced them up, one by one, but the shutters were immovable. There was nothing in the little cottage with which she could pry them open.

At last she sank down on the chair and stared blindly at the wall. Jeff, where are you?

NINETEEN

WHEN Lil reported for work at one o'clock Céleste gave her a curt nod and returned to the customer to whom she was talking. In a few moments she went into the back of the shop where Lil had stopped to exchange greetings with one of the dressmakers.

"This is outrageous," Céleste said. "You should know better, Lillian. If Constance was unable to report for work you should have done so, whether or not you had a half day coming. There was no one to model that new line of spring suits for Mrs. Whiteside."

Only one part of this tirade reached Lil. "You mean Connie never came in?"

Something in the girl's horror-struck face checked Céleste in the acid comment that trembled on her lips.

"What's wrong?" she asked instead.

"Oh, Madame, something has happened to Connie! Something terrible has happened to her."

"Don't be hysterical!"

"You don't understand. Someone tried to kidnap her last night. He got away from the police. Oh, Connie!" Lil ran to the telephone and dialed the number of Emery & Emery.

"I'm sorry," a crisp voice said. "Mr. Colin Emery is in conference. If you will leave your name —"

"It doesn't matter where he is," Lil cried wildly. "This is a question of life and death."

In another moment Colin said, "Colin Emery speaking. What kind of gag is this?"

"Colin, it's Lil. Connie has been kidnaped. She never came to work this morning."

"Kidnaped!"

"Listen." She told him what had happened the night before while they were out at dinner. "And she never reached Céleste's this morning. And there's been no word. She would have called — she —"

"Steady," Colin said, but it was his voice, confident, reassuring, that steadied her. "Now let's have it from the beginning."

When the torrent of words had stopped he said, "Now let's see if I got this straight."

"There's no time to talk, Colin. We have to hurry."

"We can't hurry until we know where we are going, dear. Now, Connie got a fake telephone call last evening, and, being one of those rare people who follow my advice, she checked on it. Then she saw the car waiting outside and called Gray. Okay so far? All right then. The police came but the guy saw the blinker and got away. Still okay? This morning she set out for work, so far as you know, and she never got there."

"She never got here." Lil's voice was shaking. "What are we going to do?"

"Leave it to me, Lil. I'll handle it. We'll find her. I'll be in touch as soon as I have any news. And try not to worry too much."

When Colin set down the telephone he found Steve scowling at him across the desk. As he started to dial a number his brother said, "What's that all about?"

When Colin had told him succinctly, Steve looked at him, appalled. Then he said, "This is awful. A terrible situation. But I don't quite see why you offered to take over the responsibility. What can you do?"

"First, I'm calling the police. That seems to be the obvious course."

Steve put out a hand to check him. "In four generations we've never handled a sensational case, Colin. We don't deal with criminals."

"I do. There's a girl's life at stake, Steve," Colin told him and his brother looked at him in astonishment. He did not know this determined man. There was nothing of the playboy about him now.

"Who is the girl you were talking to?"

"Lillian Debaney. She's Connie's roommate. She's also the girl I hope to marry if I'm lucky and she will have me."

"The girl you were with last night?"

"That's the one." Colin began to dial a number.

"Wait! If this — Miss Debaney — is right and Constance Wyndham has been kidnaped, you may add to her danger by calling in the police. Hadn't you better make sure of the situation before you start something that you won't be able to stop?"

Colin set down the telephone, staring at his brother. "But, Steve," he said at last, "I don't know where else to turn. Lil has told me all she knows. There is no one else —" His voice trailed off. "That girl you were with last night —"

Steve stiffened.

"She's Miss Kent, isn't she? She and Connie are old friends. She might know —"

"We can't involve Alexandra," Steve said sharply.

"Just Connie and Lil, I suppose." When Steve made no reply, Colin said. "Is she made of finer material than the rest of the world or doesn't she have the guts to back her friends, to help save their lives, if she can?"

Steve's fury nearly broke out. Then he remembered Alexandra saying that perhaps Connie was paying for other people's mistakes. He saw Colin's drawn face. Wordlessly he reached forward and took the telephone from him.

The maid at the Kent apartment said that Miss Kent was not at home but took Steve's message and promised to mark it "urgent."

The receptionist at Kent Enterprises demanded that Emery state his business and was finally persuaded to switch him to Kent's secretary. She, too, held him up maddeningly by demanding his name and his business.

At last Steve found himself speaking to Kent. He introduced himself and Kent merely grunted. Then Steve, who was beginning to share Colin's worry, told him that they believed Constance Wyndham had been kidnaped. Did Mr. Kent have any lead, did he know of any reason for such a situation? They had not called the police for fear of increasing any danger that she might be in.

"I can tell you exactly what is behind this, Mr. Emery," Kent said. "The young Wyndhams are completely unscrupulous. They have been attempting one trick after another to get money out of me. I do not for one minute believe that Constance has been kidnaped. I wouldn't believe it if a ransom note came in — and if they are trying this stunt I am bound to be the one to be approached. I am convinced that this is simply another attempt at extortion. And I might say that the Wyndhams are badly mistaken if they believe that I will submit to it." Kent slammed down the telephone.

Steve found himself staring at his own phone blankly. He set it down.

"Well?" Colin demanded hoarsely.

"Kent thinks it's a trick perpetrated by the Wyndhams — there seems to be another one, brother or sister — in order to extort money from him."

"Why the —" Colin broke off, staring at his brother. "I guess this is sensitive ground. You seem to like Kent's daughter. Maybe you don't want any trouble with Kent. But, honestly, what do you think of the way he is reacting, Steve? Do you believe his unspeakable implications against Connie?"

"I can't believe it," Steve said at last. "That girl — she has a quality of honesty, of integrity, of personal honor — I know something about people. I can't be that mistaken about Miss Wyndham."

"Then," Colin asked, "are you with me in this? Or are you against me?"

Steve stretched out his hand across the wide desk. "I'm with you."

ii

For the second time in two days Kent flung open the door of Jeff's private office.

Jeff looked up in surprise. Then he said stiffly, "I've just dictated my letter of resignation, Mr. Kent. My secretary is typing it now. I allowed thirty days in which to clear up my work here and, if you like, get someone else trained to handle it."

Kent blinked as though he were taken aback by the words. Then they finally penetrated. "Oh, that," he said with an impatient gesture. "Let that go for the time being. You'll get over this mood, Jeff."

"Will I?"

"You will if you have the common sense I credit you

with. Something has just happened that makes evident just how great a mistake you have made about Constance Wyndham, just how much you have been taken in by her."

Before Jeff could speak Kent described his telephone call from Stephen Emery.

"Oh, my God, they've got her!" Jeff leaped to his feet with a cry of horror.

"It's a trick, I tell you," Kent said. He turned irritably as Jeff's secretary appeared at the door.

"Mr. Kent," she said breathlessly, "your secretary has just transferred a call to my desk. It's some man who says it's a matter of life or death."

Kent reached for the telephone. A man's voice with a strong lisp said, "Kent? We have Constance Wyndham. We want one hundred thousand dollars in small bills. Unmarked. We'll give you instructions later. Tomorrow you'll get a call from her showing she's still alive. After that it is up to you. Don't call the police or you'll never see her again."

"Put her on the telephone as often as you like," Kent snapped, "but you'll never see a penny of my money. Not one cent. And don't make the mistake of threatening me again. I don't scare."

He set down the telephone. His face was almost purple with suppressed rage.

"What is it?" Jeff demanded.

Kent told him.

"They've got her!" Jeff held on to the back of his chair. "They've got her!"

"Nonsense," Kent said. "You're a young fool, Jeff. But, thank God, I'm not an old one." He reached for the telephone.

"What are you going to do?"

Still scowling at him, Kent spoke into the telephone. "Get me the police," he said coldly. When he had reached a man in authority he reported the alleged kidnaping of Constance Wyndham. "I wish to go on record," he said, "as refusing categorically to yield to extortioners. When they are discovered I want them prosecuted to the full extent of the law."

"You don't believe the Wyndham girl has been kidnaped?" the police sergeant asked alertly.

"Of course she hasn't been kidnaped. She is probably holed up right now with that scoundrel of a brother of hers and they are laughing their heads off. Well, they had better do their laughing while they can."

TWENTY

CONNIE turned on her side, pulled the thin summer blanket around her, reached for the coat she had placed at the foot of the cot. Still the cold seemed to penetrate her very bones. Why was she so cold? She remembered then that she was in the deserted summer cottage on the Jersey shore, that there was no heat, there was no escape, and tomorrow morning Holt would come back. Twenty-four hours, he had said. After that —

There was no more sleep for her now. She had not undressed, merely lain down because she was emotionally exhausted. It was a surprise to know she had actually fallen asleep.

She got off the bed, slipped into her coat, managed to wash in cold water, to get some order into her disheveled hair, and to sit down in the wicker chair in the living room, wrapping the blanket from the cot around her.

Her watch showed that it was early afternoon. There was no sound but the constant beating of the waves. Yes, there was another sound. She sat more alert, heart quickening its beat. A car approached, a door slammed.

There was a grating noise as a key turned in the lock and then a gust of cold air as someone came in. Guy Holt stood looking at her. There was something in his face that had not been there before. He was like a cornered wolf.

"Your friend Kent refuses to pay a cent of ransom even to save your life."

"I told you that would be how he felt about me."

She shrank back in her chair trying to make herself small as he came close to her. "So," he said, "you've had it."

"Oh, please — please — don't hurt me."

He jerked her to her feet, ripped off her heavy coat, pulled up her sleeve. A needle jabbed into her flesh.

ii

"If anything happens to Connie as a result of that call to the police," Jeff said, "you will be morally responsible for her death."

"You're a fool," Kent retorted. He looked at Jeff, saw that he was aging before his eyes. "You're being taken in," he added, but he could hear the uneasiness, the growing doubt in his own voice.

As the telephone shrilled again Jeff lunged for it. "Gray."

"My name is Colin Emery. We met —"

"Yes, I remember."

"Have you heard about Connie?"

"The kidnaper has already approached Mr. Kent."

"Oh God! They really have her! How much do you know about it?"

"That's all. And you?"

Colin told him rapidly of Lil's phone call. "Naturally I haven't called the police. I was afraid to increase Connie's danger until we were clear as to what the situation was, whether she had really been kidnaped or had an accident or simply gone off somewhere on her own."

"You were more considerate than Mr. Kent," Jeff said. "He lost no time in informing the police, first, that the whole matter was a hoax, and, second, that he would prosecute those responsible to the full extent of the law."

"No!"

"Oh, yes." Jeff did not look at Kent. "He might as well have killed her himself."

"Wait, Gray! There's bound to be something we can do. I'm in this to the finish. Will you help?"

"Will I!"

At the man's tortured cry Colin thought, "Poor devil! He loves the girl." He said, "I'll be with you in a quarter of an hour."

Actually it wasn't more than twenty minutes before Jeff's secretary ushered Colin Emery into his office. The secretary was wide-eyed. There hadn't been so much excitement since she had taken her job five years before. Twice Mr. Kent himself had rushed into the office. Jefferson Gray, the most attractive bachelor Kent Enterprises had ever known, the wistful focus for the dreams of half a dozen girls, and the man whom everyone expected to succeed Kent as head of the business, had written out a resignation.

Someone had called Mr. Kent, saying it was a matter of life and death. Kent himself had stormed out of Mr. Gray's office looking like a thundercloud. Now this good-looking man had raced in as though all the furies were after him.

The two young men sized each other up carefully as they shook hands. Colin was struck by the havoc wrought in Gray. He did not seem like the same man he had met at the opera, self-possessed, relaxed, on top of the world, obviously a man who had a rendezvous with destiny.

"Let's see what we know first," Colin suggested. "Pool information. You had better tell me what happened last night. Lil was so upset I couldn't get the story too clearly, but I gathered some attempt had been made to trick Connie into going out."

Jeff explained about the fake telephone call that had been designed to get Connie out of the apartment so the gangster could pick her up. Colin, in turn, described how a man had trailed Connie, how he had found him lurking outside the apartment building and had chased him away.

Together they pieced what they knew into a recognizable pattern, while Jeff explained Nick Wyndham's association with the gangsters who were undoubtedly involved in the kidnaping.

Then Colin told him that Connie had started for Céleste's that morning as usual, but that she had never reached there.

"I shouldn't have left her alone last night," Jeff groaned. "I should have camped right outside the door and followed her to work this morning." He hesitated. "Or perhaps you —"

Colin smiled. "You are on the wrong track," he said gently. "I have no claim on Connie at all except for great regard and esteem. Lil is my girl."

"Oh." Jeff's expressive face flooded with relief, and then darkened again. "But that's not quite the point now, is it? What matters is Connie's safety. Those goons want a hundred thousand from Mr. Kent. He is convinced," Jeff swallowed, "that this is a trick being engineered by Connie and her brother. He doesn't believe she has been kidnaped. He made all that clear to the police, so that when the story is made public, as it is bound to be, the police aren't going to worry about Connie, and the gangsters will know that they'll have to get rid of her fast because she can identify them. They'll never dare let her go."

Colin stared at Jeff in dismay. "That tears it," he said.

"No, darned if it does! We aren't going to give up. But what can we do now? Do you have any possible lead? Do you think it is conceivable her brother could be behind this? According to Lil he's a bad egg. If he is running this business, of course, Connie won't be hurt. That's about the only bright spot I can see."

"Nick is a thoroughly bad egg," Jeff agreed, "but he is out of the picture right now. Out of touch with his gang. In fact, they are gunning for him. Anyhow, vile as he might be, he wouldn't —" He broke off.

His expression changed. "There's just one possibility that I can see," he began slowly and then talked faster as the possibility took on coherence. "Only someone who knew Connie well would know of her association with the Kents in the past. It wasn't the sort of thing she would flaunt. Nick, her half brother, on the other hand, has always been determined to cash in on the Kents if he could. To cash in on anything if he could. It's possible, more than likely, he told his gang about Connie's friendship with the Kents. He certainly told them about the stamp albums."

He described the theft of the stamp albums and how he had traced Nick through the red-headed man and got them back. "If Nick is in this at all, we know at least where the headquarters of his gang is."

"And we know the red-headed man is the one who trailed Connie and that his name is Guy Holt. All right, Gray, let's go."

"I won't be back today," Jeff told his startled secretary as the two young men hastened past her.

As Jeff started to hail a cab Colin checked him. "Wait! We don't know what we're going to need in the way of transportation. Let's be prepared for anything. We'll hire a drive-it-yourself car and then, if we have to split up, one of us can drive and the other can go on foot."

When Colin was at the wheel of a rented car, Jeff directed him to the apartment building off Third Avenue where he had trailed Holt and had found Nick Wyndham.

"There it is. The third building on this side," he pointed out. "I didn't notice the number but —" He broke off. "Hold it."

Colin drew in at the curb and Jeff turned his head away, pulling up his coat collar, jerking down his hat brim. He did not want to be identified as Mr. Winterson.

"Someone just came out," Colin said. "Take a look. It's all right. He's getting into that battered old Chevy."

Jeff risked a look. "That's the guy who tried to sell me the stamp."

"Then it's the one I chased. I never got a good look at him. I wish now I'd followed him into the subway."

"Would he recognize you?"

"I doubt it. A street light was on his face but I came up on him so fast he never got a good look at me."

Colin followed the Chevrolet, sometimes letting a couple of cars in between, sometimes closing up the gap, but Holt did not appear to be worried about being followed.

"Where on earth is he going?" Colin asked in surprise as Holt's car turned into the Holland Tunnel.

"New Jersey, apparently."

"Suppose he isn't going to Connie. Suppose someone else has hidden her."

Jeff's jaw set. "We've got to gamble. This is the only lead we have. We've simply got to play it for all it's worth."

"He's in a whale of a hurry," Colin said uneasily. "I keep thinking, well —"

"What is it?"

"Suppose the newspapers get the story that Kent doesn't believe in the kidnaping, that he won't pay up, that he's going to prosecute?"

"They'll hold it back as long as they possibly can," Jeff said.

Colin leaned forward to switch on the radio. A jazz number came to an end. The announcer said briskly, "News flash for those who just tuned in. John Kent, head of the Kent Enterprises, informed New York police today that an extortion attempt has been made on him. A hundred thousand dollars ransom is demanded for the safe return of Miss Constance Wyndham, a former school friend of his daughter's. Mr. Kent declared that he would not pay a cent and that he would see the extortioners were found and punished."

Colin switched off the radio and groaned. "How could he? He might as well have killed her himself. Now they have nothing to hope for. They'll have to kill her now."

He looked at Jeff's drawn face and fell silent.

iii

Connie moaned. Little by little, her sluggish body was awakening, her sluggish thoughts beginning to stir. She knew that she was cold. She ought to do something about it. She moved slightly, moaned, slept again.

Her next conscious thought was that she was riding along a very bumpy road. Her eyes opened and then she closed them quickly, shutting out the red light. Fire? But how could there be fire when she was so cold? Colder than she had ever been in her life. She groped for blankets, touched rough, wet boards.

Her head seemed to expand like a balloon and then it

shrank to a knife-edge of pain. A dash of cold water in her face shocked her eyes wide open.

The light was not fire, it was the setting sun. The water was spray. A wave rocked the rowboat in which she was tossing as the wind whipped the ocean into great foaming swells.

A rowboat! There were, she realized, no oars. Lying full length, clutching at the sides, she tried to think. To remember. Holt with the needle. He had drugged her, dragged her out to the open boat, without a coat, without oars. But why? Then memory flooded back. Holt had told her that Kent refused to pay the ransom. She was no longer of any value to the kidnapers. Now she was only a liability, a threat.

As the boat rocked and pitched she marveled that she had not been tossed overboard. That, she realized, was what Holt had expected would happen. The boat would be driven away from shore; in time it would be swamped and it would sink; eventually, hours or days later, she would turn up, miles from the scene, drowned.

She lay clinging instinctively to the sides of the boat, trying to think. She was going to drown. The sun was sinking in the west, and twilight was taking the color out of the sky. In a little while, a very little while, it would be dark. She would never seen the sky again.

Drugged, shocked, chilled, terrified, her first feeling was one of despair and defeat. She wished that she had not awakened from that drugged sleep; that she had remained unconscious so that she need not be aware of what was happening to her.

Then she reacted like a normal, healthy girl. She was not going to die without making a fight for it. Anything was better than passive surrender. A French general had once said, "A lost battle is a battle you think you have lost." She hadn't lost this one. Not yet.

The shore line seemed a long way off; her chief hope lay in the possibility that the tide had turned, was coming in. She shivered as gust after gust of cold wind cut through her dress. She knew what she had to do and she dreaded it. But the longer she waited, the weaker, the more chilled, she would become. Soon the last of the daylight would fade from the sky. Never would she dare try to swim in the dark. Even now she wondered whether she could make it.

There was no choice, of course. She had to make it. She kicked off her shoes, pulled off her dress with great difficulty. It seemed to cling to her, to fight her efforts to be free of it. Then as the harsh wind struck her bare arms she began to shake uncontrollably. Slowly she made herself get to her knees, stand up. Then she plunged over the side.

For a moment as she sank in the water she feared that she had lost the use of her arms and legs. They were numbed by the terrible cold. The shock of the icy water stopped her breath. Waves pounded at her. Slowly she began to swim toward the distant shore and the last of the light.

TWENTY-ONE

ON THE Jersey Turnpike, the Chevrolet picked up speed. Now that twilight had settled down, headlights were switched on. Jeff had changed places with Colin at the wheel. Moving now and then from one lane to another, falling behind, catching up, trying not to get directly behind in the same lane, he never took his eyes off the car he was following.

"Where on earth —" he exclaimed. The Chevrolet had left the turnpike and turned down a narrow road. Jeff slowed down, allowing the other car to draw farther ahead. "I don't dare close up," he muttered. "We're too conspicuous. There isn't any other traffic on this side road."

Ahead they could see the red lights of the car drawing farther and farther away. Jeff cut down his lights, using only dimmers, and began to pick up speed. Again he had to slow down. They were approaching a beach resort that had been closed for the winter. Grocery stores, cleaners, a movie, a gas station. All empty. All deserted.

Now they were turning toward the beach where they would be even more conspicuous. There was still some light in the sky.

"Let me take the wheel," Colin suggested. "You go ahead on foot. In the dusk you are not apt to be seen if you are careful." He reached into the glove compartment for the flashlight he had purchased while Jeff was hiring the car. "Take this. Signal if you want me. Or let out a yell."

Jeff got out of the car, fastening his overcoat as it billowed when the wind from the ocean struck him, turning up his collar. He stood back against the side of an empty cottage and peered around it. The Chevrolet had drawn up at the fourth house along the beach. There were no lights. There was no sign of life.

Crouching, Jeff ran past the first cottage, hugged the side of the next one. The man had come around in front of his car and the headlights shone on his red hair. Jeff expected him to enter the cottage at once. Instead he had turned and he was staring out at the ocean. For a long time he scanned the waves.

At last he approached the cottage. He was walking heavily, making no effort at concealment. Evidently he was not afraid of anything or anyone inside; obviously he had no suspicion that he was being followed.

He had gone inside now and Jeff made a dash past the next cottage and crept up on the porch of the cottage with the shuttered windows. The door was open and he could see the man moving around inside, industriously rubbing tables, chairs, everything that could hold fingerprints. On the floor there was a discarded blanket. Across the back of a chair had been tossed the coat that Jeff had seen Connie wear. She was here! She must be here!

He stepped back to move the flashlight in a wide arc, heard the car start up. Then he plunged inside the room, hurling his weight on the red-headed man's shoulders, bringing him down to the ground. The surprise was complete.

Jeff was on top, his hands on the man's throat. The latter thrashed wildly, and Jeff let out a shout. There was an answering shout and Colin came charging up the steps, sprang forward to grab the man's wildly kicking legs and hold him down.

While Jeff tightened his grip on the man's throat, Colin pulled off his prisoner's belt and fastened his hands together behind his back. Then the two men dragged him to his feet.

"Winterson!" Holt gasped. "You sure had me fooled. I thought I could tell a policeman in the dark."

"Where is she?" Jeff asked.

"Who?" Holt was blandly innocent.

Jeff knocked the man's head back with his fist. "What have you done with her?"

"I don't know what you are talking about."

"That's her coat. What have you done with her?"

Holt, studying the angry man, realized that he would not dare kill him. First he had to be sure of the girl's safety. If he could just play for time. Time was all he needed. The rest of the gang would be here before too long.

Colin, who had made a quick survey of the cottage, said, "Someone was lying on the bed in here. She's been here. She didn't get away on her own, Gray. She couldn't have opened those shutters." He grabbed Holt, shook him. "Where is she?"

"Hang on to him," Jeff said. "He won't talk. She's — somewhere. She has to be somewhere. He made his pitch to Kent and then heard on the radio that Kent had reported to the police. He's come back to eradicate any traces he might have left. She — she's not here, Emery."

He went outside. Connie! What had they done with her? How had they — disposed of her? But the answer lay before him in the ocean whose waves were licking higher and higher on the sand as the tide came in. Licking hungrily. The ocean. That was why Holt had been looking at it so hard.

By the afterglow he could see a dark object bobbing up and down, rising on a wave, dropping out of sight. An empty rowboat. Frantically he began to strip off his clothes.

Colin appeared in the doorway. "I've got him fastened to a chair. Gray! You can't do that. You couldn't live in that surf! Not for five minutes. She — she couldn't either, man."

His restraining arm held back Jeff. Then the latter bent over numbly and picked up the overcoat he had thrown on the sand.

"Could she — that is, can she swim?"

Jeff took a long time grasping the meaning of the words. Then he began to run along the beach, the flashlight moving from side to side, shouting, "Connie! Connie! It's all right. You're safe now. Connie!"

He ran, stumbling, shouting, pausing to paw frantically through a pile of trash, racing away from the beach to explore dark bushes higher along the bank. Back to the edge, his eyes straining, looking out past breaking waves, down at the sand.

The last of the light had nearly gone. The flashlight moved from the water, across the sand, touched something white, moved on, turned back.

"Connie!" It seemed to Colin that Jeff's cry was like a trumpet sounding in triumph, in jubilation.

Then Jeff was on his knees beside the girl who lay on her face in the sand, wearing a white slip that clung to her, a pool of water soaking into the sand, water dripping from her hair. For a long sickening moment Jeff thought that the waves had washed her in, that she was drowned.

Then he lifted her gently in his arms and her lashes fluttered, her eyes were open.

"Jeff," she said, her voice a sob, "I knew you'd come. I knew you'd find me."

As he caught her against him, his lips seeking hers, Colin turned back toward the cottage and his prisoner. The latter glared at him.

"We've got her," Colin said, "and she's alive. You know, I could feel very, very sorry for you."

He released his prisoner from the chair, tightened the strap that bound his wrists behind him. "March!" he said cheerfully.

In a few minutes Jeff passed him, carrying Connie, going toward the cottage.

"Where are you taking her?"

"I want to get her inside. She's icy cold. I'm afraid of pneumonia."

"Wrap her coat around her and put her in the car." Colin switched on the heater. "We'll get her to the nearest hospital. That's best."

With Jeff in the back seat holding Connie in his arms, Colin drove through the night. Beside him he could hear Holt's heavy breathing. Behind him he could hear Connie babbling. She talked of rowboats and waves, of wind and cold. Then the words finally were silenced. Her head was on Jeff's shoulder, his arms held her, but she was not aware of their comfort. Her thick lashes lay darkly on the cheeks that were so white.

The doctor in the emergency ward looked around as a tall, tense young man came in carrying a girl wearing a wet slip under a winter coat. He took her temperature, listened to her chest.

"Oxygen," he said curtly. While people scurried around, and Connie was wheeled away on a stretcher, the doctor said, "What kind of fool idea was this — going bathing in March?"

"This was attempted murder," Jeff said, slumping against the wall. He straightened himself with an effort of will.

"Better let me have a look at you, too, while I'm at it," the doctor said. "You're out on your feet."

Jeff shook his head impatiently. "No time. I've got to get to a police station. We have a kidnaper out there in the car."

ii

The message from Stephen Emery was marked "urgent" and Sandra dialed his number at once.

"I suppose you have heard," he began.

"Heard what?"

"Constance Wyndham has been kidnaped!"

"Stephen! No. It's not possible."

"I thought your father would have told you. The kidnaper approached him several hours ago about the ransom. We — Colin and I — hoped you might know something about your friend that would help us, give us a lead."

Sandra listened, her thoughts whirling. Connie had been kidnaped. Her father knew and he had not told her.

"But what's — being done?" she asked at last.

"Colin got in touch with a man named Jefferson Gray. I don't know what they had in mind. I haven't heard since. Except, of course, your father's statement to the police. It has just been made public."

"My father?" Sandra was bewildered.

"Yes. He told them he did not believe Miss Wyndham had been kidnaped, that he would prosecute the extortioners. Of course, assuming the kidnaping was real, and her roommate certainly thinks so, he has put your friend in a — precarious position."

After a pause Stephen said sharply, "Alexandra, are you there?"

"Yes. You said your brother —"

"He and Gray seem to have gone off on some tack of their own. I haven't heard from them. I suppose Miss Debaney, the roommate, will be the first to be informed. She was greatly upset about Miss Wyndham. And Colin," for the first time Stephen sounded amused, "was upset about Miss Debaney."

Sandra sat huddled beside the telephone. She was still staring unseeingly at the wall when her father came home. She heard his voice in the foyer and ran across the great drawing room, down a corridor, up the stairs to her own room. It was absurd, of course, but somehow she did not want to see her father now.

A few minutes later she came downstairs and started quietly toward the front door. Her father was just leaving his library.

"Alexandra, where are you going? I thought you were dining at home tonight."

She looked at him as though she were seeing him for the first time. Then she said, "I'm going out."

"What's wrong? You look as though you had had a shock."

"I just heard about Connie. Stephen Emery called me."

"Surely you don't believe that ridiculous tale!"

She drew away from his restraining arm. "Don't keep me now, Father. I must go."

"Where?"

"To Connie's apartment. To see her roommate — the one who cares what happens to her. To wait for news."

"Alexandra!" Kent was impatient. "Don't you see —"

"What I'm beginning to see is what you are really like, Father. You and me both." She was gone before he could speak again. He stood staring after her.

iii

The chauffeur nodded. "Yes, Miss Kent, this is where I brought Miss Wyndham before."

Sandra looked at the shabby building, went into the tiny entrance and looked at the cards below the bells. Debaney. That must be the one.

The door clicked and she went into the dark hallway. The door at the far end opened. A girl called eagerly, "Con — oh, I thought —" She slumped with disappointment against the frame of the door.

Sandra went down the hall. "I am Alexandra Kent," she said. "Will you please let me come in, Miss Debaney."

"Of course." Lil pulled herself together. After a quick glance she knew that Sandra had brought no news.

"Have you heard anything?" Sandra asked eagerly.

The small girl shook her head mutely.

"How did it happen?"

"It goes back to her brother Nick, I guess," Lil said dully. "He's — Nick is not a good person like Connie." She described how he had stolen the stamp album and how frantic Connie had been. Her father had left them to an old friend and she had promised to turn them over to him.

"Though I must say," Lil remarked candidly, "it didn't seem fair to me. She said they were worth a small fortune and all she had was what she earned."

She went on to tell about Nick's association with the gangsters, about the red-headed man who had been following Connie; told how Colin had chased him to the subway station and concluded with the fake telephone call that had nearly led to disaster the night before.

"Mr. Gray tried to help," Lil said. "He came at once." She did not look at Sandra. "He — but if you are an old friend of Connie's you probably know about Mr. Gray. She's terribly in love with him, a one-man woman she says, but he is going to marry her best friend and she said she would ruin both of their lives if she didn't stay out of the picture. She's —" Lil gulped. "Connie is pretty swell."

I shouldn't have said all that, Lil thought. Connie is too generous to have done it. But after that broadcast I just heard, after what this girl's father has done to Connie, she deserves to suffer. I used to envy her with all her money but I don't now. I don't even like her.

Having settled this to her own satisfaction, Lil took another look at Sandra, looking desperately unhappy. She went out to make coffee.

They drank it in silence, broken only by sudden starts of attention when the outer door opened, when voices sounded in the hallway. Then they lapsed into their separate thoughts, into their eternal waiting.

Finally Sandra said, "Miss Debaney, you and Connie must hate both of us, my father and me."

"Connie doesn't hate people. When she's a friend, she's a friend all her life."

Sandra looked up from her clenched hands, straight into

Lil's level, searching eyes. "I've made a terrible mistake. I hurt Connie worse than — than my father has. But I didn't know. I didn't understand."

She found herself confiding in this girl as she never had in anyone before. She told her about her father's plans for her, about the marriage with Jeff that would have made the situation bearable for her, about Nick saying that Connie intended to marry Jeff because she needed money. "I thought if she could sell the lodge she'd let Jeff alone."

Lil studied her gravely. "You tried to make a bargain with life. And the worst of it was you didn't really want this man. He was your escape. And you don't love him or you would have cared more about what was best for him. If you had got your bargain it would never have made you happy."

"What makes you so sure?"

"Because you don't find happiness in what you get, just in what you give."

The telephone rang and Lil upset her coffee cup as she reached for it.

"Hello. Hello!" Her face fell. "No, no word at all . . . no letter. Nothing."

When she put down the telephone she said in a discouraged voice, "That was the police again. No news yet. But I suppose they are doing all they can. All they — dare do without making Connie's position any more dangerous."

The door buzzer sounded and she was across the room in a flash. She stood back in surprise as a tall, grave-looking man said, "Miss Debaney? I am Stephen Emery, Colin's brother."

Lil braced herself. "Come in, Mr. Emery."

When he had put down his coat and hat they surveyed

each other frankly. Lil took a long breath, head high, eyes level, cheeks flushed.

"I hope you don't mind my coming here. Naturally I am anxious and I thought this would be the first place to get news." There was a slight smile on his mouth. "Colin would be sure to inform you."

Wordlessly Lil waved him to a seat beside Sandra on the couch. He clasped her hand silently and then turned to study Lil who was bringing him a cup of coffee. Then she mopped up the coffee she had spilled. She did not look at him again but the color came and went in her face and her hands shook.

"I hadn't expected to find you here, Alexandra."

"I had to know. And I'm so terribly glad I came, Stephen, because I've met Lillian Debaney who is —" She spread her hands with a gesture of inadequacy. "She is — so kind, so wise. I'm glad, when the rest of us failed Connie, that she had a friend like this."

Lil flicked a surprised look at Sandra and then the big warm smile transformed her face. "I thought I'd been pretty darned mean," she confessed.

"I don't believe you could be," Sandra said. "I hope if — when Connie is found we can all be friends."

"That's nice of you, Miss Kent, but — let's be honest about this," Lil's chin tilted upwards, "I wouldn't fit into your world. I'm a farm girl from the Middle West and a model for Céleste." She shifted the talk away from herself. "But so far as Connie is concerned — Colin will find her."

"What makes you so sure?" Stephen asked.

"He told me to leave it to him."

"And you have that much faith in him?"

"All the faith there is," Lil said sturdily.

"What do you think of this dream he has of buying and running a dairy farm?"

"That's not a dream, it's a project." The telephone shrilled again and she seized it.

"Lil?"

"Colin! Colin! Where — what — Connie —"

"Hold it," he said. "You'll trip over yourself, going so fast." He was laughing. *Laughing.* "First, Connie's safe. But she is suffering from shock and exposure and she may have pneumonia. She's in a hospital and you won't be able to see her for a couple of days . . . No, all the care she needs. Round-the-clock nurses, private room, oxygen. She's going to make it, dear. But right now she's a very tired, sick girl."

"Oh, Colin, you're wonderful! How did you manage to find her?"

"Sure I'm wonderful," he said cheerfully. "But it was Jeff Gray who found her. We also found the kidnaper, who is now getting room and board at the expense of the taxpayers of New Jersey until New York decides what it wants to do about him. We're on our way back to New York now but we'll be tied up with the police for a while. I'll call you later."

"I'll wait until you call. No matter when."

"That's my girl. But first, get yourself something to eat. If I know you, you've been sweating it out without a bite of food. A real meal, promise?"

"A real meal," Lil promised.

"One more thing you could do for me. Besides eating properly. If you will call Steve —"

"He's here."

"Steve! There? He hasn't been making you any trouble, has he?"

"No." Lil looked up to meet Stephen's eyes. "He's really very nice. On the whole." She handed him the telephone.

He listened for a long time. When he hung up he said, "She's safe. She'll be all right. And Colin and Gray got the kidnaper."

"Thank God!" Sandra cried. She started to get up. "I mustn't stay any longer. But I don't want to go home. I don't think I am ready to face my father just yet."

"Why don't you stay and eat with me?" Lil said impulsively. "I promised Colin I'd eat properly. It won't be fancy but it will be good, if I do say so."

"I'd like to stay," Sandra said eagerly.

Lil glanced shyly at Emery. "Will you — I mean —"

"I'd be delighted to stay. After all, we had better start getting acquainted, hadn't we? Colin tells me he is going to marry you, if you will have him. And if you need my recommendation, I think he's rather a nice fellow. You could do worse."

TWENTY-TWO

THE ROOM was white, so was the narrow bed, so was the crisp uniform of the nurse who smiled down at her.

"I am Miss Graham," she said cheerfully. "Don't try to talk yet. I'll tell you what you must want to know. You are in a hospital in New Jersey where you've been five days, suffering from shock, exposure, and double pneumonia. But right now you have got over the hump. You'll be well in no time. But," she put up a hand warningly, "not strong for a while. You're going to need time to recuperate, to gain back all the weight you have lost. Spring is a tricky time, you know. We don't want you catching cold."

She raised the head of Connie's bed and watched approvingly while she sipped an eggnogg. "Now I'll let you rest."

Connie's head sank back on the pillows. Curious how weak she was. Her body hardly seemed to belong to her. Her legs felt too heavy to lift. Her eyes closed, opened again.

It seemed to her that for a long, long time she had been living suspended between life and death. There had been dreams, horrible dreams. There had been an icy plunge into the ocean, the long struggle to swim toward the shore that had seemed to recede, drawing farther and farther away from her all the time.

There had been a moment when she had known she was not going to make it, when she was too tired to care whether she made it or not. Then her foot had touched sand, she had made a few more clumsy, inadequate strokes, a big wave had picked her up, dumped her on dry sand. *Dry sand.* Frantically she had clawed her way, first on hands and knees, finally by dragging herself full length, until she was beyond the reach of those hungry waves.

Then there had been nothing at all except a queer dream — or was it a memory? — of Jeff holding her in his arms, Jeff with his mouth covering hers.

She must not think of that. She had been miraculously restored to life. She was safe. Or was she? What had happened to Guy Holt? If he had escaped he would find her again some day.

At the moment she was too tired to care. She could never run away again. She had no more strength to fight. Anyhow, while she was in the hospital no one could hurt her.

The hospital. She had been there for days. She had a private room, a nurse. She was not going to be able to work for a while, perhaps not for weeks. Anyhow, Céleste would not want a model who was recuperating from an illness. What was she going to do about paying for all these things? The money for Stony Brook might not come for a long time.

The nurse, who had been watching the girl's restless movements, listening to her quickened breathing, came to take her wrist in warm, strong fingers.

"There's nothing to worry about," she said firmly. "You must go back to sleep now."

Next time Connie opened her eyes there was sunshine streaming in the windows. There was sunshine on the table. No, that was a great vase of forsythia, holding golden sunlight; forsythia, the harbinger of spring.

She turned her head as she heard a slight movement and

saw Lil sitting in the chair beside her bed, her face one brilliant smile.

"Lil!" She meant it to be a word of welcome; it was little more than a whisper.

"Hello, there! Jeepers but it's wonderful to see you. I told Colin I'd break in if they didn't let me see you soon." She added anxiously, "I don't want to tire you."

"You won't." Still that strained whisper. "Please tell me what happened. I don't remember much."

Lil described how Colin and Jeff had given chase to Guy Holt, how Jeff had found her, and how Colin and he had brought back the kidnaper.

"Jeepers! I don't know when there has been so much excitement. Your picture was in the paper and mine and Colin's and Jeff's. When they came back with the kidnaper there was a regular riot. Television men trying to get them to talk, people taking pictures, the police moving in. That guy Holt is being held for the grand jury and so are the rest of the gang. They picked them all up."

"How about Nick?"

Lil hesitated as she met Connie's imploring eyes. Her hand covered the thin one that moved so restlessly on the blanket.

"He came back, Connie, when he knew what had happened to you. I guess he was ashamed. Anyhow, he made a full confession and he helped get all the evidence that was needed about the rest of the men in that racket. He's doing his best. Honestly he is. There must be more of that wonderful father in him than you realized."

"I'm — glad. What will happen to him?"

"Chances are that he will get off. If he is sentenced, Colin is going to give him a job when he is released, working on the farm until he is sure that Nick is really straightened out."

"Colin's farm?"

The happiness in Lil's face was as bright as the forsythia in the room. She nodded. "He's going to take possession next month. We — he found a place in Connecticut. Rundown and it needs stacks of work but —"

A smile flickered across Connie's pale lips. "A lot seems to have been happening."

Lil nodded emphatically. "We're going to be married," she said, "just as soon as you are well enough to come to the wedding."

"Oh, Lil!"

"Colin's waiting down in the car now. They said only one visitor at a time but he said to tell you his name is on the waiting list and there's to be no shoving."

Connie laughed softly.

"Did you bring me the forsythia?" she asked.

Lil shook her head. "Jeff Gray left it for you — he's terribly attractive, isn't he? — just before he went away. He said it was to remind you."

"He — went away?"

"He resigned from Kent Enterprises and he has left New York. No one knows where he has gone."

"Oh."

Connie's nurse opened the door quietly, took a look at her patient and said briskly, "That's enough for today, Miss Debaney. We don't want to tire her."

ii

"I'd like to talk to you, Alexandra."

"Sorry, Father, but I have a dinner engagement."

"Emery again?"

"Stephen Emery. Yes."

"You can sit down for a few minutes, can't you? We don't seem to have had much time to talk lately."

"We never have had really, Father."

Kent looked at his daughter. She had changed a great deal. It agreed with her, of course. He had never seen her so glowing. He had never before realized that she was a pretty woman. But the change had made her a stranger. Courteous but aloof, avoiding him when she could.

It all went back to that unfortunate business about the Wyndhams, of course. He had blundered badly there, a blunder that had caused him the first unfavorable publicity he had ever received from the press. As a rule, newspapers are careful not to criticize men in his position.

All that could be handled, of course, when the advertising appropriations for the following year were decided upon. But it wouldn't be so easy to handle Alexandra. In fact, it might not be at all easy to handle her. So far he had been patient; he had been more than reasonable. Not once had he reminded her of that inexcusable outburst when she had said — how had she put it? — "I am seeing what you are really like. You and me both."

She was waiting now for him to talk to her but waiting in a manner he did not altogether like. There was no passive acceptance about her these days.

"I suppose you know Jefferson Gray resigned and that he has gone away."

"Yes, I know." Seeing the question in her father's face Sandra said, "He came to see me. We had a long talk."

"You did nothing to try to prevent him from destroying his future?"

"He isn't destroying it, Father. He is trying to rebuild it."

"And where do you think he can do better than with Kent Enterprises?"

"In the life he chooses for himself." As her father started to speak Sandra said quickly, "It took me a long time to know that. It cost a lot, too. Before I had learned a very simple, human bit of wisdom I did the cruelest, most unforgivable thing of my life. I hurt Connie."

Her father looked up. Hesitated. Constance Wyndham was one person he would be happier not to discuss.

"And I did it for an unworthy reason," Sandra went on. "You see, Father, I was trying to live my life as you had it all worked out for me. I intended to marry Jeff, knowing perfectly well that he wasn't in love with me; knowing that I wasn't in love with him. But that's what you wanted. So I did it. Then I learned the hard way — as I suppose we all learn — just how bitterly wrong I was. I was unfair to Connie. I would have cheated Jeff."

"*Cheated* him!"

"Married him without love; marrying him so as to deprive him of love. To fit in with your plans, your ambitions."

"You've never dared speak to me like this before, Alexandra."

"I've learned courage as I learned honesty. And I didn't learn it, Father, as I should have learned it, through my own conscience. I learned it by falling in love with Stephen Emery, by having a glimpse of happiness. Have you ever had a glimpse of happiness, Father? It's so bright that at first it blinds you and then it teaches you to see clearly. It taught me that the integrity of human relationships is the most important thing there is. I don't know whether Stephen will ever ask me to marry him. If he does I'll say yes. And I'll try all the rest of my life to earn the happiness he has it in his power to give me. If he will."

"Alexandra —"

"But all the rest of my life I'll feel guilty for the things we — you and I — have done to Connie."

"You are overwrought." Kent felt totally inadequate to meet the situation. "So far as Constance is concerned, I have taken over all her hospital bills; I will see that she has money for as long a recuperation as she needs."

"Money isn't enough. Don't you see that?"

He moved one hand uncertainly. He looked at her with a kind of pleading. For the first time Sandra was sorry for her father.

"Then what is enough?"

"Human kindness. Just plain simple human kindness. I should have learned that from Connie. I didn't. But I've learned it now, partly from her roommate who is deeply wise; partly from falling in love and learning that other people matter."

She got up and for a moment her hand rested on his shoulder. "Good night, Father."

"Good night, my dear." After a moment he added heavily, "Give Emery my regards. Tell him I hope he'll dine with us some evening before long."

She turned to smile and her face lighted up. She blew him a kiss. Why she is really lovely, he thought in surprise. The door closed behind her.

iii

The Emery brothers were dining with Sandra and Lil. Colin had finally worn down Lil's resistance.

"I won't fit in," she kept saying stubbornly.

"Look here, wench, speaking as your lord and master — that's correct, isn't it?"

"Aye, aye, sir."

"You'll come along and get acquainted with your future brother-in-law and your future sister-in-law. At least, that's what I read in the tea leaves."

"I'll disgrace you," Lil said glumly, and even Colin's laughter did not cheer her.

An hour later, sitting between the Emery men, she wondered why she had been afraid. For some reason that she could not grasp her simplest remark seemed to throw everyone into gales of laughter. The stiff Emery had unbent unbelievably. Sandra rocked with laughter.

It was Sandra who said unexpectedly, "I've laughed so much I almost forgot this was to be a serious occasion. Let's get down to business."

"Business? Tonight?" Lil wailed.

"Silence, woman," Colin told her sternly. Under the table his hand reached for hers.

"Let's plan your wedding," Sandra said. "If you and Colin are going to be married in three weeks there are a million things to be done."

"Oh," Lil said, "I have no family near enough to come, you know, so we'll probably just go out some morning and get married."

"You'll do nothing of the kind," Steve told her. "You are going to be married from the Emery town house as you ought to be."

"Your house?" Lil faltered.

"Colin's and mine."

"But I couldn't, Mr. Emery — Steve."

"You'll have to get used to it," Steve told her. "After all, you and Colin can't spend all your time on the farm. When you come to the city you'll naturally live there." He smiled and touched her cheek lightly. "So I want you to start feeling at home."

"Oh, Steve!" For a moment tears blinded her and then she blinked them away.

"And," Sandra said, "I'm going to provide the trousseau and Céleste is going to design it. For those New York trips, of course. You can buy your own blue jeans for the farm."

"Sandra!"

"You're spoiling the wench," Colin grumbled. "Just when I had her ready to take orders."

"Anything you say," Lil agreed. "All I insist on is that we wait until Connie can come."

"Of course we will."

"Have you seen her yet, Sandra?"

"Not yet. I was — afraid."

iv

Colin and Lil left early — "I'm still a working girl," Lil reminded them — and Steve drove Sandra home. The air was unexpectedly mild, with a hint of spring in it, but the ground underfoot was treacherous and slushy, a sordid reminder that winter was reluctant to be dispossessed.

"They are going to be riotously happy," Sandra said wistfully. "Can't you imagine them? Laughing through the days no matter how hard they have to work? Laughter bubbles up in Lil like a fountain."

When he made no reply she touched his arm lightly. "You don't still disapprove of her, do you?"

"No, of course not. She's a fine girl and she is making a man of Colin. I'm still continually surprised to discover, day after day, how much drive and ambition he is developing."

"I'm glad. They are right for each other."

"Let's forget them for now. I want you to think about me, Alexandra. About — us."

She was very still.

"Of course I'm not the man to fit into your father's plans, any more than Colin was the man to fit into mine. Besides that, I am years older than you are. But I love you very much. I'd do anything in my power to make you happy. Will you marry me?"

She gave a long contented sigh. "I was so afraid I'd have to do the proposing."

The car swerved violently, then steadied.

"Alexandra!" He added unsteadily. "I'll teach you to love me."

"I've already learned. And love has taught me how to forgive my father. It has even taught me to forgive myself. Now if only Connie —"

TWENTY-THREE

THE NURSE had helped Connie to dress and now she was resting in the big chair beside the window. She was dismayed to discover how weak she still was, how easily she grew tired. The doctor, too, was uneasy about her condition. By this time she should have recovered fully except for regaining weight, but for some reason her progress was slow. Much too slow. She was a good patient in a way. She did passively whatever was asked of her. In another way she was a bad patient. She seemed to lack the will to get well.

Her suitcase had been packed and was standing against the wall with her coat and hat. She was waiting for Lil and Colin to come for her, to take her back to the apartment. She would have at least two more weeks of rest before she could return to work, the doctor warned her. Then she would have to find a new place to live. It was going to be lonely without Lil.

She leaned back in her chair, hands clasped loosely on her lap, looking indifferently out of the window. It had still been winter when she entered the hospital. Now, in the Garden State, it was spring. She could see forsythia like bottled sunlight; daffodils waving their golden heads in the light breeze; crocuses sprinkled like stars on lawns.

Spring always comes. She shook her head, trying to drive the words out of her mind. Not for her. Never again for her. Jeff had gone without a word.

The door opened and, instead of Lil and Colin, she saw Sandra Kent and her father.

Sandra came forward slowly, looking as though she feared a rebuff, uncertain of her welcome. "Connie, I was afraid to come before. I wanted — can you forgive me? Can you forgive the words — the angry words —" Tears spilled down her cheeks.

Connie summoned up a smile. "What words?" she challenged her.

"And me, Constance?" For the first time in his life John Kent was humble.

"It was a natural mistake," she said. "Shall we — just start over?"

"You are a very generous woman, Constance." He picked up her suitcase. "Ready?"

With Sandra supporting one arm and the nurse the other, she made her slow departure from the hospital. The chauffeur took the suitcase from Kent and the latter and Sandra helped Connie into the waiting car.

There were light clouds scudding across the sky and wild azalea making a purple mist on a hillside. The air was so balmy that Kent rolled down a window after making sure that Connie would not be in a draft.

"We both think you need a change of air," Kent said at length. "I wanted you to come home with us but Sandra thinks you might prefer going back to Stony Brook for a while."

"But it doesn't belong to me any more."

"The new owner hasn't moved in yet, and I understand your old housekeeper, Mrs. Kennedy, is working there.

Sandra inquired and found that you'd be more than welcome."

"I'd — like that," Connie said unsteadily. She found tears welling up in her eyes, blinked them back. It was just weakness, she assured herself. She wasn't in the least unhappy. She tried to fix her attention on something else.

Suddenly she was aware of Sandra. There was none of the unhappiness that might be expected over Jeff's disappearance. Instead there was a radiance, a glow that made her lovely, a kind of inner light.

"Sandra," she exclaimed, "it's happened. You've found yourself. Your real self. And someone else has found it, too."

Sandra gave a quick glance at her father. "Well—"

Kent chuckled. "I think my daughter is afraid I'll continue to be the heavy father. But I've learned my lesson, too. She hasn't told me yet but I think Alexandra is on the verge of announcing her engagement. Right?"

Sandra laughed happily. "Right. Stephen Emery, of course. And, Father, you're going to like him. Honestly."

"Honestly I'm going to try."

"That's all I ask."

An hour later Connie unfastened her seat belt and leaned back in the plane. How many months had passed since she had made this trip? Perhaps it was a mistake to return. It would only open the wound that had begun to heal.

This time it was daylight when she landed at the airport. No lisping man with a revolver lurked in shadows. There were no shadows anywhere. The sky was bright though snow still lay on the ground in sheltered places.

There was no Cadillac to meet her, either, with a tall, fair-haired driver with narrow eyes. Stop it, she told herself firmly.

"Nice to see you, Miss Wyndham," the taxi driver said cordially. "Hear you had quite an adventure in New York. Papers were full of it. You look kinda tired."

Connie murmured something inaudible.

"Hear you've sold Stony Brook," he went on. "Sorry to hear it. The day when people put down roots seems to have gone forever. Oh, well, it may work out all right. I hear the new owner is going to build some rustic cabins for hunters and vacationers. Maybe he'll make the place boom."

Stony Brook looked just the same. Smoke curled up from the chimney. Mrs. Kennedy opened the door and took the girl in her arms.

"Connie, my poor lamb. It looks like I'll have my work cut out, putting weight on you. Like a frozen little ghost you are."

As usual, logs crackled cheerfully in the great stone fireplace. "You just sit there by the fire and I'll bring you a bowl of chowder. You can't beat my chowder in New York. Why I hear they even put *tomatoes* in it."

I shouldn't have come, Connie thought. I shouldn't have come. The room was as dear, as familiar as it had ever been but there were changes. A sturdy chair was drawn near the fire and on the table beside it was Louise Dickinson Rich's joyous book about life in Maine, *We Took to the Woods*. In a heavy ashtray there was a pipe. The new owner had apparently been here.

On the big table there was a roll of blueprints and she opened them, bent over to study them. This was the plan for the new Stony Brook. It wasn't, she saw, going to lose its character, but cabins were to be erected in the woods. As footsteps sounded behind her she said, without turning, "This is going to be just the way Dad planned it. I'm so glad."

"I'm glad you are pleased."

She whirled around to find Jeff standing behind her.

"Jeff! What are you doing here?"

"At Stony Brook? I bought it."

"You?"

As Mrs. Kennedy bustled in with a tray holding a bowl of steaming chowder, he cleared away the blueprints.

He let her eat in silence. Then when she had finished and Mrs. Kennedy, beaming with pleasure, had taken away the tray with the empty bowl, he said, "You didn't know?"

She shook her head. Swallowed. "They just told me — you had gone away."

"I learned that Kent Enterprises had nothing to give me that I wanted. All my life I've watched people starting out with dreams and ending with something they didn't want at all. I intended this dream to come true. So I bought Stony Brook and I'm going to live here. It — wasn't an easy decision to make, Connie."

"I suppose not. You had to give up a lot for it."

"Did I?" His face was grim. "I lost the possibility of having great wealth and glamour and prestige."

"But what do they matter?" she asked.

He laughed shortly. "You say that to me? *You?* Changed your mind, haven't you?"

"Never. Only I thought — Mr. Kent — and Sandra — and —"

"Did I lose you, Connie? That's all that matters?"

So it was Connie who completed the cycle, who finished the pattern that was to make her life. She put her arms around his neck.

"Jeff, I don't know what I would do without you. I don't want to do without you. Not ever, so long as I live."

He crushed her to him. It was a long time before she released herself gently, half laughing, half crying.

He eased her into the deep chair near the fire and knelt beside her. "I forgot how weak you still are."

"I'll get stronger every day. I'll hurry and get well. Because one of these days soon we'll have to take a long walk in the woods and look for the first robin. Even in Maine, spring always comes."